The London Reaction

Altered State 2
The London Reaction

J. G. Jenkinson

PRESS

PRESS

Published by Vulpine Press in the United Kingdom in 2023

ISBN: 978-1-83919-489-4

Cover by Claire Wood

www.vulpine-press.com

This book is for Cassie; beautiful and intelligent, it is her strength that I admire most.

Prologue - Berlin, 1945

Olga watched the collar of the oberleutnant's greatcoat flapping rakishly in the wind to reveal glimpses of a medal at the neck, just like the Iron Cross her father had won in a war he'd fought before she was born.

The boy had his back to her as he looked from the officer to the men.

"I am looking for another unit to join," he said, his voice small and uncertain.

"You can join us, junge," one of the soldiers said. He jerked his head to one side making Olga notice the men strung up from the lampposts. They were swaying with the wind, with signs describing their crime of desertion hung about their necks. She stifled a cry because some had been there for a while and putrefaction had well and truly set in; the hungry carrion of Berlin already having helped themselves to the eyes and cheeks.

"What is your name?" the officer asked.

"Rudi, Rudolph Kessler." Olga's hand shot up to her mouth to suppress another cry. She had found him, the boy who would be Doktor Rudolph Kessler, the boy who would become the man she loved. The man for whom she'd traversed deserts, oceans and the vast gulf of space and time.

"Where's your rifle?" demanded the oberleutnant.

"There weren't enough, Herr Oberleutnant, they said because my job is to load the shells into the gun, I don't need one."

1

"Well, I'll tell you what, little Rottenführer, we've run out of rope," he said, turning to smile at his men.

"I will fetch you rope, Herr Oberleutnant," Rudi said eagerly.

"No, no I have a far more expedient plan. See that rifle?" He pointed with his riding crop at a weather-beaten Gewehr leaning against the wall. "Go and get it."

Rudi carefully laid his bike down and ran over to the weapon. He picked it up with the care one might afford to a new-born baby.

"Do you want it?" the oberleutnant said. Rudi nodded.

"This man is a deserter." He pointed at the dark-suited man. "He left his post and tried to run away from defending the Fatherland. You know what happens to deserters, don't you, junge? My men are tired. It's been a long war, and if you help us out by shooting this man, I'll let you keep the rifle."

Olga watched as Rudi staggered backwards at the thought of shooting this man in cold blood. The rifle seemed to shake in his hands, his head hung and his shoulders slumped.

"Okay," he said after an apparent emotional wrestling match.

"Stand back, boys, this one is a steely-eyed killer," one of the soldiers said, his rotten teeth revealed as he roared with laughter at his own joke.

Rudi was inexpertly checking the weapon, struggling with the weight of it, as he prepared to perform this heinous act. Now he stood with his back to her again and the officer began reading some sort of hackneyed litany.

"In the name of the Führer and of the Reich…" Olga let her coat drop to the ground as she swung her Galil around and brought it up into her shoulder. She was lightning, two shots into the centre of mass, first the officer, then each of his men. They folded up where they stood, not knowing what had hit them. Rudi turned, and locked eyes with Olga. Was there some recognition there? He brought his rifle to bear slowly, clumsily.

The shot rang out but he missed.

"Rudi, stop," she yelled as she let the Galil fall to her side. "Please listen…"

BANG!

Olga spun around to the right and hit the ground, the shot rang out in the square and Rudi ran over to her, tears in his eyes and panic on his face. Their eyes met, and he let his rifle drop loudly onto the cobbled street.

"Olga?" he said and the word felt strange in his mouth, like he'd never said it before but also that he had said it a thousand times. It felt right, like a pair of well-fitting shoes or a home-cooked meal. Where was the blood, he'd seen plenty of wounds in his short life and there was usually a lot of blood by now, wasn't there?

She looked up at him, breathless and confused.

"I'm sorry, I thought you were a Russian. I thought you were going to kill me too. Why aren't you bleeding?"

She was winded and tried in vain to catch her breath as she watched the horror on his face slowly abate.

"The vest," she panted. "I'll have a nasty bruise, no more." She placed a hand on his grubby little face and nearly passed out, the dizzy sensation, that of falling. He too looked confused, somehow older, but still a twelve-year-old boy. She could imagine the man she loved if she forced herself to, but what she really saw was the boy, a scared little boy who needed to be rescued, cared for, and loved. He would need an education too, one appropriate for a child of such high intelligence. So that was what she would have to do.

She wept, imagining the next years as she would play mother to this adolescent, the love she felt dying by degrees with each painful year of waiting.

The sporadic rifle fire and not so distant shelling shook them from their reverie. "We need to get off the street, these flying tribunals are everywhere and, this," he gestured towards the dead soldiers, "will have the whole of Kreuzberg up in arms."

"Hello? Am I still to be executed?" The voice made both Olga and Rudi start, the corpulent deserter still standing blindfolded against the wall. They led him, still blindfolded to the edge of the square and told him to walk one-hundred paces before removing it.

"I have an idea," Olga said, still breathless. The men had not run out of rope, and soon all three were strung up alongside their victims, with equally damning signs covering their gunshot wounds.

"Where do you live?" she asked.

"Just around the corner."

"Is there food there?"

He shook his head, staring at the ground. Then he looked at Olga, a light in his eyes as he ran over to the neatly folded coats and haversacks of the men Olga had killed. Inside they found food, ammunition, and most surprisingly, a small tin of tiny, oddly shaped pieces of gold. They put everything useful into one pack and walked away, Rudi pushing his bicycle and Olga in her huge coat.

Sabotage – Suffolk 1915

Sydney Vittel paddled his inflatable dinghy for two kilometres after the *U-Boot* had dropped him in a spumy sea off the coast of Suffolk. He'd pitched and rolled on the heavy swell, his tiny boat taking on a dangerous amount of water, so by the time he reached the estuary of the River Debden he was shaking violently with hypothermia and his wet hands were raw from the effort of rowing.

As he entered the estuary, the merciful pull of the ebb tide offered some respite, and Vittel slumped into the stern where he was able to rest. Using one oar like a rudder to steer the boat he rode the ebb upriver, reaching the town of Woodbridge just before dawn.

He foundered and sank his dinghy, then made his way to 14 Kingston Road while struggling with a large plastic bag of dry clothes in the English fashion and a British-style suitcase containing the tools of his trade. At the house, the broad frame of James Jack Gleeson filled the open doorway, his face showed no signs of tiredness; he was keen-eyed and fully dressed as if he had waited up all night for the contact. Without an introduction, he ushered the sodden man inside and instructed him in broken German to strip in front of the fire.

Gleeson was a veteran of both Boer wars and sported the scars to prove it, in fact it was the British treatment of the Boers that had led him to this work. When he arrived home, he bought himself out of the Army and began looking for a way to fight the British and bring about Irish home rule. After messing about with his local Dungannon Club, he eventually found a home with the Irish Volunteers. Gleeson was instrumental in developing their training and tactics, before eventually moving into agent handling, human intelligence and espionage.

When the German secret police had approached bearing gifts in early 1913, Gleeson agreed to be part of the fifth column, one of scores of agents along the south and east coasts of England. Now he had been at 14 Kingston Road for nearly two years, posing as an artist, the cover story and materials provided for him.

They'd outlined their plans for him at the start, with someone on staff in Berlin who would produce the paintings. They would arrive by post in various stages of completion, expertly done so that people would buy enough to supply him with a modest living but lacking the true genius that would get him noticed and blow his cover.

They were mainly coastal scenes, which gave him the perfect excuse to stare out to sea where he could monitor the shipping and naval activities for hours on end. Now he was waiting to assist German saboteurs in whatever way they needed and then after the invasion, he would finally go home to his family in County Clare.

Vittel was the first of five such men. He stood now, unashamedly naked and shivering, practically inside the inglenook fireplace.

"Bist du hungrig?" Gleeson ventured, with some hesitation.

"I speak English, pal," he said in a strong Mancunian accent as he threaded a pale, swollen foot into a suit trouser leg.

"You can call me 'Handbuch'," Gleeson said, surveying his latest charge, a gangly German chemist with mismatched features who had studied at the University of Manchester and spoke English like a native.

"'Kamel'," Vittel said, his trembling hand outstretched.

"Jesus, man, you're shaking like a shitting dog." He threw Vittel a towel and proceeded to rub down the man's bony shoulders. Vittel allowed Gleeson to do this and after considering the metaphor, laughed, explaining the joke to the teller.

"Did you ever see a whippet take a shit? They really do shake!" chuckled Vittel.

"Listen, there's porridge on the kitchen table. I'm going to run your case upstairs before I break my neck tripping over it." He grasped the case by the body effortlessly in one spade-like hand, towelling off the seawater as he turned it, while more dripped onto the carpet. "Couldn't stretch to a watertight case?" he said, shaking his huge head.

"It was easier to make the contents waterproof," Vittel said apologetically.

When Gleeson left the house, the starving Vittel found the bowl of what could only be described as goo on the kitchen table. He prodded it as a pathologist might prod the skin of a corpse and taking a tiny amount of the grey sludge on the tip of his spoon, he tasted it. It was sweet, but the texture was unpleasant. He forced the first few mouthfuls down before he began to find it less disagreeable, eventually deciding he did not much mind it after all.

"I managed to get some coffee," Gleeson said as he walked into the kitchen via the backdoor.

~

That evening just after dark Vittel took his suitcase and began his work, setting off on a bicycle borrowed from Gleeson with his suitcase strapped to the luggage rack over the rear wheel. He cycled all over the Suffolk heathland, surreptitiously poisoning the water supplies of the many Ministry of Defence installations in the area. Upon locating the supply, he added a tiny amount of a water-reactive chemical agent that after twelve to twenty-four hours would render any size of reservoir undrinkable. And after thirty-six hours, the water would be pure poison. His orders were to take minimal risks and return each morning to 14 Kingston Road before first light.

It was three in the morning when he reached the final target on his list: an army barracks with watch towers and roving patrols. This was the closest Vittel had come to action and he felt nervously for the dagger at his waist. He left his bicycle in a nearby wood and lay at the extreme edge of the treeline, watching the hastily erected camp through a monocular. Rows and rows of prefabricated huts punctuated by brick-built ablution blocks filled the space, and in one corner he made out the shape of the cistern. Vittel recalled his training, hours spent identifying the various types of water storage tanks in use by the British army, so he could now recognise a tank by its silhouette alone.

There were four towers, one in each corner, but the fence line in between was a considerable distance. Vittel supposed that a quiet man could enter at the midpoint unseen. He looked up at the patchy cloud cover which occasionally revealed strong light from a full moon. He studied the wind direction and tried to estimate how long he would have to cross the expanse of waste ground between him and his chosen entry point.

Hefting his wire cutters and tapping the phial of poison in his pocket, he watched the moon disappear and silently jogged the fifty metres to the chain link fence. He threw himself down at the foot of the fence just as the clouds parted, illuminating the ground he had just traversed. Working hard to control his breathing he began to cut a horizontal line in the fence as close to the ground as possible. A slit like this would not be discovered by accident. Each time he brought the handles together he flinched against the noise, because to Vittel it was a sound like thunder. After each cut, he would glance furtively around, looking for the roving patrol or movement in the tower. He nearly had a slit he might squeeze through when he heard it.

"So, says I, just let me feel 'em over the top of your shirt then!" It was little more than a whisper, but for Vittel it might as well have been gunfire. He reached for his dagger and held it under his chest in both hands as he lay face down and waited for the soldiers to pass.

"That don't count, mate," came a second voice.

"What d'you mean it don't count?"

"I mean that feeling a bird up over her clothes is nuffink, you're still a virgin and I suppose you'll eat a German bullet before you get any.

"Don't be like that, mucker, anyway I'll get a brass if it comes to that, you watch me."

"That wouldn't count, neither…"

The voices trailed off and Sidney Vittel dared to breathe. He made two more cuts and rolled through the slit. On his back his stared at the watch tower for a moment, no sign of movement, then adjusting his position he stared at the other. Satisfied, he rose carefully and in a crouching run, made for the nearest building.

Vittel moved from hut to hut, nervously tapping the pocket containing the poison as he went. It wasn't far and the task itself was easy as the inspection cover wasn't even locked. He tipped his poison in and closed the lid, jogging back the way he'd come. As he rolled through the slit in the fence he became entangled, catching his clothing on the jagged edge of the wire. The entire length of chain link rattled, alerting both towers and the nearby patrol. He struggled to free himself, only making more noise until he eventually tore his sleeve and broke away.

Panicking, he ran without thinking. He ran hard until his lungs were fit to explode. Shots rang out behind him and he soiled himself as the terrifying thwomp of lead on the ground near his feet made him zigzag. It was this that saved him, for this hard targeting prevented the soldiers from training their rifles on him and he reached the treeline as the sound of dogs erupted in the distance. They would run him to ground, torture him and expose the cell before it had even formed. He flew through the trees as the air he was so desperate to consume burned his lungs. His legs felt like lead and his pulse reverberated in his skull as he began to pedal his bicycle.

He rode as he had in childhood, hunched over the handlebars, arse in the air and flying along at twenty-five miles per hour along the dark country lanes. He wouldn't beat a motor car, but he could outrun the foot soldiers.

As Vittel cycled for his life, an engineer called Webber paddled a similar dinghy up the Debden to Woodbridge and knocked on Gleeson's door. This time the Irish giant, although dressed, was visibly shaking off sleep and smelled faintly of whisky. Webber was somehow even wetter than Vittel and his English suit had been lost overboard when a freak wave had nearly sunk him. Gleeson looked skywards and cursed, before appraising his charge in a new way.

"I'll see what I've got, you're not that much smaller than me." Webber scoffed at that.

"Sure, I've put on a few pounds since I moved into number fourteen... or is it stone?" Gleeson rubbed his belly, feigning embarrassment.

Webber stripped and dried while Gleeson rummaged and cursed upstairs, and when he did not reappear, Webber began to sort through his suitcase. He was a demolitions man and he had been equipped with a suitcase full of the latest in compact plasticised explosive. The Germans called it Hexogen, but the British knew it as RDX. He had a list of bridges, gas installations, and railway tunnels to be rigged on timers and he was bursting with excitement to begin.

Gleeson came downstairs carrying a pile of old clothes and looking annoyed until he caught the smell of almonds.

"Here," he said as he dropped the pile in the middle of the parlour, hesitating when he noticed the suitcase.

"Is that RDX?" he said, all annoyance gone from his voice.

11

"Hexogen," Webber replied curtly as he shut the suitcase. "Do you have a tool bag?" He asked in perfect English, while sizing up a pair of old overalls.

"You know, I think I do," Gleeson scratched his head and trudged back up the tiny staircase.

Just as Webber placed the last of his hexogen discreetly in his new tool bag, Vittel walked through the kitchen door looking pleased with himself.

"Codenames from now on, fellas," Gleeson said before either had the chance to compromise the other. "Everyone talks, eventually." A flash of darkness crossed Gleeson's amenable features as he remembered something painful.

"Kamel," Vittel said, his hand outstretched.

"Roheisen," Webber said taking his hand as he rose from kneeling over the tool bag.

The three men drank Gleeson's whisky and smoked his cigarettes in silence for a while. Gleeson became aware of Webber staring at him and he caught his eye.

"Yes?"

"I was wondering. What did they offer you?"

"Your masters?"

"Yes." Webber's middle-class London accent clashed completely with his overalls.

"Well," Gleeson explained, "they assured us that after the war the British will be forced to leave Ireland once and for all allowing us to reunify, and they have also said that *my* masters will be installed in power and supported as much as necessary."

"And you believe that?" Vittel scoffed.

"My masters believe it," Gleeson said.

Webber's reply was cut off by a knock at the door and Gleeson raised a hand for silence as he crept towards the window. Through a tiny chink he could see another soaking wet German standing in broad daylight and dripping onto the pavement outside his house. When he opened the door, he seized the man by his lapels and pulled him bodily through it, giving a couple of furtive glances up and down the quiet road. A short, severe-looking man with a thick, black, pointed moustache and striking grey-blue eyes stood awkwardly in a pool of seawater on the parlour rug.

"Handbuch," Gleeson said, giving his codename and offering his hand.

"Künstler," the new man said in a strange mix of Austro-Bavarian

He took the proffered hand, shaking it limply without making eye contact.

Künstler gave a barely perceptible nod to the other two men and marched into the kitchen, closing the door behind him. He emerged in a dry suit of clothes in the English style, while Gleeson craned his neck to see the discarded wet clothes in a pile on his kitchen floor.

Gleeson gestured to the chair he had occupied and Künstler took it, thanking him as he turned down the offer of whisky and a cigarette and asking instead for water and perhaps a piece of fruit. The others attempted small talk but Künstler was awkward and reticent. When he finished his apple, he stood abruptly and tossed the core into the fire before walking silently upstairs.

"He's a strange one," Gleeson said, raising eyebrows and turning down the corners of his mouth.

13

A few minutes later, Künstler came back into the room.

"I'll need you to clear out the larger bedroom for my operations room," Künstler announced in terrible English and turning his gaze to the kitchen, he added, "and I need that table too."

"You can have the smaller bedroom and I'll give you a folding card table," Gleeson responded firmly.

"Very well," Künstler said uncertainly, then he recovered slightly and said, "we can your way try."

Gleeson looked at the other two men in turn and then back to Künstler.

"I take it you're some sort of intelligence officer?"

"Something like that." He then spoke in German to Webber and Vittel.

"I report directly to the office of General Field Marshall von Ludendorff. Make sure that this man and anyone else arriving understands that." He paused, watching for their reaction, then continued. "After the invasion, they will want a list of who was the most useful, the most effective, and the greatest imperial servant and a separate list of who cowered in a house until the cavalry arrived." Without waiting for a response, he turned on his heel and headed back upstairs.

The two Germans explained to the Irishman what had been said over the sound of furniture being dragged around above their heads. Webber stood up and announced that since he now had a disguise that offered some level of legitimacy, he would carry out his work during the day.

"You'd better run it by *der Chef* upstairs," Gleeson said with a wink.

Webber rolled his eyes, put down his bag and plodded up the stairs.

They could hear the muffled voices discussing the merits of Webber's plan for some time before he reappeared looking dejected.

"He said that generals do not make plans for soldiers to ignore them."

Webber sank into his chair and accepted more whisky and another cigarette from Gleeson. "What's for breakfast, Paddy?"

"Porridge, me old mate," Gleeson said and hauled himself out of the chair. "I'll get it on."

Webber looked at Vittel, who pulled an 'it's not that bad' face. The four men sat around the kitchen table where Gleeson ate hungrily, Vittel ate mechanically, Webber ate tentatively, and Künstler ate another apple.

"It's not that bad," Webber said in an effort to encourage Künstler.

Gleeson only hearing the German word for bad glared at Webber before returning to his glutinous breakfast. Künstler rolled his eyes and turned his head away in something akin to disgust.

"I found these," Gleeson said through a mouthful of porridge and tossing two tarnished metal discs across the table to Künstler. They clinked as they hit his untouched bowl. "You know, when you left that pile of wet clothes on my kitchen floor?"

Künstler's hand darted for them, thrusting them straight into his pocket.

"That was a serious breach of security!" Künstler snapped.

"Yeah, deploying behind enemy lines without sanitising your kit *is* a serious breach of security!" countered Gleeson.

"Were you at the front?" Vittel asked, curious at the age and condition of the discs.

"Ja, I was in France and then the *Ost*," Künstler said, trying not to seem eager to boast.

"How did you end up in the SB?"

"I simply demonstrated the kind of attributes they look for in an officer of the Security Bureau. Someone decided that I would be more useful in intelligence than as *Kanonenfutter*," Künstler said pompously. He stood from the table, dropping his apple core into the cold porridge.

"I suggest we all get some sleep, it will be a long night," he said authoritatively.

The next two agents offered no specialisation, neither were they merely acting as couriers for Webber's plasticised explosives and Vittel's water poison. Experienced covert operators, they were both well versed in the local cartography. So, they were given wire cutters and crowbars and sent out into the night to wreak havoc on the local infrastructure. The plan was to start with safer, less immediately noticeable targets, like damaging train signal boxes and swapping around the cables in telephone junction boxes so that calls did not connect correctly.

While 'Rübe' was tall and wiry, with thinning hair and a cleanly shaven face, 'Pastinake' was a short, stocky man with a beard that made his age difficult to place. He smoked a pipe, and wearing his tattered rollneck he gave off the air of an old mariner. Both spoke faultless English with entirely forgettable accents.

"Don't you worry that you'll stand out? You know, with that great beard?" Gleeson asked him, rubbing his jaw.

"Ah," Pastinake said, unconsciously stroking his beard with one hand, while shaking his pipe with the other, "so, what happens if they are looking for a man with a big bushy beard and I shave it off?" He snapped his fingers next to his face. Gleeson nodded in deference to the man's dedication to the craft.

"Please now, come in stairs, you all!" Künstler announced in halting English.

"Why could you not have given him the larger bedroom?" Webber asked Gleeson as they squeezed around the card table to see the map.

"Where is Rübe?" demanded Künstler, looking for the other agent.

"You sent him to establish the O.P.," Pastinake said, impatiently.

"Ja, genau," he said curtly and continued in German, much to Gleeson's chagrin.

"Please take the opportunity while I am speaking to study the map, note the gun emplacements marked with red and with green. Note the number next to each which denotes the priority with which you will attack them. It is my intention to go from here tonight at 2100 hours and destroy or otherwise render useless as many of these installations as possible. We will deploy in two teams, red and blue; red will attack the targets marked red and blue, blue." He looked around to assess the comprehension on their faces.

The first team was to be led by Künstler, with Gleeson and Vittel, now referred to as Handbuch and Kamel. The second was to be led by Pastinake, with Rübe and Roheisen. They planned to spike the gun batteries and destroy the pillboxes along their section of coast. Each emplacement consisted of two pillboxes, a coastal gun, and an anti-aircraft gun. With this done, they were to split up with a map of various targets collated by Künstler. These included power supplies, telephone and telegraph lines, and the tyres and fuel tanks of vehicles outside the known addresses of any police or army officers. Once finished, they were to go into hiding at a new safehouse which was not marked on the map, the grid reference committed to memory instead, in case of capture.

The summer sun rose early over Suffolk, giving the cell a little over six hours of dark. However, the naval bombardment scheduled for midnight would bring the local garrison down on them within the hour, giving them only three hours to spike as many of the long-range guns and defensive positions as possible.

Gleeson produced six MP40s and spare magazines, while Roheisen doled out the hexogen and gave a short remind and refresh on its use, mainly for the benefit of Kamel. He demonstrated how to set the detonator and the most effective place for a small charge. They cleaned their weapons, checked their equipment, and waited for dark. As the sun disappeared in the west, they smeared coal dust on their faces and hands, synchronised watches, and as the last vestiges of light faded away they headed silently out of the back door and down the alley that ran between the houses.

"This is where we leave you," Künstler placed his mouth so close to Pastinake's ear that the whisper was barely more than the buzzing of a mosquito's wings.

The only sound for miles was that of waves breaking gently on the beach and the wind rustling the leaves of the trees. Roheisen led the red team south along the coastal path past three emplacements before reaching their first target. Künstler did the same to the north with blue team. Webber had rigged the timers for each and clearly marked them, with the idea of a near-simultaneous explosion offering the greatest chance to get all six installations and make it out to continue their work inland.

Red team found the first gun unmanned, so they placed the charge and rigged the longest fuse. They worked in complete silence, Webber desperate to earn the approval and respect of these professional agents and doing everything exactly as they did. The drill followed a set pattern: the first man cleared, the second man set the charge and the third kept watch at the rear. In a normal formation, they would have rotated, but as Webber was the explosives expert, he was always number two.

Blue team lacked the professionalism of Red because Künstler and Gleeson were conventional soldiers come to espionage later in life and Vittel was a chemist doing something extraordinarily brave for his country. They moved tactically enough into the first emplacement; a piece of hard standing surrounded by sandbags with a huge gun in the centre. The gun was an ancient Howitzer and would have embarrassed all involved if it were stood next to even the worst that Krupp had to offer, its presence on Britain's front line of defence was reassuring to those of the cell that knew about such things.

Künstler decided that because Vittel was a scientist and that engineering was the practical application of scientific principles, he should set the charges while Gleeson cleared the area. This left Künstler with the safe job of lookout. The first two emplacements went smoothly, suggesting that Vittel's poisoned water had kept the men of the Essex and Suffolk Royal Garrison Artillery away from their posts. When they came to the third gun, however, Vittel watched as Gleeson came up behind a smoking Tommy and ended his short life. It was not violent, the soldier had no opportunity to struggle, Gleeson simply placed one shovel-like hand over the man's mouth and nose, and with the other he coolly inserted a long stiletto blade into the soft skin at the base of his skull – the human off switch. As this was happening Künstler made his way in a flanking manoeuvre to take out the second gunner before his friend could alert him. He fumbled, dropping his knife and cursing, so the bombardier was alerted and went for his rifle leaning against the sandbags. Before he could reach it, Künstler threw himself wildly at the man and stabbed him repeatedly in a fit of silent rage. The scene was horrifying and grossly unprofessional, it confirmed to Gleeson what he had guessed all along. This man was a charlatan and a liability.

Vittel rushed forward to place the charge just as the first two exploded.

"Shit and corruption," Gleeson whispered as Künstler said something similar in German and they both turned to Vittel, who looked shamefaced but continued to rig the last charge.

Red team's charges and blue's final charges detonated just as the naval bombardment began. By which time the six agents were observing from the safety of the high ground nearby before their extraction inland. Künstler had ditched his blood-stained jacket to avoid looking too suspicious and they waited quietly at the edge of a forestry block, watching the pale-faced soldiers run from their barracks to man the now useless guns. When the roads were clear again, they went their separate ways, agreeing to meet at 0300 in the woods near the new safe house.

Gleeson decided that he would not reprimand Künstler, who, according to his own proclamation could make things either very easy or very hard for him. He placed a huge hand on the man's shoulder.

"Listen, Künstler," he said, pausing as the others jogged out of earshot. "Good work back there, you really know how to handle yourself."

He was, after all, a terrorist and master of deception who lived unnoticed in the enemy's country and had done for nearly two years.

"Thank you," he said, adjusting his collar and thrusting his jaw forward, "although it's a little different to the trenches. The noise is deafening there, I am not used to working in the quiet like this."

"Well, you did a fine job. I'll see you on the other side."

Gleeson jogged off without waiting for a reply.

"The other side of what?" Künstler mumbled to himself, thinking that Gleeson was an alright fellow after all. He had marked him out as questionable before, but he would be sure to single him out in his report later.

The towns and villages were busy now, the residents had not yet learned to hide in their cellars from bombs or shells, and they wanted to see some of the excitement for themselves. Künstler silently cursed their stupidity as he waited for an opportunity to slash a tyre on one of the staff cars across the road. He watched as an elderly couple complained about the bloody Boche and their bloody war, whilst walking painfully slowly past the car. When they were out of sight, he walked casually across the road and pretending to tie his shoelace, he stabbed the inside wall of the rear-right tyre. The noise came as a surprise to him, because he had always imagined it would be silent, but he had foolishly stabbed the knife into the bottom of the tire and so now the weight of the entire car prevented him from extracting the blade. Forced to leave it, he ran down the nearest alley and watched as the officer and driver whose car it was came out to investigate the noise.

"Oh bleedin' 'ell, Sir," the private whined, "the tyres gone flat."

"Gads, man," exclaimed the colonel. "Get it changed, tout de suite!"

"Yes, Sir!"

Künstler was satisfied that it wouldn't be long before the young Tommy would find the knife, so he decided to put as much distance between himself and them as possible. When he emerged from the other end of the alley, he started to run up the street.

"Here, where you going, mate? The action's that way," a man said walking casually in the direction of the bombardment.

"Zee Germans, zay are in-wading!" Künstler called out in his best impression of an Englishman, but he did not stop. Among the tactics recommended to the saboteurs was the creation of panic and hysteria. Shouting, arguing, and behaving stupidly were also on the list. As he rounded the corner, he heard the man take up his cry and he smiled.

The news of the invasion spread quickly through the civilian population after the church bells began to toll and soon the roads were blocked by hundreds of families fleeing Rudyard Kipling's fabled Hun.

They had all read the newspapers. They knew they were ruthless, raping and killing indiscriminately and torturing people for fun. There were even rumours in some of the less reputable rags that they had killed babies. Now horse-drawn buggies, hand carts and even the odd motor car stretched the length of all the major east-west roads in the region, preventing reinforcements from reaching the coast. Not that they were coming, all the telegraph lines had been cut hours ago and the telephones had not worked properly in days.

It was a similar scene up and down the coasts of Sussex, Kent, Essex, and Suffolk. One particularly vicious and daring agent had cut the chain-link fence of an army barracks and burned the accommodation blocks while soldiers slept inside. He was caught and beaten to death by the grief-stricken Tommies before he could be interrogated. The War Office in London was in full panic mode, with no means of communication, runners were returning with their messages undelivered, and carrier pigeons became their only effective means of communication with coastal defence. King George reached out to his cousin the Kaiser in a communique that never reached him.

Invasion – 1915

The wind bit mercilessly and men curled up tight against the cold to huddle together, covering the deck of the tightly packed landing craft. The high sides offered some protection, but at this altitude it was painful to breathe and the lack of overhead cover meant that the icy air swirled around the craft and sucked the heat from men's bones.

Oberleutnant Otto Kessler wore every piece of winter clothing he owned, as well as some that he did not, such as a pair of aviator's goggles and some sheepskin gloves taken from a careless Zep officer in the mess. He stared out at the approaching British coastline, attempting to identify prominent features in the hazy pre-dawn light and maybe figure out where exactly they would land. He looked up above his head at the huge silver beast that carried their landing craft. They were suspended from the Zeppelin by steel wire ropes that would release them just above the water at the opportune moment to motor onto the beach. He looked around him at the shivering men of his company, seeing a mixture of hardened veterans from his former parole battalion and fresh-faced youngsters sent direct from the depot.

Otto's debriefing in Pskov had been painstaking, with the same information raked over and over again.

"Describe the blast? How long was the shock wave? How many dead? How many injured? How hot did it feel?" Felsen and Geiger took turns questioning and seemed to really enjoy the details and the evident success of their monstrous creation.

When they were finally released it was heavily implied that in order to receive ongoing medical care, the men of the eighty-fourth must continue to serve, at least for the duration of the war. Most men were promoted by one rank, the most notable exception the old Bavarian Feldwebel Leutnant, who was told that he would never commission with his record.

The survivors numbered enough to fill most of the officer and NCO appointments for a full-size Storm company and Otto was able to secure a week's leave for every man Jack. The train journey west from Pskov was a long one, but the carriages occupied by the eighty-fourth were perpetually rowdy. The unit seemed to cycle through melancholy, drunken revelry, sleep, and upon waking sink back into a collective depression occasionally singing dirges until their spirits lifted once more.

Otto did not want to go to back to Gutersloh. His adoptive parents were dead, the town bored him, and all of his friends would be away in the army. So, when the train pulled in at Berlin Hauptbahnhof, he simply followed some of his men onto the platform. The city was teeming with soldiers in transit, horses and wagons, and more motor cars than Otto had ever seen in one place. He found a cheap boarding house, and when the landlady showed him around, he discovered that the place was filthy, every surface coated in a veneer of grime. The rooms and corridors were filled with emaciated prostitutes and gaunt-faced transient workers who eyed him contemptuously from the shadows. The only room she had available was a tiny garret at the top of four flights of stairs. It smelled damp and the bedlinen was stained yellow.

Otto felt compelled to accept because he knew that this was all he could afford and probably, given the number of troops on leave, all that was available. He left ten pfennigs, all he had, to secure the room and set out for the paymaster's office at the regimental headquarters, but he kept his small bag with him. Otto had not been entitled to pay in the parole battalion, but he calculated that he would have a few months of leutnant's pay and most of his NCO pay due to him from before that dark time.

The sprawling regimental headquarters was a throng of activity, with recruits moving about in squads, both running and marching. Newly commissioned leutnants saluted Otto with the vigour that came with all things new and shiny. As he returned the compliment, he could see the clarity of skin and the innocence in their eyes.

Meat for the grinder, he thought, knowing that most of these men would not see twenty years of age.

As he drew further away from Petrograd and the horrors of the Ost front, he had felt his humanity slowly return to him. He noticed it on the train, where he would find himself empathising with a young soldier over a trivial matter that before the atomic bomb he would have dissected mercilessly, destroying the boy's confidence and candour. The aftermath of the bomb and the sights he had seen would live with him for the rest of his life, but he genuinely believed that the ordeal had gone some way to healing him. To giving him the opportunity to get some of the old Otto back from before the punishment battalion and before von Bock's revenge. He felt a renewed faith in humanity after seeing the reactions of his men that morning in Petrograd, and the strange feeling he had experienced when shaking Major Felsen's hand still bothered him.

He was dreaming again, where before sleep had been no more than darkness followed by waking. Now he dreamt of children in uniforms carrying guns, of women fighting wars and of a man he somehow knew to be his grandson.

The paymaster's clerk rummaged for some time to find his records and referred back to Otto's dog-eared paybook several times before writing down a sum for him to consider.

"There must be some mistake, this is far too much." He had seen what happened to soldiers who received too much pay and spent it, only to have it recalled months later, leaving them unable to fulfil their obligations.

"I assure you, Herr Oberleutnant, this is accurate. You see here is your pay for three months as a feldwebel, three as leutnant, and four as oberleutnant." He jabbed at the entries as he talked him through his calculations.

"Interesting, do you have my promotion history on file?"

"Ja, Herr Oberleutnant." The clerk disappeared for a moment and returned with a grubby file. "You must be popular, Herr Oberleutnant, this file has seen a lot of traffic."

"Something like that, show me the entries please?"

"Here, Herr Oberleutnant." He pointed at the lines and one entry was redacted where it lined up with the date of his sentencing and below that was a fresh entry marking promotion to oberleutnant. That one was backdated to the start of his tenure in the parole battalion.

"Is this there a disciplinary record in there?" Otto asked.

"Here," the clerk produced a comparatively clean document with no entries, "clean as a whistle, Herr Oberleutnant."

"Curious. How much is a suite in the Adlon?" Otto asked, rubbing his jaw.

"Ach so, I'd say you have enough here to pay for a few nights with dinner and dancing two or three times over, Herr Oberleutnant." The clerk smiled, happy to live vicariously through these men who amassed sums like this only through months of prolonged hardship and exposure to mortal danger. "Do you need a female companion, Herr Oberleutnant?"

"Just the Marks, thank you," Otto said, admiring the man's enterprise.

Otto strolled through the camp gates, his pockets bulging with half of the cash he'd accumulated over a period during which he'd thought he was earning nothing at all. The Adlon was a short walk north through Kreuzberg and Otto took his time, absorbing the vibrant atmosphere of the new capital of Europe, thriving as new trade from new colonies filled the Chancelry's coffers.

At the Adlon he strode across the marble floor of the cavernous lobby, the sound of his hessian boots echoing in the muted milieu. Otto's uniform was clean, and he bore the badges and piping of an oberleutnant in one of the elite *Sturmbataillon*. He belonged in a place like this, he knew it, but he could not bring himself to feel it. His accent was not correct, and his education was that of a farm hand, but he had earned this commission and the perquisites and social standing that accompanied it, so why did he feel like such an imposter? Why was he slowing down, reluctant to speak with the clerk at the front desk?

"May I help you, Herr Oberleutnant?" asked the uniformed clerk. Everyone in Berlin seemed to have a uniform of some description.

"Ja, I'd like a junior suite with a view of the Brandenburger Tor, bitte."

"Naturlich, Herr Oberleutnant, how many nights?

"Three."

"Thank you, have you come from the Ost front?"

"Ja," Otto felt embarrassed, like he was bragging by simply answering a question.

"Let's see if we can't do something for one of our brave war heroes," the clerk said, keen to impress Otto with his patriotism and respect for his service.

"There, I have billed you for one night in our least expensive room and booked three nights in a suite. I hope that adequately conveys the hotel's appreciation for your service, Herr Oberleutnant?"

The exchange had buoyed Otto's mood and he stared about him at the decadence of one of the finest hotels in Europe as the bellboy led the way to his room.

The suite was larger than he could have imagined and more opulent than anything he had ever known. Everything was imported or handmade, or handmade and then imported. He tipped the bellboy and waited for him to leave before drawing a bath and stripping off, relishing the prospect of his first bath in over a year and the first private bath of his life. The clawfoot rolltop sat upon marble in a spacious, tiled room lit perfectly for the occasion.

Otto luxuriated in French bubbles, sipping German Sekt and allowing months of Russian filth and grime to soak away only to wake several hours later in cold water. The sun had set, and someone was rummaging around in the next room. He rose silently from the water and wrapped the softest towel in the empire around his waist. He approached the door carefully and burst into the room, hoping to catch whoever it was off guard.

The maid dropped her basket as her hand flew to her mouth and she let out a muffled scream. She was about Otto's age and taller than most women he had met. Blonde ringlets escaped from under her cap, dancing around in front of her green eyes and caressing her high cheekbones.

"I did not mean to frighten you, Fräulein," Otto said, whose towel fell to the floor as he extended his arms in a placatory gesture. She screamed again and he fumbled to re-cover himself.

"No, I am sorry, I should not be in here." Then her eyes fell upon Otto's uniform and a look of comprehension crossed her face. "Ach, so, you are a soldier. Did the desk clerk give you a special price?"

"Maybe."

"Well, if he did, that means that the room appears as empty on the maid's rota until he can get away to update it, but sometimes he forgets." She shrugged and Otto was mesmerised, for she was the most beautiful woman he had ever seen. She giggled and he realised he was staring.

"Sorry."

"Don't worry, it's fine, I'm sure you have seen so few women recently, I cannot be angry with you." Her smile blew his mind and he found himself crossing the room towards her. She looked at the ground shyly and giggled again.

"Please, mein Herr, put on some clothes. I could lose my position here if somebody saw us like this."

"Sorry, I... Of course... I'll get dressed right away," he said, struggling into his uniform trousers and becoming more naked in the process.

"I should continue with my work," she said, and Otto thought he caught a hint of reluctance in her voice.

"What is your name?" he called before she had opened the door.

"Brunhilda," she said, turning.

"Ich bin Otto," he said, pulling his braces over bare shoulders as he made for the door.

"It's nice to meet you, Otto."

"Do you *have* to go?" he whispered.

"I do," she said regretfully. Otto looked at her and then at the floor, then back to her, and he wanted to kiss her, he wanted to pull her towards him and wrap his arms around her. So why was he so scared? This was ridiculous, he was being ridiculous, he took half a step, and she didn't recoil in disgust. So he leaned in, he could smell her now, feel the warmth radiating from her and hear her gentle breathing. She must have grown impatient because she took his face in both hands and kissed him. Otto was transported back to France and the only other girl who had ever made his head swim like this. Why was he thinking of her when this beautiful woman was here in front of him, right now?

He placed his hands on her waist and drew her to him, wrapping his arms around her and pressing his body to hers.

Eventually, she broke away, breathless and flushed.

"I must go back to work," she panted.

"How long for?" croaked Otto.

"What time is it?" Otto looked at his watch and told her.

"One hour," she said.

"I will order some food and then afterwards, maybe we can go dancing?"

"I love dancing," she beamed.

Brunhilda's friend at reception fixed it so that Otto could have the suite for the entire week of his leave. She and Otto did very little dancing, but on the morning of the third day they found a priest and Otto burned his photograph of the girl in Bordeaux. I won't ask how long you will be away because I know that not even the Kaiser could say. So, I will only ask that you write to me and take this." She pressed a locket into his hand as the whistle sounded and a conductor announced that the train for Cuxhaven was departing. Through the window they kissed again and Brunhilda ran alongside the train, frustrated because her long legs should have kept pace for much longer, but the skirt she wore hobbled her movements.

~

The fresh meat joined the newly formed Z company 15th *Sturmbataillon Leibstandarte* Erich von Ludendorff at the staging area near Cuxhaven on Germany's west coast. The Fifteenth were notionally Ludendorff's personal guard, but as far as the order of battle went, they were no different from any other *Sturmbataillon*.

Z company spent June rehearsing amphibious beach landings with the rest of the Fifteenth and the youngsters began to overcome their fear of the scarred convicts that made up their chain of command. Otto reminded his men that they were new once, and for most of them it was not that long ago. He drilled them hard because the British were excellent fighting men and the beaches of East Anglia well defended. When some of the older men became sick, Otto had to order them to see the medical officer, and the diagnosis for all but one of them was a form of cancer. Hugo Schwab, an unteroffizier from Kassel had a new kind of illness that left his face covered with purple spots and his once thick hair patchy and thin. Otto sat at the man's bedside as he spoke to him through bleeding gums, managing only one-word answers to his oberleutnant's questions.

"The MO says that this is radiation sickness from the bomb." He held Hugo's hand and looked into his glassy eyes. "You don't have long to live, my friend."

"I'm so…tired," Hugo croaked.

"Shh," he cooed, "don't waste your energy trying to speak."

"What…what have we done?" he whispered, using his last ounce of strength to grab Otto's sleeve.

Otto imagined he was looking directly into Hugo's soul before the light in his eyes was extinguished and he was gone. His warm, limp hand rested in Otto's, who sat for some time before fetching a nurse and leaving to see another of his sick men. By comparison to poor old Hugo, they seemed well and were lamenting their misfortune at missing the great invasion, some sarcastically and others genuinely. He decided not to mention Schwab's death just yet, leaving the men in reasonably good spirits.

June 1915 – Loshavn, Norway.

The old man was strong. Stronger than he'd expected and now, as he watched the light fade from his eyes, he was glad for the respite. These last few years had made him soft, weak and most disturbingly, sentimental. He stripped off his feldgrau tunic and trousers, roughly grabbing one of the old man's limp, heavy legs to offer up a boot.

This is my lucky day, he thought wryly as he stripped the old man and dressed in his clothes.

Looking in the mirror he assessed his new appearance, he'd grown to admire his tailored German officer's uniform and the ill-fitting, cheaply made clothes hung about him like sacking.

Major Heinrich Felson watched as the flames licked the rim of the oil drum, devouring his uniform and as he sat in the dunes, he stared down at his faithful P08 and thumbed the knurled toggle button. The beach was empty, this was the back of beyond and he hadn't seen a soul since Kristiansand.

He rubbed his chin, feeling the stubble that was quickly becoming the beard he'd need if anyone wanted to see the old man's papers, because his real identity could not appear on any official record for either leaving Germany or entering Britain.

He'd arranged a flight with a pilot, only to find that he'd been shot down over the Channel hours before their rendezvous.

As the last vestiges of Major Heinrich Felsen were devoured in the flames, Henry Clive rose to his feet and hefted the Luger one last time. He drew his arm back to throw it far into the surf but changed his mind and pocketed the weapon instead.

His watch, a Lange & Söhne he'd bought in Berlin to replace his anachronistic Judex, told him that it was time to go. He kicked the barrel over and inspected the contents, it showed no signs of the artillery major's badges and piping and only an expert could guess it had ever been a German uniform. He walked briskly from the beach to the deserted jetty, admiring his new yacht as it grew closer.

A thing of beauty, with fine lines and a bluff bow, the blue hull complemented the teak deck and brass fittings. The old man certainly had taste; it was a shame he'd had to die. Clive had done his best to convince him to join him for one last voyage, offering to pay his passage back to Norway when they reached Aberdeen. Of course, he would never have reached the coast, but Clive thought a burial at sea was the least he could do for the ancient mariner.

As he watched Norway disappear over the horizon, Clive attempted to calculate the time that had elapsed since he last went home. Five, perhaps six years? He had a plan and it involved fooling Winston Churchill. He thought himself a capable liar, but could he weave a tapestry worthy of the bulldog himself? As long as the naval airship division bombed London enough to cover his tracks, he could make anything true. If he could reach the outskirts of London before the invasion began, then the journey south would be much easier.

Clive adjusted the sails and put the helm over, trying to get the most out of this unfortunate westerly wind. If he could luff and touch until it backed around, he might make a straight run of it without messing about tacking upwind. He tied off the tiller and went below.

The passage to Aberdeen in northeast Scotland would take at least fifty hours and he was not confident enough to trust in Joshua Slocum's mythological pilot of the Pinta and leave his post for any longer than a few minutes. So he cleared the saloon table, tipped the contents of a small tin out and began to arrange it into lines with a business card before producing a silver straw and snorting a small amount of the cocaine into his nostril. He sniffed, not bothering to wipe his nose as the chemical taste hit the back of his throat. He left the lines racked up and planned to go below for a bump whenever he felt drowsy.

The sun tracked across the sky providing a brief period of warmth at the zenith, then cooled again until it was gone behind the waves to the west. Uneventfully, the night ran on, the dawn broke in the east and with it came the wind.

Clive hove to, tied off the helm and lay forward to reduce sail. With a storm jib on the forestay and two reefs in the mainsail, he put the boat back into the wind and began again, westwards to Aberdeen. He clambered below and took a morning hit of cocaine, before donning oilskins and taking a long drink of water.

A gentle rolling swell began and Clive sighed. He could feel the storm in his guts as he watched the horizon, the sea, and the grey sky without shifting his gaze. White horses came to nudge the hull as he ate breakfast, again he hove to and reduced sail.

By lunch the waves were frothy hillocks, forcing the little boat to climb and drop, climb and drop. Clive did not eat; he had lost his breakfast overboard and could not face the thought let alone the action of refilling his stomach. As the hillocks grew to walls of sheer, green water, he clung to the helm and screamed at Poseidon, Manannan, and at Neptune, gritting his teeth each time he crested the waves and wincing as he hit the trough. By the second nightfall the cocaine was half gone and Clive was howling at the moon, soaked by spray and sick as a dog. He had never known fear like this, never known such a complete lack of control at the mercy of the gods he invoked, naked before the elements in a tiny blue boat.

He awoke with a start, heart pounding and terrified. The sun had dried him and he still clung to the tiller with both hands. The boat was hove to, bobbing gently on a much-diminished sea, perhaps the pilot of the Pinta had come after all. He rose from his seat in the cockpit and vomited over the side.

Below he found all was adrift, nothing had remained in place but for the three lines of cocaine on the saloon table, untouched and beckoning his beleaguered brain. He devoured it, drank whisky, and changed into fresh clothes.

On deck he ran forward and found that he could see land. He had no idea what land, so shaking out the reefs he'd put in the mainsail and bending on a larger jib, he set a course for the land. The wood of the cockpit smelled of urine where he'd soiled himself so he rinsed it with a bucket and put the boat before the wind once more. He began to sweat, hot and anxious, this was the cocaine, too much with no sleep, but still, he sailed on as his stomach growled and his head span, the land growing larger on the bow.

~

The naval bombardment of Suffolk, Essex, Kent, and Sussex began at midnight on Thursday, the first of July 1915. Once again U-boats played a pivotal role, with crews either laying mines or spending nerve-wracking hours in absolute silence waiting for the ships of the Royal Navy to scramble in defence. The submariners in their iron coffins sank a devastating number before they were even in range of the German surface vessels. The mine layers concentrated their efforts on the area to the east of Lincolnshire where they created a vast field of mines to prevent the British from counterattacking from the north.

The zeppelins that were not landing troops began to drop bombs at one in the morning. They focused on military targets highlighted by the agents on the ground with fires. Further sabotage of AA guns meant their only real concern lay with the fighter planes of the Royal Flying Corps, and these were met by German fighters and drawn away from the bombers.

Church bells rang throughout the home counties as the men of the Fifteenth *Sturmbataillon Leibstandarte* Erik von Ludendorff waded through the surf under covering fire from a machine gun mounted to their landing craft, only to be greeted by a hail of lead from the brave British defenders. These men, despite suffering the effects of poisoned water and with nothing heavier than a maxim gun, had taken up positions determined to defend their island home. The men of the British Expeditionary Force, slipping on vomit-soaked duckboards, fought tirelessly with shit running down their legs, as the Huns on the beach swelled and began to overwhelm them.

Otto Kessler judged that Z Company had found the bravest, healthiest, and best-equipped Tommies on the entire coast, and they knew their trade. Calling out to the other guns, staggering reloads and actually hitting what they aimed for. Otto once again found himself in a shell hole, trying to pick which one of his brave, beautiful boys to send over the top to certain death.

"Kellerman, Jansch, you're the fastest, you go, everyone else fire on my command."

He was in charge of the company and fighting like this was not his job anymore, but there were no cosy headquarters on a beach landing. Not until his men secured the beach and established one. A few of the new boys had not learned the difference between taking cover from effective enemy fire and sitting in a shell hole waiting to die, although watching the head of the man next to you explode mid-way through the punchline of a Rosa Valetti joke usually provided an invaluable learning experience.

When it happened to the man on your other side too, a soldier quickly found novel ways to become an even smaller target.

There was a break in the dunes to the south and Otto planned to exploit it, but first he would need to even the odds. They waited. These Vickers guns rarely jammed, but when they did, the other gun would usually need to reload by the time it was operational again. That was their opportunity and they would grab it with both hands and shake it until the loose change fell out. They seemed to be waiting forever and began to think that perhaps they would run out of ammunition completely before the Tommies suffered a stoppage.

"GO!"

They all gave covering fire as Heiny Kellerman set off, followed by Bert Jansch, a primed stick grenade in each hand. They ran directly into the jaws of the momentarily disabled beast, posted all four bombs and threw themselves desperately into cover.

Immediately the blast was seen, Otto gave the order to attack and the whole shell scrape charged. They overran the position and continued through it, turning south to attack the line from its vulnerable left flank.

This kind of thing was what the *Sturmbataillon* was made for. Fast, aggressive fighting with relentless momentum. With every Vickers gun they disabled, they allowed more of their comrades to approach from the beach, and soon every living man of Z company was back in the fold, screaming, killing and high on adrenaline. The long barrels of the Lee Enfield did not stand a chance in these confined quarters, and the only injuries came from the gun crews and subalterns firing fat slugs of showstopping lead from their Webley Mark V Service revolvers.

Within three hours, the enemy on either side of Otto's target was neutralised, and he began to establish a beachhead, launching a sequence of coloured rockets to invite the *Sturmbataillon* commander to join the party. The morning's fighting was successful in most areas, and where it was not, the naval gunners simply waited for the first wave of troops to die and then softened it up some more for a second.

By the time Oberstleutnant Helmut von Klempthofen landed with his staff and personal guard, Otto had used his initiative to push the whole battalion out to the limit of sight and sound, so that they occupied a huge but manageable area of the Suffolk Coastline. The Oberst rode ashore on a magnificent white charger. Adorned with the dress uniform of a Colonel of the Guards, he looked better suited for a portrait sitting than a largescale, multiservice invasion of an island whose defences had not been breached in this manner for nearly nine hundred years.

"Herr Oberst," Otto greeted as he strode over to his CO to give him the good news.

"Kessler!" the Colonel snapped. "Do you not salute your commanding officer?"

"Not in the field, Sir," Otto said, confused, "it draws snipers, I have see—"

"Nonsense, man," he cut in, "look at me, I just rode through the surf on a *Verdammt* white charger. If some cowardly *Engländer* with a scope bandaged onto his Lee Enfield was waiting to see who was in charge, I would be dead already!"

41

"Ja, Herr Oberst!" Otto said firmly as he threw up a parade-ground-perfect salute.

"*Vielen Dank*," he said sardonically, returning the compliment with about as much lustre as the turd his horse had just deposited on the sand.

"Where are my men?"

"I took the liberty of pushing out the limit of sight and sound as per the di–"

"Get them here now, I want every man jack assembled in front of me in ten minutes." The Colonel cut him off again, "Do not just stand there like a fish, Oberleutnant, get my *batailon*."

"Ja, Herr Oberst!" Otto said, saluting again.

Before going to find the other company commanders, Otto spoke quietly to the adjutant, a sensibly dressed man with the air of a combat veteran if Otto had ever seen one.

"Does the Oberst know how many men are in his unit?"

"I doubt it, he put his boots on the wrong feet this morning," the adjutant said with a wry smile.

"Thanks," he said, returning the smile with a knowing look between warriors.

Otto arranged for enough men to be recalled so as to maintain the line and to appear complete to the colonel on the beach. He crossed his fingers against an English counterattack as he listened to the pompous address of a man so detached from the realities of war, that he had been overheard arranging for his private yacht to be sailed to Chichester when the army had taken the Solent. He feared for the fate of these men and hoped, for the sake of the empire, that indifference such as this was not common.

Mercy – Berlin 1945

The six-story apartment building wasn't unusual and it didn't particularly stand out, but when Olga was forced to consider that this was home to forty or fifty people, their possessions either intact and visible to the world or destroyed and buried under tons of rubble, the implications of the scene suddenly became apparent to her.

"That's ours on the fourth floor," Rudi told her as he pointed to half a living room and two-thirds of a kitchen. The sink and associated plumbing remained fixed to the wall while the floor beneath was gone, and Olga could see the pots and pans in the cabinet next to it.

"Who else do you live with? Why hasn't your mother taken you somewhere else?" she asked.

"She is in hospital and my sister Carla is a *Flak Helferin*. She will be home later, hopefully with some food." He looked at her with his big eyes, like he knew that he had lost the love of his life before he even got her. At the same time, he was completely unable to process these emotions and confused about the feelings he had and how to act on them. He began to walk and then stopped, lifted his foot again like a malfunctioning robot, then he turned and kissed Olga on the cheek before scurrying off in the direction of the lobby.

"We can't stay here," Olga said through a mouthful of the black bread they had found on the soldiers.

"I know," he said, swallowing his bread, "my mother will probably take us to her sister's in Aldershof when she is discharged."

Olga turned to look him directly in the eye.

"That's not what I mean, Rudi. We can't stay in Berlin, it's not safe and you are too important to be risking your life like this."

"What do you mean, too important?"

"Don't you feel it, Rudi? That sense of wisdom, like you've done this all before many times, like you know what it is to be old and sore, to love and to grieve?" Olga implored.

"I…" he paused, turning a piece of bread over in his hands as if it alone contained the answers to all the questions in the universe.

"I guess I thought it was growing up in this," he waved an arm at the missing wall and the scene of destruction beyond. "The hunger, the loss, the uncertainty. I have been told by the *Opas* on the gun line that I have an old soul, but I didn't understand, I didn't really pay it any mind. I know that I'm not like other boys and it has always worried me, and I speak my mind too often." He held out his hand to show scarred knuckles, presumably from the rulers of sadistic teachers or overzealous Hitler Youth leaders.

"Tell me, Olga, what's it all about?" He looked at her now and she saw the ancient man behind those youthful eyes, ringed through lack of sleep and malnourishment, red from the ever-present dust, but deep and wise, like a shrivelled monk or a frail priest buried in layers of robes.

"You're very intelligent, Rudi," she said with a sympathetic smile. "You are driven and fearless, you have an enduring will, an undying desire to right injustices. It was these admirable qualities that led you to this life of many lives, this pseudo immortality, this quest for a twentieth century that isn't blighted by the suffering and mass genocide committed by a handful of despots." She took his hand in both of hers. "What I'm saying, Rudi, is that in your desperation to make the world better, you invented a device capable of time travel."

He wasn't incredulous or surprised, he didn't spit his bread across the room or pace about proclaiming the absurdity of the notion. Instead, he smiled solemnly and nodded. He found that he already knew, already possessed the dormant knowledge, like a sleeping beast was stirring in the depths of this twelve-year-old boy. He looked at her seriously and spoke a single word.

"Torsten."

"What?"

"I don't know why, but that's really important, that name is significant to this whole thing. Have you heard it before?"

"Yes," Olga said," and she rifled through her sheaf of papers and found a page of calculations. "Here, Torsten Schweighöfer, does this mean anything to you?"

She handed Rudi a page, fully expecting him to say no.

"I feel like I have seen it before, but I don't understand any of it. I know that we should make a copy, though."

He immediately began to scrawl out the calculations on a blank page and as he did, he seemed to release something within himself. It did not give him the knowledge of quantum mechanics to make sense of the formulae, but he knew that one day he would and that inside him was the impetus to reach that level of education and to build this time machine.

"We have to leave Berlin," he said, looking up from the page.

"We can't take your mother," Olga said ruefully.

"We can't just leave her here for the Russians," Rudi said, standing from where he sat on the floor, and just as he didn't understand why this made him irrationally angry, nor did Olga.

"What do you think you know, Rudi? What will become of her if she stays?"

He closed his eyes, linked his hands behind his neck, bringing his elbows together.

"She is destined to lead a horrible life, all I remember is hospital visits and pain, shame over something I let happen, and pity. I pity her, that is my abiding emotion." He looked at Olga, pained and glassy-eyed and asked, "What kind of life is that?"

"What if she never leaves the hospital?" Olga said solemnly.

Rudi did not want to acknowledge what she meant by this, but he knew somehow that it was right. He also knew that if the overriding emotion over lifetimes of knowing this woman was pity, when he thought now of his mother, *Mutti* lying in hospital with Russian shrapnel in her chest, then the only word for this tacit agreement, the only one he wanted to accept, was mercy.

"I don't want to know. Just stop the pain, okay?" He broke down, the boy he was physically took over, and he rocked in his former lover's arms as Olga stroked his hair and thought of her little brother Klaus for the first time in months.

Rudi woke to find his sister snoring nearby and Olga gone, and assuming she was relieving herself, he rolled into a more comfortable position and went back to sleep.

Olga moved inconspicuously through the dark streets wearing Carla's *Flakhelferin* uniform complete with blue *Stahlhelm*. She was carrying Carla's papers, her own Jericho and Rudi's knife in her shoulder bag. Just another loyal German on her way to help defend the Fatherland from the British *Terror Flieger*. She skirted the edge of the hospital and made her way along the banks of the *Landwehr* Ship *Kanal* until she reached an unguarded service entrance. She had surreptitiously gleaned the room number from Carla when she came home from her shift on the guns at Zoo Tower. The Berliners were afforded no rest from the bombs, suffering attacks from the Americans in the day and the British during the night.

Rudi had spent the better part of an hour talking Carla down, convincing her that Olga was no threat and her presence was sanction by their mother.

Olga watched the entrance for an hour before risking entry. There seemed to be no formal security and the hospital was so busy that no one challenged her as she wove a path through the beds and bodies in the poorly lit hallways. She found Emma Kessler in a ward of maybe twenty snoring patients with various ailments, and when she thought she was looking at Rudi's mother, she checked the chart to be sure.

Emma lay sleeping, her white hair a halo and her expression pained, if it hadn't been for the wet, rasping breaths, Olga would have taken her for dead, such was the pallor of her skin and the stillness of her repose.

This is it, thought Olga. *Either the cold-blooded murder of a helpless woman in her bed, or merciful euthanasia, a kindness, a reprieve from a life of untold suffering.* Olga tried breathing deeply, tried picturing the Emma Kessler of 1961, the woman with filled with opiates and regret, her translucent skin and tiny frail form beneath the covers. Was she really going to do this? Was this right? Was it truthfully a kindness, or was it to be rid of dead weight, a burdensome old woman who would slow them down?

"It's you," Emma Kessler said in her strong Berliner accent as she woke to see Olga standing over her bed. "You usually come sooner than this."

"I've done this before?"

"Oh, yes, I know what you're thinking and yes, this is a mercy, a kindness. Please…" she jerked upright in a fit of coughing, and Olga slipped into the shadows lest a nurse appear.

"Don't worry *Schatzi*, nurses do not come for something so trivial, not anymore." Olga stepped back into the light from the door and Emma grasped her hand with surprising strength.

"Listen to me, *liebling*, we've done this many times and in many ways, so I know how I like it, and I want you to do exactly as I ask." Olga nodded as Emma continued. "I want you to find me enough morphine to drop a horse. There's a cupboard down the hall, you can get it from in there." She let go of Olga's hand and seemed to shrink before her eyes.

48

Olga moved quickly and quietly, her heart pounding in her chest. This was a foolish, sentimental risk, but it was the dying wish of the mother of the man she loved. She spotted the cupboard and used Rudi's knife to force the lock. Inside she searched frantically for the right phial, knocking over several boxes as she searched. Every sound she heard could be a nurse or a doctor or someone to whom she would have to try to explain this rummaging. She found a phial of morphine and a hypodermic needle and shoved them into her pockets, but just as she closed the door she heard footsteps growing louder, so she moved away and cast about for what to do. On the floor she saw a bucket of bloody bandages, and she picked it up just as a petite matron with a face like a miller's shovel came around the corner.

"What are you doing here, girl?" she demanded, eyeing her *Luftwaffe* uniform suspiciously.

"I was sent to help *Schwester*, I am taking these to be cleaned," she said, desperate for a reason to leave.

"Cleaned? This isn't the Great War! These must be disposed of properly and new ones taken to the ward." She produced a key and made for the cupboard. "I will give you a box of new bandages to take back with you, and you can toss that bucket into the *kanal*."

She was going to see the mess Olga had made and even if she did not suspect her of stealing, she would cause some sort of fuss and papers would be checked, questions would be asked, and Olga could not risk that happening.

"What ward have you been assigned to? This is ridiculous, clean the bandages? We used to do that, you know." She opened the door and cried out, "*Oh, Mein Gott…*" Olga shoved her bodily into the store and spun her around. She grabbed her by the shoulders and straightening her own arms as she brought her helmeted head back, she drove the rim of it into the nurse's face as she drew her in. The rim of the helmet left a nasty gash in the nurse's forehead, and she slumped down to the floor. Olga grabbed some more morphine and a handful of other drugs and supplies, shoving them into her shoulder bag before locking the nurse in and hurrying back to the ward.

Emma was dozing, but she started when Olga approached her.

"Oh, well done, *Schatzi*." Emma pressed a locket into her hand, saying, "Give this to Carla, it was my father's. Now, you take the phial and stab it with the needle, that's it, now turn it upside down and draw back the plunger." She was smiling, a truly happy smile of anticipation. "That's good, now get it all, excellent, now stick it into my drip. Thank you so much, just give that knob a twist anticlockwise. Perfect." Emma eyed Olga with a look of genuine contentment on her face. Her proximity to Rudi, the bond between mother and son, the unending carousel of living and dying had taken its toll.

"You might want another for your friends on the way home," she said dreamily. Olga shrugged, loaded another phial, corked the needle, and dropped it into her pocket.

She had given Emma a lot of morphine and it looked as though she had already gone when she grabbed Olga's wrist again and fixed her a with very different expression, ominous and dark.

"Beware of *der Engländer*!" she hissed, her intense gaze holding Olga's.

"Who? Olga asked, desperately.

"*Der Engländer*," she gasped, her grip loosening before her hand fell limp at her side.

Olga kissed her forehead, closed her eyes, and shot a few furtive glances around the ward before leaving quickly, pressing a hand against her bag to stop the glass phials from jangling. She left via the canal exit unhindered and made her way back to Rudi and Carla.

It was only a short walk to the apartment and Olga cried silently as she thought of what she had just done. She could not decide if it had been good or evil and doubted that she would ever truly come to terms with it. As she walked south along Baerwaldstraße, three teenagers in the uniform of the *Volkssturm* appeared from a side street and seemed to be staring at Olga. She could not run; she would have to try and bluff her way out of this on fourteen-year-old Carla's papers.

"Evening, *Fräulein*," the tallest said, a spotty youth with irregular features that his mother no doubt assured him he would grow into. He smiled, showing nicotine-stained teeth. Olga looked up from a partially bowed head, trying to appear younger and in fact appearing rude.

"Papers," he said laconically, holding out his hand.

She produced the Luftwaffe document and smiled shyly, the way she had in her old life, when she lived in London and with the Altstötters.

"Long shift?" he said casually.

"You know how it is, those *verdammt* Amis won't let up," she said nervously, throwing in a chuckle for good measure.

"I'm sorry, did you say you were on your way to report or on your way home?" the boy asked, sounding aggressive now, challenging her, testing her story.

"Home," she said without missing a beat, and she really smiled now, her most dazzling smile bearing her shining white teeth.

"This says you live in Prenzlauer-Berg and your duty station is Zoo Tower, so how have you ended up this far east?" His tone was almost triumphant now, like he had caught her in a lie.

"Listen," she said, placing her bag carefully on the ground, kicking it under a bench and making eye contact as she stood. "I went to see my boyfriend, but he couldn't make me happy." She frowned playfully, "I bet *you* three…" she ran a finger down the front of the boy's tunic, pushed through them and turned, "big, strong, men could, couldn't you?" She walked into the side street backwards and as she turned again, she hitched her restrictive skirt up.

Olga walked several metres into the dark street and the young men followed, leering and lupine as they stalked towards her, laying down their rifles, until the leader spoke.

"No, Dieter, keep yours handy, just in case." He smiled at Olga, revealing those awful teeth, and she returned it with the most salacious grin she could muster.

"Okay, Udo," Dieter said, disappointed to be missing out.

"You'll get your turn," he breathed, eyeing his prey less than a metre away now.

Olga looked at Udo, all skin and bone, with no conditioning and the most important years of his young life on starvation rations. She had the hypodermic needle in her left hand, hanging limply at her side while she took her helmet off and held it with her right. Olga waited until she could smell the cigarettes and halitosis on Udo's breath while she pretended to look about for somewhere to put her heavy steel helmet. Using the ruse to put her entire body weight into the blow, she struck. He staggered, and she was on him, pushing him bodily towards Dieter, who was desperately trying to get a bead on her without shooting his friend. The bodies collided, Dieter's rifle was forced upwards, and he fired into the air as she reached around and stuck him with the morphine. The third boy grabbed her from behind, lifting her in a rib-cracking bear hug. She kicked out forwards at Udo, causing his nose to explode, thick red blood spreading all over his face. Again, she kicked him, this time in the chest, throwing her assailant off balance and causing him to stagger back. His grip loosened just enough and she was able to wriggle free.

She spotted the rifles leaning against the wall and brought one to bear, training it on the hugger and glancing at the other two. Udo stirred but Dieter was out cold, perhaps even dead. Olga advanced on her prey, and it was her turn to glower, to instil fear, to exploit perceived weakness and to feel powerful. She turned the weapon, striking him sharply with the wooden butt and opening a livid wound on his forehead which knocked him to the ground.

Olga rounded on Udo who was struggling to stand, tears streaming down his teenage face, and she became aware of the adrenaline coursing through her as she loomed over her quarry. Udo knew now that he had bitten off more than he could chew and finally, after years of bullying, he knew what it was like to lose, to have the shit beaten out of him and most humiliating of all to have this done to him by some *Schlampe Flakhelferin.*

Olga moved quickly, removing the bolts from the three rifles and tossing them, then she searched the boys and found bread, a lighter, and a Swiss army knife. She composed herself, stepped back into the main street and retrieved her bag from under the bench. She walked quickly back to the apartment and silently removed Carla's uniform, before lying down in the bedroom they were all sharing, the only room with four walls, and pretended to sleep as her heart pounded in her chest.

Army – 1915

Captain Sir Gerald Clive was not a highly trained professional soldier but a landed aristocrat with the power, influence and means to receive a King's commission based on his time in the Officer Training Corps of his boarding school. He'd once heard a man he respected say, "Never mind manoeuvres, just go straight at 'em!" He was misquoting Admiral Lord Nelson, the famous naval commander, and this was the extent of the good captain's tactical awareness.

Through sheer luck, he now had command of an entire battalion of men on manoeuvres in Thetford, Norfolk. Lieutenant Colonel Henry Bradshaw, an old school friend who had just returned from Ireland with the Norfolks, invited him to come down in uniform for the weekend and dust off the cobwebs before he was called up proper. The plan was a night in the mess in Bury St. Edmonds, then a weekend observing the professionals in Thetford.

"Don't worry, Gerry, I won't let on that you're a territorial, it'll be our little secret," he'd said with a conspiratorial tap on the side of his nose.

When he woke in the early hours of Thursday morning to the sound of church bells, he found that all the field officers had been called to an emergency orders group in Woodbridge. He now had a crowd of subalterns around him asking the senior captain and de facto local commander for orders of their own. He excused himself into a side room to collect his thoughts.

Right, Gerald, you were born for this sort of thing, it's in your blood, now get out there and take control.

Gerald had a great many shortcomings, but despite these he had charisma in spades and an uncanny knack for names. Only the previous night he'd charmed and schmoosed his way around the mess, gathering information and collecting useful allies.

"Company 2 ICs," he said firmly and four captains with more experience than he possessed in any one of their little fingers emerged from the crowd of nearly twenty officers. He turned to a young second lieutenant with further orders.

"Go and find the company sergeant majors and any other warrant officers and bring them here."

Gerald invited the captains to join him in the side room. Gerald was an intelligent man, he could be cunning, and he had no intention of showing his inexperience.

"Look, I don't know any of you from Adam," he said as the door closed, "but if Henry saw fit to give you a command in his battalion, then you must be damn fine officers." He used the CO's first name intentionally to demonstrate their familiarity.

"Now, let's just make sure we're all on the same page, what?" He led them to a map table. "Now, err, Marjoribanks, show me our position and the likely direction of the enemy threat?"

"We are here, and the likely threat would either be east or south," he said, eager to impress his colonel's old school chum.

"Jolly good. Boydell, mark for me friendly units in the vicinity that we could rely on for mutual support," Gerald instructed, handing the man a pencil.

"Well, Sir," he said, smiling, "Division has been in the process of forming since the Christmas day attacks." He pointed to the surrounding towns. "We form part of 208th, 2nd/1st Norfolk and Suffolk Infantry Brigade, as you know, and we have the 2nd/3rd Howitzers to our west at Blenheim lines."

"Excellent. Brokenshire? Features on the map that stand out to you as potential defensive positions?"

"It's pretty flat around here, Sir Gerald, so might I suggest we nip across the road to the Keep?"

"Capital idea, it's not err, *occupied* as it were?"

"No, the majority of Two Battalion are on manoeuvres in Thetford already."

"Well, might I suggest we reconvene this in the Keep?" suggested Gerald congenially, while rolling up the map. "Have the NCOs and subalterns get your men and equipment over there, then meet me in the operations room in ten minutes."

Gerald's mind raced as he walked alone across the road to the Keep, where the gate guard saluted him.

"Thank you," he said, returning the compliment. "Listen, Private, how many of you stayed behind to guard the camp?"

"Ten, Sir. Eight Toms, a screw, and a sergeant."

"Jolly good, carry on." The soldier relaxed ever so slightly.

Gerald was up on current affairs, and he knew what the Germans had been doing all over Europe, he also knew that the once-great Royal Navy was on its knees. An unprepared force was not going to repel this invasion, but they might hold some ground that offered no immediate tactical significance to the Boche. And a man with the right attitude might build himself a little enclave in which to ride this mess out.

He took out a notepad and began to list ways the Germans could attack this walled compound with its Keep and armoury. He wrote: ground, artillery, air, poison gas, starvation. Next to these he wrote suitable countermeasures, and soon he had a list of tasks for his new battalion.

"Listen, chaps," he began. He now had the four 2ICs and their Sergeant Majors, as well as the machine gun lieutenant and the quartermaster. "The Hun is at the gate!" He felt very pleased to quote Kipling so aptly, but no one else seemed to appreciate it.

"QM, I need you to send out some men who know about these things and find healthy livestock. Get horses if you have to, we may be here for some time. You'll need to source water, obviously a well within the walls would be ideal and whatever else you think you may need to outlast a prolonged siege."

"Lieutenant Bathurst, place a machine gun in each of the guard towers and then occupy the topmost window in any buildings with a vantage point. Rather try to avoid uniformity."

"Brokenshire, send a platoon of A company with some pioneers from HQ and improve our line of sight, we want to get rid of any trees and even tall buildings that will prevent us from seeing the enemy. Put the other half on guard and absorb the Two Battalion men into one of your platoons. Then I want you to think on the problem of communication… I intend to bring the other battalions up on our left and right to form a line, keeping the Bosh in the southeast if we can." As he spoke, he paced the large operations room with its views of both the camp and the outside world.

"Boydell, try to link up the Howitzers, establish reliable communications and get a battery of the smallest guns they have here." He looked out of the window at the parade ground and the expansive park area and continued. "Set them up wherever they think is best in the middle over there."

"Marjoribanks, I want anti-aircraft guns." He looked at the captain and blinked. "Take who and whatever you need and work it out, and if you do leave anyone behind, have your CSM put them on the guard list."

"Gower, take the remaining pioneers and push out to the, the err…"

"The limit of sight and sound, Sir Gerald?" offered Captain Gower, a chinless coat hanger in a beautifully tailored uniform.

"Yes, that's it, do that, then get yourselves dug in or find a nice tall building if Brokenshire hasn't blown it up yet, what?" He laughed at his own joke. "And see if you can't get hold of some machine guns, have a poke about in the armoury." He turned to the assembled men with hundreds of years of combined experience, all hanging on the word of a jumped-up officer cadet and smiled. It was the smile that had masked a thousand lies, stayed schoolmaster's canes and parted many a pair of fair legs. Gerald was not particularly handsome, but he understood how to learn what people wanted, to listen and to speak the words they craved with such conviction that his silver tongue was often worth its weight in gold.

Henry Clive swore that he would never take cocaine again after his landfall and subsequent journey had been a waking nightmare. Eventually running aground on the beach at Seaton Carew near Middlesbrough he'd had to walk six miles through marshland to reach the nearest train station. In the town he had sought out a pawnbroker and sold the gold and jewellery *acquired* during the last year of war on the eastern front. He wasn't proud, but he was glad of the money which provided train fare, board and a most welcome change of clothes. Suitably dressed for London, he had boarded the train only hours before the invasion began, arriving at Euston to the sound of bombs falling and planes buzzing overhead.

With an attaché case containing the carefully doctored files, he made his way to Whitehall and the offices on Cannon Row, simply stepping into the chaos where, if forced, he planned to give the name Jones. Mandarins and agents rushed in every direction, gathering files either to be taken north or burned.

This is what it must have been like in Berlin, at the end, Clive mused.

He'd been in Hamburg, denazifying teenagers who hero worshipped Hitler and believed in *Der werwolf.*

"Don't forget this one," Clive said to a reliable looking clerk in his mid-forties. "That's to go to the First Sea Lord you understand?"

"Yes sir, anything else?" he asked, pushing his glasses up his nose.

"Yes, I need the list."

"Sorry sir? The list?"

"Damn it man, the list, Winnie's list," Clive said impatiently.

"Oh, of course sir, right you are." The clerk returned a minute later with a fat envelope stuffed full of files, paperclips and the corners of photographs protruding from the top.

"Very good, err—" he eyed the man, waiting for his name.

"Bain sir."

"Ah, yes, good work Bain and the best of luck," Clive winked and made for the door. He couldn't believe that had been so easy, even if those files didn't make it to Churchill, this little treasure trove was enough to see him through the war and the occupation with his skin intact.

The Clive's London house in Mayfair appeared to be let, but on closer inspection it seemed that the tenants had fled. Clive found the key in its usual place under a pot of rosemary and let himself in. Some minutes later with a cup of tea in hand, he sat to read through the files.

"Good God, this is every thug, villain, rabble rouser and political dissident in London," he said aloud. One in particular caught his eye, Harrold Percival Tench, formerly of the Royal Navy, quartermaster aboard the HMS *Indefatigable.*

"Dear me Harry, you have been a busy boy…and you might be just the man I need."

Occupation – 1915

The British fought like lions, but against overwhelming numbers, a sabotaged infrastructure, and inferior technology, it was less than a week before Hindenburg was accepting the sword of Sir Charles Douglas, a man who had not commanded men in battle since he was a captain during the first Boer war, over twenty years previously.

The ceremony took place on The Mall under the shadow of the Victoria Memorial and in clear view of Buckingham Palace. The Kaiser flew out on the inaugural Zeppelin flight to accept his cousin's subjugation. King George V was asked to kneel before Wilhelm II, kiss the ring and relinquish his right over British imperial interests abroad. He arose King of only the *Grosse Britische Reich*, which did not include Northern Ireland or any other landmass outside of British national waters, and the word *imperial* was to be struck from all official communication and future publications. At the time of the subjugation, the occupied zone only covered the home counties and the five original invasion counties.

Some said the ceremony was premature, numbering among these the government-in-exile, including Prime Minister Hubert Asquith and First Sea Lord Winston Churchill. They fled to Birmingham as the German army marched through Trafalgar Square. Further west, The Battle of The Solent raged on for nearly two months. The horseshoe of water that lay between

Portsmouth, Southampton and The Isle of Wight was easily defended, and the sailors and soldiers stationed there fought to the death with every last bullet and bomb in their arsenal.

Once the Germans had taken The Isle of Wight, however, the battle was all but lost.

The bravery of the men in Hampshire bought crucial time for the burgeoning resistance movement and they used it to coordinate the evacuation of the southwest of England, spoiling any food they couldn't take with them, scorching the earth and destroying road signs as they went. The combination of a wall of AA guns along the south coast and the Royal Flying Corps, prevented Zeppelin raids and slowly, the millions of inhabitants of Cornwall, Devon, Dorset, Somerset, and Wiltshire were safely behind the line of defences that ran roughly along the route of the Old Bath Road, from Aldershot to the shining River Severn.

The Battle of Aldershot was the first victory for the British resistance, and the first major instance of civilians taking up arms against the German invaders. The counties to the west of London had time to react, not to defend their homes but to run. Their flight blocked the advance and bought time for the border of the unoccupied zone to become a substantial wall between the newly appointed garrison towns of Bristol in the west, Swindon, then Reading, and north to Milton Keynes and Cambridge, then east to Bury St. Edmonds and finally north again to Kings Lynn. Anywhere between these towns and the sea fell under German occupation and Martial law.

The British still controlled almost all of Britain's natural resources and manufacturing plants, and without the most densely populated areas in London and the southeast to feed, there was a chance they would not starve. British manufacture and conscription had increased to a war footing seven months before the invasion and raw materials had been stockpiled in ports and major manufacturing centres all over the north and midlands of England, and the whole of Wales and Scotland. They concentrated on producing for defence: AA guns, barbed wire, rifles, Vickers guns and ammunition. Every major town and city was fortified and every scrap of land set to growing food. Despite the might of the Reich, with the right leadership the British still had an outside chance of repelling this invasion.

While the maniacal driving of millions of Russians thousands of miles to the foothills of the Urals had taken a severe toll on the German army in both manpower and resources, this invasion of England had cost far more lives and taken far longer than Ludendorff had expected. This meant they were forced to simply hold the ground they had taken in a frustrating stalemate, while training more conscripts from Germany and the increasing European empire in order to acquire much needed resources.

~

"Leutnant Hitler, congratulations on your promotion." The codename Künstler was long dead, consigned to the annuls of the secret section in a records department somewhere on the outskirts of Berlin.

The office was sparse and utilitarian, on the wall was the usual portrait of the Kaiser, a map of Germany and a citation for an Iron Cross second class towards which he followed Gleeson's gaze.

"Ah, my Iron Cross First Class is with the framers. What can I do for you?" His English had improved vastly over the last months and now there he was, sitting behind a real desk; a substantial improvement from the back bedroom of number fourteen.

"Well, sir," Gleeson rubbed the back of his neck, having never imagined he would be apprehensive when speaking to this man. "Webber is back at his factory, Vittel has returned to his Lab, and I haven't seen the agents formally known as Turnip and Parsnip since Tag-X."

"Ja, ja, out with it, you oaf." Gleeson was not used to being spoken to like this, even in anti-Irish England, as his size and obvious ability to scrap afforded him a certain level of wary respect. Back home he was a lieutenant of the Irish Volunteers and would not, under any other circumstance tolerate such affrontery, but he bit his tongue, and somehow, still felt like he was behind enemy lines.

"Sir, I want to go home. It's been nearly two years and I long to see my country free, which hasn't been the case for nearly three centuries."

Good, Gleeson reassured himself, *measured and deferent, just play his game.*

"My dear fellow, the Reich still needs you for one last thing."

"Name it," he said, repressing a sigh. He had seen this man in action, and he did not mean the fiasco on Tag-X. He meant his counter-insurgency work, the lengths he would go to, the brutality of the reprisals. No one was safe and everyone was a

65

potential spy, resistance fighter, communist or degenerate. That was his latest favourite. God himself knew how he came up with it all, but once he got started that was it, his rhetoric was intoxicating and seemingly endless.

"It's simple really, I want you to pretend to escape. I'll have some men chase you, firing to miss, of course." The ghost of a smile crossed his lips. "But we will let you get away and then you will give the English some false intelligence about, among other things, Stalag 102."

"That all?"

"You will be using the name Connor. I knew you would be accommodating." A painfully forced smile now. Had the sarcasm gone over his greasy black head, or had he chosen to ignore it? Gleeson was unsure.

He was too old for this malarky, he was cold and damp and his muscles ached from sleeping rough for too long. He felt the tips of the fingers of his right hand. One was bandaged, and the rest were smooth, no nails, not even the thumb. Those English bastards had managed to do him over one last time before he would be allowed to finally enjoy the fruits of his labour in a self-ruled, unified Ireland. The image of that prick Clive smiling at him, so civilised, would be clear in his mind's eye for years to come.

"There's a good chap. Now listen, of course I believe you, Connor, but I can't quite convince Sergeant Grimes here. You don't mind putting his mind at ease do you, old bean?" He always left the room before the unpleasantness began.

66

Grimes was an accomplished sadist, deftly pulling Gleeson's fingernails out with a deliberate slowness Gleeson hadn't known was possible. Of course, he had been interrogated before, beaten, bound, even a staged execution, but never this. They had already broken the index finger on his right hand.

"In case you was to join the rebels or something, you know when you gets 'ome, can't shoot none of us wiv a broken finger now, can you?"

The pain was excruciating as Grimes used a clamp and slowly closed it to the point of acute discomfort before calling to Clive.

"Sir, I has 'im by the toe, in a manner of speaking!"

"Ah, thank you, Sergeant Grimes." So polite even when overseeing the torture of a human being. "Now, Connor, tell me again about this camp, Stalag... what was it?" He rubbed his thumb and forefinger together, feigning absent-mindedness.

"Stalag 102!" Gleeson slurred through his swollen jaw and lips.

"Yes..." Clive sounded bored now. "And who did you say was there?"

"Colonel Henry Bradshaw... and five others from his unit." He spat blood and Grimes turned the vice ever so slightly, driving Gleeson into an entirely new realm of pain, but the Irishman refused to cry out.

"Sergeant Grimes, do you think he's telling the truth?"

"Hard to say, Sir, seeing as we've barely laid an 'and on 'im yet, you knows what these micks is like, they does whatever they wants and just confesses it all away to the priest."

"Break the finger," he said impatiently. "But wait until I've left the cellar, for God's sake."

It didn't matter, however, because he could hear Gleeson screaming all the way to the mess.

Finally, an open-top truck appeared. Gleeson had been living in this shelled-out hole since the bastards turned him out, back into the occupied zone. He'd had to walk for nearly ten miles before he found a German patrol and they only wanted to shoot him. The English bastards had kept his papers, and he had to beg the Germans to be taken to Woodbridge where people knew him. They took him and Leutnant Hitler was sitting behind his desk as if he had never moved, not a flicker of emotion when he saw Gleeson's face, just banal pleasantries.

"You've trimmed your moustache." Gleeson proffered, but no reply came. "It suits you." Still nothing, the man simply continued with his paperwork.

"I'll need a car."

"You can have a motorcycle," the leutnant said without looking up from his work.

"You can't sleep on a motorbike."

"And you can't conduct operational briefings from a small bedroom using only a card table," countered Hitler curtly as he signed a document with a flourish and blotted it.

"Here," he said, holding out the paper, still looking down as he started on the next task, "orders for a motorcycle and suitable stores to sustain you for a few weeks on OP."

"Thank you kindly," Gleeson said sarcastically. He was taken aback when Hitler suddenly stopped what he was doing and looked him in the eye.

"Goodbye, Herr Gleeson."

And there he was ten days later, watching the lorryload of troops disappear as he scrawled notes on strength, weapons, direction, and dress. He released the carrier pigeon he had brought with him to warn the Germans to stay clear of this particular truck. This part of the occupied zone was a wasteland, people had either fled to the English free zone or gone to the major population centres in search of food, but some buildings were still standing and the closer they got to the sea, the more Gleeson saw.

The Germans needed headquarters, messes, brothels, and barracks, but building these things was a costly and time-consuming business and they were never as comfortable as the hotels and private houses they could simply take.

He watched them embark at Stowmarket and guessed the rest of their plan, then doubling back, he raced along the main road to Woodbridge. The Germans loved a well-maintained road. Hitler had placed a company of soldiers on standby and introduced him to Hauptmann Otto Kessler, officer commanding Z company Fifteenth *Sturmbataillon*.

"Call me Otto," he said wearily.

"Gleeson. Do you speak English?" he replied as they shook hands.

"I will act as interpreter," Hitler interjected.

"Right, I'd say we have about an hour," Gleeson said slowly. "I want your best shots to replace the guards on the towers, and the men you feel most capable of killing with their bare hands to lie in wait here." He pointed to the woods in between the Alde River and the camp. "The rest will wait in the sleeping huts." He waited for Hitler to translate.

"Now, the plan is to let them come into the camp, that way we can take them all prisoner. Sure, I used to be one of these Tommies, so I know that they will leave a rear party in these woods and possibly some fire support around here." Gleeson pointed to the map again.

"So, tell your men that we want as many alive as possible," Hitler said and added in English that if he did not get at least ten men including one officer and some NCOs, then Gleeson was going nowhere. "Do you think you can manage that?"

"It sounds pretty straightforward," Otto said. "Allow me to deploy the men who will need to reach the woods and we can discuss it further. They don't have much time." He strode from the room, evidently pleased to be doing something.

Flight – Berlin 1945

Olga must have slept, but it seemed to her that she had spent the time reliving the previous few hours. Emma and her eagerness to die, Udo and Dieter... *Udo and Dieter!*

She sat bolt upright and recalled that they had seen her address, read it, considered it in relation to Zoo Tower and known her name, had known *Carla's* name! The clock on the wall said only one hour had passed since she arrived home.

"Wake up, wake up!" she screamed. "We have to go now!" She shook Rudi and Carla until they were fully awake.

"They know this address and they will be coming for us," she said, unable to hide the panic in her voice as she pulled on Carla's uniform and stuffed useful items into bags.

"Who is coming, what's happened? Why are you dressing in my uniform? Why is there blood on it?" Carla demanded as she held her tunic up to the light of a candle.

"I went to see your mother, but I could not go out without a reason so I borrowed your uniform and papers, but on the way home I was stopped by some boys from the *Volkssturm* and they tried to... and I had to... that's where the blood came from, and the knife I left in the pocket," she blurted apologetically, before taking the tunic from Carla. "I'm so sorry, but I have a plan and you need to be in civilian clothes for it to work."

She was dressed now, fidgeting impatiently while she waited for the others to be ready.

"Why would you go to see *Mutti*?" Carla demanded, dressed now and inspecting the knife. "How do you even know her?"

"She was very kind to me once, and I wanted to say goodbye, but–" she broke off. "Rudi, will you hurry up!"

"But what?" demanded Carla, giving Olga her full attention now. Olga looked at Carla, her face shadowed by the dancing flame, and she realised that she was ignorant. Not in general but of the time travel business.

But perhaps her memories unlocked when they touched?

The sudden knowledge would have serious consequences for Carla, and she resolved not to let that happen until they were safely out of harm's way.

"I'll explain on the way, but we have to get moving. Rudi, will you stop playing with that?" She took the Swiss army knife from him and stuffed it into her coat pocket. He only had his shirt, socks and pants on still. "You know what, Rudi, do you still have your Hitler Youth uniform?"

"Ja, why?"

"If you wear that, people won't ask so many questions, they will think you're a messenger or something. We all need spare civilian clothes. Carla, can you throw in something practical for me please?"

Carla had grown up in Nazi Germany and she understood why they must run but *she* had managed to keep her nose clean for years without bringing trouble to the door. "Who *are* you?" she demanded, stamping her foot with impotent rage.

"Carla, she is a very old friend, and we must let her help us," Rudi said, hopping on one foot while he tried to pull his trousers on.

"A very old friend?" she echoed incredulously. "You are a twelve-year-old boy, you don't *have* very old friends."

"A very old friend of *Mutti's*," he said quickly. "She made me promise to listen to Olga and let her take care of us." He was dressed now, pulling on his satchel.

"When, when did *Mutti* tell you this?" Carla stood in the doorway, arms folded, making it clear she wasn't going to play along without some answers.

"Listen, Carla, we need to go. I promise to explain everything on the way," Olga implored.

"Or," Rudi cut in, "she can tell you through the wall of your cell in Prinz-Albrecht-Straße?"

That was enough, Carla picked up the clothes she had taken cycling last summer and packed them into a bag while Olga blew out the candles and grabbed the matches, stuffing them into her bag too.

Olga peered out over the edge of the floor and down at Schliemannstraße, but there was no sign of an arrest party or three vengeful boys, not yet. They walked briskly westwards in total silence.

"Do you even know where we are going?" demanded Carla as Olga slowed to check a street sign.

"No, not really, but I know that Russia is that way," she jerked a thumb eastward, "and they are bad." What she didn't say or know, was that after a period known as the rape of Berlin, the Russians imposed an oppressive communist regime on Germany and the only way to escape it was to get as far west as quickly as possible. The last time she'd had to run from the

73

Reich, she had done it by boat and that was all she could think of every time she saw a vehicle checkpoint.

"How far is the sea?" she asked after a few minutes of silence.

"There's the Grosser Wannsee?" offered Rudi.

"Great, we'll head there." Olga said.

"And then what?" Carla asked.

"Then we steal a boat and sail to safety," Olga said with far more conviction than she felt.

"You want to go to a lake in eastern Germany and sail away from a Reich that stretches from Czech in the east all the way to the Atlantic Ocean? Didn't you hear of Fortress Europe?" Carla was sneering, an angry teenage girl who had been forced to flee her home in the middle of the night by some idiot who stole her uniform and got blood all over it. This idiot was now trying to say that they could sail about on the Wannsee to escape the Nazis.

"The Havel connects the Wannsee to a lot of other lakes and eventually the Elbe-Havel-Kanal, which leads to the Deutsche See," Rudi said, trying to be helpful, but only upsetting Carla further.

"So, the plan is to escape via the Elbe-Havel-Kanal?" She sounded even more incredulous.

"We don't have to get that far, the war is nearly over, we only have to survive a few weeks and then we can start afresh, wherever we want," Rudi said, annoyingly optimistic.

"With what?" Carla demanded. "What are we going to use to pay for all of this?"

"Gold. I stole some gold from the soldiers that Olga saved me from."

"Which they probably stole from people like you and me," Carla said, haughtily.

"Well, I can't very well find them and give it back to them now, can I? Besides, we need it, we have to…" Rudi trailed off, because his sister was not ready to listen to a story about time travel from her wise, old, little brother and his soulmate from 2036.

"There's a checkpoint," hissed Olga. "Remember, we were bombed out of our home and I'm your cousin Annelise Schneider. I'm taking you to stay with my family in Dahlen, tell them your mother is in hospital."

Shadowy men lurked in the shelter of the tiny guard hut, stirring as they approached and stepping out to meet them.

"It's late to be out," croaked a man in his sixties, his breath misted on the frigid air. He wore an Iron cross on his left breast pocket, and he probably won it in a war long before this one.

"Our home was destroyed by a bomb," Rudi blurted out, his nervousness manifesting as a rather convincing excitement.

"He's never had such an adventure," Olga chuckled. "Their mother is in hospital, I'm taking them to stay with my family," she said, offering the papers. Carla was silently channelling years of anguish to cry, and it was working a little too well, as loud sobs caused her to convulse as she threw her arms around Olga.

"She's not taking it well," Olga said, shielding her eyes as the guard shone a torch in her face and back down at the identity papers.

"These are civilian papers, but you are wearing the uniform of a *Helferin?*"

75

"Ach so, my Luftwaffe papers have not come through yet, I only started last week." She smiled her most convincing smile and looked pleadingly into the eyes of the old man.

He met her gaze with scrutiny and then looked back down at the papers, then at Carla, still sobbing on her shoulder. He turned to see what the other soldier was doing and looked back at the *Kenkarte*, then he smiled sympathetically at Olga.

"Everything is in order here," he said loudly enough for his colleague to hear. "Hurry along home, you never know when the terror flyers will start bombing again." He handed back the papers and tousled Rudi's hair. "You remind me of my grandson Walter, it was only three years ago he was running around dressed like you, and now he is fighting the Amis in the Rhineland." He turned away, perhaps to hide a tear.

When she was sure that they were out of range of the checkpoint, Carla rounded on Olga, stopped with her arms folded and spoke slowly.

"My mother, I want an explanation, I will go no further until you give it to me!"

"Okay," Olga sighed. "Step into the park up there and we can take a rest amongst the trees, eat something and I'll tell you everything about your mother."

They sat down on a bench in a secluded area of the park beneath a magnificent willow which stood over them offering its protection. Olga handed around a chunk of black bread and some water. Rudi and Carla each broke a piece off and drank thirstily.

"Your mother was very kind to me once, she helped me when no one else would," Olga lied, trying to make something up that might sound believable to Carla. She did not have to worry about Rudi, whom she knew would not challenge her because they shared a bond that transcended space and time.

"Ja, you said that." Carla was not going to accept such a vague explanation; she was going to make this difficult for Olga.

"Carla, please, why don't you trust her? She is trying to help us," Rudi said feebly.

"She is hiding something, I know it," Carla was staring at Olga through narrowed eyes.

"Your mother is dead," Olga blurted out. She had meant to deliver the news with more tact, more sensitivity, but Carla had forced it from her and now it was said. The war had raged for years, Carla remembered little else about her short life, other than death and grief and hunger, by now old friends. As such, she did not react in the way Olga had expected. In fact, she simply nodded as if Olga had merely confirmed a suspicion.

"Were you with her, at the end, I mean?" Carla asked calmly to which Olga simply nodded.

"Did she suffer?"

"No, she was on a lot of pain medication, but she told me that you and Rudi were the most important part of her life and her greatest achievement," Olga said emphatically.

"Liar!" Carla shouted, causing Olga to glance around, in case they were heard.

"She was, I watched them give it to her," she said.

"Not about the drugs, about what she said, she would never speak like that, what did she really say?" Carla demanded.

77

"Morphine can make people say and do strange things, reveal truths that they would not normally."

"What did she really say?" Carla insisted.

"Carla, you can't speak to Olga in this way." Rudi stood from the bench and appealed to his older sister, desperate to explain their intimate, age-old connection and how much she meant to him.

"No, it's fine, right before she died, she grabbed me by the wrist and told me to beware of *der Engländer*," Olga confessed.

"What is that supposed to mean?" demanded Carla, but Rudi thought he knew. He was reminded of a British spy who he tried to kill but… he could feel a sharp, searing pain in his right hand and he clutched it to his chest, as the feeling brought tears to his eyes and he inhaled sharply.

"What's wrong with you?" Carla sneered, incapable of understanding the phantom pain her brother was experiencing and unable to empathise with anyone. Olga was beginning to see Carla for who she was, and she did not like what she saw.

"He just found out his mother is dead, perhaps he is grieving?" Olga said this questioningly over her shoulder as she embraced Rudi. "Has this got something to do with *der Engländer*?" she whispered to him.

"I'll tell you later, thank you for making *Mutti* comfortable," he whispered back.

"Okay," Olga said as she drew away, placing a hand on each of his shoulders and looking at Rudi. "Will you be okay?"

"I think so," Rudi said, meeting Olga's eyes and smiling weakly.

"Come on then, let us keep going to the Wannsee to find your magical boat," Carla said sarcastically.

The three of them left the park and continued southwest towards the lake and hopefully to safety. The signs of the destruction wrought by the daily American bombing and the nightly British raids were everywhere; piles of rubble, craters, overturned trucks, and gaps where houses once stood. The bombing had slowed over the last few days and so had the Russian advance. The allies seemed to be consolidating for a big offensive, a final push to defeat Hitler once and for all.

Another hour of walking and they reached the leafy residential area on the banks of the Wannsee. As they walked along a tree-lined boulevard with palatial houses on either side, no doubt home to high-ranking Nazi officials or even *Reichsministers*, the masts of watercraft became visible over the rooftops against the predawn sky.

"Do you even know how to sail a boat?" Carla asked in a contemptuous tone that was becoming her normal mode of address for Olga.

"Yes, I have sailed passages in the Atlantic, the Mediterranean, and the Red Sea. I have led watches and I can navigate using the stars." Carla chose not to respond straightaway, then she said,

"Well, don't expect Rudi or me to be of any help, we've never even been on a rowing boat." Rudi wanted to say that he had, that he had escaped the Stasi with Olga and a priest called Lorenzo in a rowing boat on the Spree, but he could not explain that to his sister and he did not want to try.

79

"Don't worry," Olga said, ruffling Rudi's hair. "I'll show you both how and you'll be tacking and jibbing and shaking out reefs before you know it." Rudi's spirits were lifted at the thought and he began to look expectantly for a suitable yacht.

"What kind of boat will it be?" he asked.

"A small, inconspicuous one, just big enough for the three of us to live below in relative comfort for a few weeks. We will also need to get hold of some food along the way," she mused.

"Yes, but will it be a sailing boat or a fishing boat or a... a red one?"

"You really know nothing of boats, do you, Rudi?" Olga said affectionately.

"No, but I cannot wait to learn!"

As they followed the grand sweep of the road, they found themselves on the lakeshore. The grey half-light from a sun that was threatening to rise any minute, showed dozens of boats. Beautiful teak-decked gaffs, sleek cutters, and a multitude of small yachts, perfect for the task at hand. Olga would have loved to explore each one, checking their rigging and equipment, but there simply wasn't time.

She spotted a well-maintained 25-foot gaff sloop with a white hull and tan coloured sails. Sailing yachts were not built with motors in this time period, but lashed to the port shroud was a pole that the British called a quant. This was used to propel the boat along, much like a Venetian gondola, and it could also be used to get the boat out of trouble or to push it clear of a Lee shore.

"This one," she whispered, after briefly looking it over. The clouds in the east were beginning to turn pink and orange, they

80

had to get underway before the daylight came and the risk of discovery became too high. Rudi leapt aboard and took everyone's bags, while Carla stepped gingerly from the jetty to the stern of the boat. Olga inspected the mooring lines and rigged them to slip. This wasn't a vast marina with endless jetties and a complicated route into the open water, it was a single line of yachts moored stern-to, facing the expanse of the Wannsee. Olga planned to simply punt the boat into the open water and around the headland before setting sail and drawing too much attention from the shore.

"When you push this, it's called the tiller, push it away from you and the front of the boat will go in the opposite direction. Pull it towards you and it will come back, I will provide what's called steerage way, by punting the boat along using that stick, the quant."

"Got it," Rudi said, nodding enthusiastically.

"Carla, could you untie the ropes at the front there, the ones holding us to those piles, please?" Olga instructed, receiving a grunt in reply.

She unlashed the quant and tested the depth of the water, which was surprisingly shallow. She handed Rudi the two stern lines and told him to let go and grab the tiller when she said, then she looked forward to see the two bow lines disappearing beneath the surface of the water. Carla had untied the wrong ends of the rope.

"Okay, Rudi," she said as she pushed the boat forward using the quant. Rudi dropped his lines and took hold of the tiller as the boat lurched out of its moorings and into the lake. Carla saw the two stern lines trailing and realised what she had done.

"You should have been more specific," she said, sitting down in the cockpit and folding her arms. Olga did not answer because she was punting for all she was worth and struggling to retrieve the quant as it was sucked into the muddy lakebed. She began to get a rhythm and Rudi's steering grew less erratic as he became more familiar with the concept. Olga nearly fell overboard when she didn't feel the resistance she had come to expect. She lost her balance and only by grasping the backstay was she able to remain aboard. Nevertheless, she swung around the outside of the wire and back onto the other side of the boat, her hand blistered from the friction. The quant, however, was lost beneath the gently rippling water.

"Quick!" she shouted. "We must make sail before we lose steerage way, or it will be very difficult to control the boat." She showed Rudi the small flag at the top of the mast and told him to keep it facing rearwards. Then she ran forward and started to release the ties that stopped the sail from flapping about in the wind.

"Carla, help me with the sail ties, please," she said, patiently.

Olga left her to it and studied the halyards at the mast, ropes that raised the sails, two for the mainsail and one for the jib. When she'd identified the peak and throat halyards, she waited for Carla to release the last of the ties and began to pull both ropes. The sail flowed in the headwind and the spar at the top of the sail rose up the mast. When the throat halyard was tight, she made it fast and continued to pull the peak halyard, watching the creases on the sail for a guide. As she did this, the boat lost steerage way and turned out of the wind onto a starboard tack, the boom swung out to port with some force and rocked the boat, scaring the children in the cockpit. Olga rushed back and took control of the sail with a rope called the mainsheet in one hand and the tiller in the other, as she steered for the headland and brought the sail to meet the wind on a close reach.

The process took her back to the *Herev* and to thoughts of the happiness she had known aboard it in the endless blue of the Atlantic. To Yael and Ruth, Daniel and Chaim, their horrific deaths, and her forty days adrift in an inflatable raft. She thought of Ibrahim and his sacrifice, of the *Veritas* and sailing to freedom with Yael. When she pictured Yael's body in the dusty cellar in Mitte, she began to cry.

"What's wrong with you?" demanded Carla, disgusted at this display of emotion, this admission of weakness.

"Will you just fuck off!" Olga said, flatly, concentrating on trimming the mainsail. She'd worry about the jib later, when she had shown Rudi how to work the sheet and the tiller at the same time.

"You can't talk to me like that," Carla said indignantly, and then she rose from her seat and opened her mouth to say something else.

"Ready about," Olga said through her teeth, "stay there, Rudi." He was sitting in the front of the cockpit opposite Carla and down out of the way.

"What?" Carla said.

"Helms a-lee!" she called as she pushed the tiller away from her, putting the boat through the wind and on the opposite tack. With the tiller between her legs, she quickly pulled in the mainsheet.

"Boom," she said, smiling cruelly at Carla and when they made eye contact, Olga flicked her gaze to Carla's left, the girl turning just in time to see a heavy wooden boom swinging around, pushed by the new position of the boat in relation to the wind. She ducked just in time, but the message was loud and clear.

This is my world, and in it you will play by my rules.

"You have to watch out for the boom when we're tacking and jibing, Carla dear," Olga said, her words dripping with insincerity.

Carla stood up and glowered at Olga before turning on her heel and rattling the doors of the companionway that led below deck.

"Yes, could you try to get that open, please? That would be great," Olga said, her head craned upwards, watching the wind indicator.

It was Rudi who eventually got the two wooden shutters open and slid back the hatch to reveal a cosy but well-equipped cabin. A small galley consisting of a gas stove and little else, sat opposite a tidy navigation table with the charts, books, and instruments neatly stowed in wooden compartments. Forward of that was a saloon comprising two cushioned benches that doubled as berths and a folding table, and beyond that was a small triangular space called the peak, with a cushion-topped locker.

Olga showed Rudi the fundamentals of steering and trimming while Carla sulked in the peak cabin. The smart little craft zig-zagged westwards up the lake all morning, until eventually they hanked on and hoisted the jib, adding an extra element to the tacking procedure and challenging Rudi further. As they glided along silently, Olga gazed at the skeletal trees on the shore, tiny buds offering a glimpse of the verdant beauty that was to come.

By lunchtime, they had navigated some thirty kilometres of lakes and waterways in the Havel basin and were now ploughing a frothy furrow through the Göttin See. Olga was pleased to see that Rudi seemed to have the hang of it and she ventured below to find Carla snoring in the forepeak. She discarded the *Luft-waffe* uniform in favour of Carla's practical cycling clothes and inspected the cabin and its various equipment. Then she took stock of their food. They had a loaf and a half of black bread, three apples and six tired-looking potatoes. This would not last long at all and Olga began to think about where they might find some more food. She looked through the galley and found a kettle, which made her think of the water situation, and she was again reminded of her sheltered upbringing.

"Rudi," she called, clearly indifferent about disturbing Carla. "Ja?"

"Do you think that if we boil the lake water, we can drink it?"

Rudi laughed, "I have been drinking boiled water from the Spree since before *Weihnachten*, surely this will be far safer."

Olga re-joined Rudi and took over the tiller to give him a break.

"You should eat, have an apple." It seemed that Rudi had only been waiting for permission and flew down the ladder to select the finest apple, but then he looked guiltily to Olga, and reluctantly proffered the prize fruit.

"You have it, just bring me a piece of bread, please." She hated the tough, dry bread. Of course, it was popular among the Brits of her time, Germanophiles and social climbers who embraced all things Teutonic. But her mother had baked soda bread, a recipe handed down through generations of Lynch's from mother to daughter, and soft fluffy farmhouse loaves eaten with lashings of rich, creamy butter. But she was grown and developed, malnutrition in a boy as young as Rudi could stunt his growth and lead to illness later in life. So, she gnawed at the unpleasant, crumbly hunk of joyless bread and pretended to relish it.

When Rudi had nearly finished, she pointed at the apple and then said the English word for it, going on to point at other items around them. It had occurred to her that if they ditched their papers and uniforms, and she did the talking in her native London accent, they might be left alone. She certainly knew enough about being an army brat to pass for the errant child of an indulgent British officer.

"I will teach you and Carla the very basics, but more importantly, I will help you to learn the accent that will convince people that you are English."

"Apple," Rudi said, dangling the core by its stalk.

"That was awful. *Ah-pull*," she said slowly. This time he got it, and they spent the afternoon practising basic phrases and answers to likely questions. She'd say something and then Rudi would have to repeat it until he sounded like the twelve-year-old son of a British officer.

A thought struck her as they tore through the calm lake, the only sound the water creaming at the bow. A memory of her and

Rudi in a boat came to her; not like this though, a smaller boat rowed by a priest. She strained to remember and realised it had come to mind because of Rudi's clumsiness with weapons.

That was it! First, she thought of that awful business in the square a few days ago, then of that night on the canal when he had not known what to do. Had she taken the time to teach him, that poor priest might have lived. She must have been close to him, for tears flowed readily and she sighed as she did sometimes when the weight of the centuries was too much to bear.

"Rudi," she said after a few minutes of quiet reflection. "I saw you with that rifle in the square." Rudi stiffened because he had been about to kill that man in cold blood. He hadn't wanted to, but he had just about talked himself into it when Olga had started shooting. Then he'd turned the gun on her. He looked at his feet, afraid of what she would say next.

"You were useless," she laughed, "and although you clearly understand the very basics, I think that in a pinch you should know what to do. So, later, we'll get my Galil and my Jericho out and discuss what to do if there is any trouble." Rudi struggled to contain his excitement because he coveted those futuristic weapons and longed to hold them, to understand how they worked, and to be trusted to use one was a dream come true.

When Olga saw that they were sailing along a quiet stretch of water, she ducked down and re-emerged with the weapons. They spent the next hour talking through basic handling and various scenarios, what Rudi might do to help and where she would hide the guns. She held up the pistol.

"The Jericho will be loaded, a round chambered with the safety on, always in the rear starboard cockpit locker." She placed it there now. "And the Galil, loaded but made safe, will go in the forepeak locker under the bed. Understood?"

Rudi nodded and wondered if he had it in him to kill a man, his vivid nightmares said yes, but his heart had doubts.

Blitz – 1915

Kathleen Lynch was late. She was always late, though her employers never seemed to mind because she was polite, helpful, excellent at her job, and beautiful. With dark brown curls that hung over high cheekbones covered in porcelain skin, her long eyelashes caressed blue eyes like tiny planets, swirling and deep. Her broad shoulders and curvy hips suited the driver's uniform she was wearing these days and she could not get enough glimpses of herself in that peaked hat on the way to work.

Born and raised in Mile End by Irish immigrants Branagh and Domhnall, Kath was the second youngest of five. When the Zeppelins came that day in July, her father and two elder brothers were away with the army somewhere in that vast expanse of land she only knew as "the north." Her mother was a nurse and her little brother James was still at school. Kath had been home on her own, too old for school, too young for nursing college and terrified. The news she did not bother to read, had warned of invasion and it was the reason Dad was away, but somehow it had not seemed real.

Through efficiency rather than respect for human life, the German raid focused on the docklands and military targets like Woolwich Arsenal and naval buildings in Greenwich, but bombs did not always go where they were sent, especially when the Zeppelins were harried by the brave boys of the Royal Flying Corps. Those pilots flew sortie after sortie until finally they came back to find their airstrip destroyed by German bombs, and had to glide further north on fumes, desperately searching for a safe place to land.

Kath paced the tiny kitchen of their terraced house trying to decide if she should get James and take him to the shelter. She thought that surely the school would know what to do far better than she would, and her mother would be at the hospital all day and well into the night. She thought about grabbing James and getting out of the city, but where would they go?

All their family lived either here in the East End or back in Dungarvan. She decided to make tea because the familiar ritual calmed her nerves and when she finally sat down at the kitchen table, she took a sip and said aloud in her East London accent, "I fucking *hate* tea!"

She asked herself why she drank it and realised it was a choice between that and whisky. No one drank water and fruit juice was not for the likes of her.

"Bollocks to it!" she exclaimed.

Kath stood and walked over to the dresser, reached on her tiptoes for the key and unlocked the cupboard where her father kept the spirits. She sniffed at it and decided not to drink it straight, so with no other option, she poured some into her tea.

"Ahh," she said, "that's better." It wasn't really better, but that was what her parents said after a drop of the hard stuff.

Fortified, galvanised, and emboldened, Kath pushed her chair back with her hands on the table and stood. She resolved to get James and bring him home, then she would pack them a picnic to take into the cellar. She might even have some more whisk-tea. She placed her hand on the doorknob and turned it, just as the shockwave hit the partially open door and threw Kath to the ground.

At the same time, a young pilot called Godfrey Freemantle was haranguing a Zeppelin over Poplar. The Bombardier was about to take the best shot of his career on Canary Warf itself when some of the ballast bags were hit and the Zeppelin lurched upwards and to the north. The bomb was released, and it plummeted from the Zeppelin, landing at the far end of Kath's Street.

She lay there dazed but not unconscious for some moments before getting up, then she took a slug of Tullamore D.E.W. and marched towards the door. The ringing in her ears affected her balance and she stumbled down the steps to the pavement. As she looked up, the scene around her was one of panic and confusion. No one on the street owned a car and all the vans were out on deliveries during the day, so she had a clear view up and down the road. At the far end, where the bomb had landed, she could see water gushing from the broken pavement into a crater no deeper than three feet. Beyond that, a double-decker bus listed to one side, roof missing and windows destroyed, while the driver lay covered under a blanket on the pavement as people still worked to get the passengers out.

Kath walked towards the trouble the way that she always had, and as she grew nearer, she noticed more and more broken windows. When she reached the crater, she saw that the terraced houses surrounding it looked like a giant had carefully removed them from the row without wanting to disturb the neighbours. She could hear screaming and sobbing and knew she should look for something to do, but everybody seemed to have all the important jobs covered and…

"James!" she said a little too loudly. She began to walk quickly away from the bombsite towards the primary school her brother attended. As she drew further from the epicentre, unbroken windows became more frequent and by the end of the road, things seemed almost normal. Except for the fighter planes buzzing like mosquitos around giant grey behemoths intent on blowing her up *again*.

The school was untouched and apparently unoccupied, and after a moment of confusion she realised the children must be in the cellar. Was she really going to take James from the relative safety of the cellar to…to what? She still did not have a plan. She stood in the playground watching the scene above, mesmerised beyond fear, beyond anything but the desperate struggle between plane and Zeppelin.

The fighter she was watching scored a hit, but one of the airship's guns got a bead on him and tore his left wing to shreds. The Zeppelin dropped ballast and lurched upwards, disappearing into the clouds and away from trouble as the tiny biplane spiralled towards the ground. She watched him falling ever closer to his death, unaware of the tears in her eyes for the unknown pilot. It seemed now that he was gaining something like control, his descent slowed, and he began to level out.

He was headed right for the school playground it seemed.

It was the largest open space in this direction that he might reach, she tried to move but her feet were frozen to the ground, while all the time he was getting closer, engine roaring, billowing smoke.

Move! she told herself, *why don't you just bloody well move?* She thought of the people she loved. Of her parents and brothers.

Oh God, if I die James will be on his own! Mum works the clock around and Dad and the boys are away.

The tiny biplane was really quite big now, pitching and weaving just above the rooftops. She forced herself to move, running for the cover of the teacher's bicycle shed just as the plane came crashing through the fence and onto the tarmac playground. Momentum kept it moving at a horrifying speed all the way to the front entrance where it finally stopped. As a final act, it took out the portico before its engine coughed and sputtered, giving up.

Kath picked herself up and ran over to the wreckage as thick grey smoke filled her eyes, nose, and mouth, but she pressed on.

"Hello?" she called as she approached the cockpit, standing on tiptoes and peering in. "Are you alright?"

He wasn't alright so he just groaned. She looked at the harness holding him in and started struggling to unfasten it.

"It's alright, love, I'm just trying to get you out," she coughed. She was up on the wing now, leaning right over with her legs in the air.

She got it loose just as he came around, and he groaned again, giving her a shock.

"What, what are you doing?"

"Oh, you're awake, I'm trying to get you out," she said indignantly.

"I...I think I can move, argh!" he cried out with the pain, but still he managed to stand.

Kath hitched up her skirt and with a sort of leap and a strangled yelp, she was sitting astride the fuselage facing the cockpit.

"Right," she said, "let's get you out."

Another scream of pain and he was clinging to the wing. Kath moved with an agility she did not know she had, to get behind him and help him to the ground. She grabbed the man under his armpits and dragged him away from the wreckage to the bike shed. He was a slight young man, but Kath still struggled with his weight and had to stop frequently to catch her breath.

It was only when she reached the shelter of the shed that she looked back and saw the drag marks. Dark red blood trailed across the playground in gruesome contrast to the children's chalk drawings of yellow stick families, trees, and houses. She knelt beside him and began to strip away his greatcoat when she felt something hard; a piece of shrapnel the size of a carving knife was protruding from a hole in his stomach. Blood oozed from the gaping wound in pulses that matched the beating of his heart. She knew he was going to die and all she would be able to do now was to make him comfortable. She made a pillow of her jacket, placing it carefully under his head as she wondered whether moving him had been the right thing to do. But the question was answered for her when at that moment the fuel tank caught fire, engulfing the cockpit in flames, and turning the remaining wing to ash. Kath tutted, "Fucked either way, I 'spose."

"What?" he croaked, his breathing wet and shallow.

"What's your name, my love?"

"God..." he gasped.

"God?" she said incredulously.

94

"Godfrey," he rasped, trying to smile.

"That's a lovely name. Have you got a sweetheart, Godfrey?" She had no idea what she was doing so she just held him and stroked his hair.

"I never did…"

"Never did what, darling?"

"With a girl, not even a kiss. But how many men get to fly?" he said, smiling weakly up at her. "I've flown up so high that I've touched the heavens, seen the sunrise over the Atlantic and travelled at speeds most only dream of."

"Some men will say anything to get what they want," she chuckled weakly, her voice breaking as she spoke. Then she shifted her weight, bent over him and closing her eyes, she gave him a gentle kiss on the lips.

"There," she said, "and that's all you're…" she stopped mid-sentence because he had not reopened his eyes, the sound of his breathing was gone and to Kath, he looked peaceful. She covered him with his greatcoat and stood over him for some time, until a bomb landing nearby reminded her of why she was there.

Kath went down into the shelter, found her bother in the flickering light and after a brief argument with the teachers, she took him home. She dragged him by the arm through the streets as he tried to watch the air battle raging above. James did not look scared at all, just fascinated by all the violence and destruction, gawping open-mouthed at the ethereal airships and the impossibly brave fighter pilots locked in a sort of aerial ballet.

Kath and James spent the rest of the raid in their cellar, eating the picnic she had promised herself and waiting for the bombs to stop falling or for Mum to come home.

95

The bombing of London and the southeast continued for two more days and nights.

Branagh Lynch snatched an hour or two of sleep in the hospital's duty room when she could, working tirelessly to deal with the endless stream of casualties. On the third day of the bombing an Airship called the Franz von Hipper dropped three six-hundred-pound bombs on and around Mile End Hospital.

She never came home.

~

"These reprisals are getting hard to stomach, John,"

"I know, Sir, but what can we do?"

"You bloody well tell me, you're the General!"

Sir John French sat in the new cabinet building on Corporation Street in Birmingham listening to the Prime Minister's daily moan. It would last a few minutes and then he would get his turn. Today he planned to bemoan the weak civilians who had decided to chance it with the Germans instead of moving north to fight. This had been Sir John's attitude since he had run and left the divisions under his command to fight a losing battle without their General.

"Good morning, gentlemen," a balding man in his early forties greeted them as he walked in, hung up his bowler hat and fought his way out of an unseasonably thick coat.

"Good morning, First Sea Lord," French replied companionably.

"Morning," Asquith said, distractedly. "Listen, Winston, I wanted to talk to you about these reprisals. Is there nothing we can do?"

"Prime Minister, by our very existence we anger the Hun, so the unfortunates in the south of England incur this horrific punishment *because* we resist. Therefore, we have only two options. Capitulate..." he said, pausing for effect, watching both men and studying their reactions, before shouting, "or... *or we fight!* We take back this green and pleasant land and we meet the Hun with steel and lead to break him and to bind him and to drive him into sea!"

"Yes, yes, but how? What is your big plan?" Asquith demanded.

"Londoners."

"Londoners?" Sir John asked.

"I had the boys over at naval intelligence speak to their counterparts in the Secret Service Bureau. Together they drew up a list of the roughest, most dangerous men London has to offer. Anarchists, radicals, and downright brutes."

"Your plan is to put the future of the nation in the hands of those who would see it burn?" Asquith scoffed.

"I must say, Winston, this is beyond the pale!" added Sir John.

"Think about it," Churchill enthused, "they'll be the front line, grist for the mill, fodder for the German guns while we regroup, rearm and regain our strength. Remember," he fixed Asquith with an unreadable expression, "this has the added advantage of removing all of the thugs from the streets of London."

"Fine, draw something up and I'll take a look," Asquith said noncommittally.

"It's already happening, Prime Minister, that's what the reprisals are about. Their leader…" Churchill checked his notes unnecessarily, "…Harry Tench, under the guidance of a very reliable man of mine, has rallied these ruffians into something of an organised force. Using guerrilla tactics, they're really giving Fritz a headache, hence the reprisals."

"You've gone too far this time, Winston," Asquith reproached.

"You do not go far enough, Sir!" Churchill countered. "You sit here hundreds of miles from the front and do nothing but complain. You dither and delay while our army languishes in barracks and our people are slaughtered in the streets of the capital."

"Really, Winston—"

"I can speak for myself, Sir John," Asquith interrupted, holding up a hand for silence. "As Prime Minister, I speak for the entire country, in fact. Now listen here, you jumped up…"

"What? What were you going to call me, Asquith? Because I've heard it all before, and it's this sort of thing, this, this, this name calling and pettifogging that has led us down this ruinous path!" Churchill inhaled deeply and looked from the soldier to the statesman and back again. "I simply do not have time for it," he said, throwing up his hands in exasperation, before turning on his heel and striding from the room.

When Churchill had left, Sir John spoke quietly.

"I try my best to like the man, but he really knows how to make a chap feel rather foolish."

"He's a damn cad, he… he's a cad!" Asquith said, unable to finish his sentence.

~

They came in the night, Churchill's men. They snatched Asquith and his unpleasant wife, Margot, from their beds along with his most vehement supporters of whom there were few. The party was whisked away to a large country residence and held there.

"Wipe his hands, man, we can't have blood stains on the letter," Churchill said, pacing the cellar impatiently and stopping occasionally to inspect an interesting looking claret or a particularly dusty burgundy.

Asquith was sitting slumped in a low wooden chair, his face bloody and beaten. The only thing preventing the Prime Minister from falling to the floor were the ropes that bound him. The shock of the ice-cold water caused him to convulse, sitting upright again and squinting through the blood and snot that covered his swollen eyes.

"Sign these and it will all be over. Nursey can draw you a nice hot bath and you can finally take up painting or work on your backswing."

Churchill proffered the sheets of paper, copies of a resignation, naming himself as successor. Asquith capitulated because he knew they would just kill him and forge his signature anyway. He wanted to say something now, something fine and memorable, statesmanlike and cutting. He wanted to compare Churchill to the Germans, say that by ignoring the due process of the law he was no better than the Hun, but he simply signed the letters and lamented his own mistakes and inaction and the inherent weaknesses that had led him to this point.

"Jones?" Churchill barked.

"Yessir?"

"Take these and have copies made. Make sure the resistance understands just who is charge now."

Henry Clive took the documents without saying that he didn't think Harry Tench would care either way who was prime minister.

Rescue – 1915

Captain Sir Gerald Clive stared out across the grey wasteland that two months ago had been the charming market town of Bury St. Edmonds. Using the sewers under the town, they were connected to satellite positions that kept the enemy from ever actually reaching the Keep. The pioneers had dug a well in the park and the rest was either grazing or arable land now. His plan for a line of defence had worked and held, drawing the attention of those in Birmingham. They were occasionally supplied from the west with ammunition, food, and even fresh troops.

"Sir, a dispatch for you."

"Thank you, Bates," he said, taking the packet and tearing it open. "Gosh!"

"Good news, Sir?" enquired Stanhope, an impossibly young Lieutenant acting as a sort of Adjutant to Gerald.

"Well," he said, smiling. "Captain Stanhope, let me be the first to congratulate you on your promotion and your official appointment as my adjutant."

"Thank you, Sir," he said, shaking the proffered hand and pointing at the dispatch. "May I?"

"It's not about you," Gerald said, still grinning.

"I don't understand."

"Well," he said, clearing his throat. "A proper CO needs a proper adjutant."

"Oh! Sir, may I be the first to give you joy of your promotion!" They shook hands a second time.

"The dispatch tells me that I was promoted to major some time ago and lieutenant colonel effective yesterday."

"Oh, I am pleased, Sir."

"Who is that Stanhope?"

"Who, Sir?"

"There," he pointed to a sangar tower. "That man is not watching his arcs of fire, he's, he's amusing himself."

"Oh, I rather believe you're right, Sir. Shall I have him brought before you?"

"Absolutely. My office in ten minutes," Sir Gerald agreed, strolling off in the direction of the Headquarters building.

"Private Savage, you were seen failing to adhere to the duties of a sentry."

Lieutenant Colonel Sir Gerald Clive was peering at the man disdainfully from behind a vast mahogany desk. "This action is in direct contravention of King's regulations section forty, neglect to the prejudice of good order and military discipline, paragraph twelve, subsection four, with reference to the behaviour of men whilst carrying out the duties of a sentry in war time. Do you contest this?"

"Yes, Sir." The young man appeared to quiver in his desperate attempt to remain still, arms by his side, shoulders back, chest out and staring at the wall above his CO's head.

"What *were* you doing then, Private Savage? What required such *vigorous* attention?" Gerald asked incredulously.

"I had spilled gravy on my trousers, Sir, and my Mum always said to wait until the offending material was dry and scrape it off with the nail, Sir," implored Savage.

"Convenient," mused Gerald. "I do not however see a stain."

"Me old Mum was a lot of things, Sir, but she knew how to shift a stubborn stain," the young man risked a smile, which was his undoing.

"Something funny, Private Savage? Is the dereliction of a man's duty to King and country a matter for light-hearted witticisms? I am sure that when this is over and the nature of your disgusting little crime is common knowledge there will be much laughing and joking, but until then, until you have learned that vigilance on sentry duty is all, you will not laugh, you will not smile. In fact, I wouldn't be surprised if you are reduced to tears over the coming months. I sincerely hope that your moment's *relief* was worth it, Private Savage." Gerald looked down at the papers on his desk and sighed. "I find you guilty of the charge. You will be taken from this place and subjected to Field Punishment Number One for a period of ninety days. Do you accept my award?"

Field Punishment Number One sounded innocuous enough. Soldiers under sentence were tied to a gun wheel or similarly immovable object for up to two hours in a twenty-four-hour period, for three days in four. The rest of the day would consist of hard labour, with nights spent in the cells. These guidelines were often ignored and with the complete lack of command structure outside of the battalion, anything went.

When Savage hesitated, Gerald took on a fatherly tone and said, "Look man, you can either take it on the chin or wait in the cells for a court martial to be assembled. That could take months, do you understand? The men will see it as shirking, things could become quite difficult for you."

"Yes, Sir," Savage finally said.

"Very well. RSM, get this man out of my sight."

"A-bout turn!" balled the regimental sergeant major. "Quick march, left, right, left!" The corridors and offices of the head-quarters building reverberated with the sound of the RSM's unique drill voice. Gerald reclined in the soft leather chair and closed his eyes for a moment while he pushed thoughts of young Savage from his mind and focused on the Irish prisoner.

Later in the mess, Gerald ensured a few more brother officers shared in the promotions. He made all his company commanders Brevet Majors, as he could do no more without higher authority, and found suitable company seconds from the Warrant Officers. When duties were handed over to the sergeants' mess for the night, the officers did their very best to put a substantial dent in the Keep's champagne reserves.

He had learned recently that the field officers of the 2nd/1st Norfolk's had all been interred as POWs. The same source had said that they were only twenty miles away in Woodbridge. He thought about Connor now, a lovely chap, really, jolly brave to escape like that. It was a damn shame what the lads had done to him in the cellar, but still, you couldn't just believe some paddy off the street. He believed him now, however, and the seed had been planted.

Gerald had often thought of a rescue mission, but he worried that their return would mean that he would lose his new calling. He loved being an officer and he often asked himself *why*.

Why did I not go with Henry to Sandhurst all those years ago?

Now though, now he could save them, and they would probably need to go to Birmingham for medical treatment and debriefing. He could keep his command, or perhaps be given another after proving himself here.

"Right, chaps," he announced. This was not blustering anymore, he was no longer trying to bluff his way to power, now he felt worthy and capable, ensuring that most of his men had survived the worst loss of British life and territory since the Romans.

"We have sufficient of everything. Correct, QM?"

"That's right, Colonel."

"I have said it before, there is no Division anymore, no one sends us orders, we simply tell Birmingham when we've put on a good show or if we need a hand with something, what?" The assembled field officers and warrants murmured assent.

"So, if we have everything we need for the winter, and the Hun, according to intelligence anyway, is waiting for more men and supplies before they reveal themselves, then I propose a mission, one that should be close to the hearts of us all." He looked around the operations room at the men he had come to admire over the last eight weeks.

"I want a course of action from every company commander for a rescue mission and from every warrant, I want an extraction plan." Again, he searched the faces of his men for the realisation of what he was saying, and he began to see reserved smiles on their faces. "Stanhope?" The adjutant pulled down a large-scale map of Bury St. Edmonds and the area to the southeast.

105

"Stalag 102, Woodbridge." Gerald pointed with a golf club at a red X on the map to the north of the market town of Woodbridge. He proceeded to describe the map and its prominent features, pointing out obstacles and known enemy locations. Then he nodded at a pile of papers on a side table.

"Intelligence report from Stanhope. Reconvene at fifteen hundred to review courses of action." With that, he strode confidently from the room.

The intelligence contained in reports came from Gleeson, the Irishman they knew as Connor who they had tortured, interrogated, and then thrown back to the wolves. It showed guard numbers, changeover times, mealtimes, and the armament in each sangar tower. After he had confirmed that Henry and some of his comrades were definitely resident, he had divulged plenty more. Patrol density and concentration of enemy forces were all in the report.

Brokenshire's plan seemed to have the most merit, requiring a single platoon handpicked by the most competent NCOs.

"The plan is to move by truck fifteen miles through the quiet part of the occupied zone, directly to the east of the Keep into the River Gipping at Stowmarket." He pointed with Gerald's golf club.

"Once there, they will either find a boat or use the inflatable's they will carry with them. The men will then navigate the inland waterways to the point at which the Alde passes within two miles of Stalag 102." He indicated this point on the map also.

"This is conveniently the side of the camp that is least defended and the only tower whose changeover coincides with the guards' evening meal. From the river, the platoon will move into the fire support position, four-hundred yards from the wire."

He pointed to the edge of a forestry block near the camp.

"They will leave Corporal Pope's three-section in place, comprising all the crack shots in the battalion. These are men whose accuracy means that they can take out the sentries with no difficulty. They are to lie in wait for signs of our being compromised, only opening fire if absolutely necessary."

"One and two-section will proceed to the form-up point. Here, we will leave the platoon sergeant and two-section, comprising the men with the highest rate of fire." He looked around to make sure his audience was following him.

"Lieutenant Kellard has agreed to lead the raid on the camp. He is our most experienced subaltern and I believe he has shown himself to be brave beyond doubt. The men will follow him anywhere." This was met with nods and murmurs of agreement from the gathered officers.

"They will cut the fence and proceed into the camp, and from here they must work it out on their own, I'm afraid, but they will have cover from darkness and fire support from two points."

His CSM offered an equally creditable extraction plan, involving a stolen German truck or, failing that, a return trip upriver in either the stolen boat or the inflatable boats. One Platoon A company was reorganised and briefed, they rehearsed the plan on the parade ground, they practised the various formations and the use of the boats. They studied the manuals and memorised some useful German phrases, just in case.

A harvest moon hung in the September sky, ethereal in pale orange and twice the size of the last full moon. The boys in Scotland still managed to put out a shipping forecast and conditions looked perfect. That evening, before it was truly dark, the men of A company sat silently or talking quietly, the gravity of the coming night's raid palpable. They were not only risking their lives, but their objective was also a personal one, because it was *their* captured colonel and company commanders that could be rescued tonight.

—

Corporal George Pope lay prone, his position built up and comfortable. One of the boys had placed ponchos over the backs of the four sharpshooters to give them some protection from the elements. Pope had watched the rest of his platoon move through the position and drop off two-section at the form-up point. He'd had an eye on the party cutting the fence, but he was more concerned with the northeast watchtower. The guards were so unprofessional, they had smoked three cigarettes since he'd taken up this position. Something wasn't right, he could feel it. One Section had been inside the camp for four minutes now and every so often he could hear a door open or see a silhouette between two huts. How did the guards not notice?

He felt the warm hand as it clamped over his face, hard like Krupp steel and smelling of tobacco and wet leather. He felt the blade on his throat and he was gone. So taken up was he with the strange behaviour of the sentry that he hadn't heard the squad of German *Sturmtruppen* moving silently through the trees. The grey-clad men with coal-blackened faces enveloped them like a cold dark mist. The rear-facing sentries died noiselessly, then the Germans descended upon the sharpshooters. The whole of three section died without a sound.

Obergefreiter Bert Jansch sent word for the Maxim gun to be brought up and trained on the open ground between them and the camp. Somewhere out there was a British infantry section waiting in vain for their comrades to return. While the *Sturmtruppen* waited, they searched the dead men and helped themselves to their personal effects. George Pope lost his DSO and a silver pocket watch.

Somewhere in the darkness a German voice snickered.

"Look at Bäumer in the tower. Is that his fifth cigarette? He doesn't even smoke."

"Shut the fuck up," hissed Jansch. This was his first mission as squad leader, and he was feeling the pressure.

Lieutenant Tom Kellard had felt honoured to be chosen over fifteen other subalterns for this raid. When the colonel had said he was the most experienced, all that he'd been referring to was a year or so of policing in Ireland, not real fighting. Nothing like this. He worked the knurled grip of his Webley service revolver as he waited for Jones and Parker to cut the fence. That sentry was a bloody disgrace, smoking, and dancing around to keep warm, and he could swear that he was reading something by torchlight too.

The chain-link clattered and they were in. He led from the front like all good officers should. He signalled a halt against the first building and looked up and down the line of nine men he had brought with him. His eyes fell upon the likely culprit, the only one he'd taken under sufferance. Carter, a recent conscript with a slow west country accent. He moved silently over to where he knelt and put his face right in Carter's.

"Can you hear me?" His voice was so quiet that the men on either side of Carter did not realise Kellard was even speaking. Carter nodded, frowning slightly.

"If you can't be quiet, you non-ferocious waste of skin."

Kellard grasped the jaw of the young man firmly with one powerful hand

"If you bugger this up, Carter, if you get one of my blokes killed and *you* make it back to the keep, I'm going give you to Sergeant Grimes. Do you know what he does down there in his cellar? Have you heard the screams?"

Carter nodded mutely, his face a mask of pure terror, drained of any colour.

"Good, now keep quiet and do your job you fucking screamer."

He gave him a light slap to the face and stood up, giving a silent signal for the section to move. Conveniently, the ultra-efficient Germans had labelled the doors of the huts, so they easily found the senior officers' accommodation and read the names. Bradshaw was printed clearly in chalk, second from last. They had no reason to believe that they would find anything but sleeping officers within, but the last two men needed some help through the door from Otto's *Sturmtruppen*. Kellard still thought it was going well until the blankets were thrown off the horizontal Germans and he had twelve submachine guns pointed at him.

He thought quickly. Just because Kellard was an arsehole, it did not mean he was slow, this was capture or he would already be dead. He looked around at his men and down at the Webley shaking in his hand, and he started planning fast.

Six shots. Who will talk? Carter obviously, and five others or one for myself? No, this is it then.

He knew they would rather have him alone than all nine of the others, so he turned to face them, raised his pistol, and started executing his own men. The men he had trained, fought alongside and to some extent cared for over the last two years. The British platoon commander is mother, father, financial advisor and relationship counsellor to the men under his command. Kellard was a callous, uncaring bastard, but he understood his duty and he had carried it out. Now though, he emptied all six chambers of his service revolver into the faces of these innocent young men, even as the Germans wrestled him to the floor, he was still squeezing the trigger.

Click. Click. Click.

When they heard the shots, Sergeant Grimes and the fire support section ran for the fence, confident in the knowledge that Corporal Pope and his section would deal with the guard, and sure enough, shots came from that direction and ricocheted off the tin roof of the tower.

"He needs to get back on the range," Grimes said under his breath as he loped along behind his small band of men. Ape-like in appearance, he was tall, with long muscular arms and side-whiskers reminiscent of a nineteenth-century ostler. He sent two

111

men forward to widen the gap in the fence and they piled through into the cover of a hut wall.

"Come out into the open and place your weapons on the ground," shouted a heavily accented voice from the guard tower, just as a powerful spotlight burst to life blinding Grimes and freezing him to the spot.

"Best do it, lads. Look."

Figures emerged from the shadows, submachine guns pointing from the hip. Grimes lowered his rifle, stepped gingerly into the open and watched as the others followed suit, the spotlight moving with them.

"Kneel slowly, place your hands on your head and look at the ground."

Otto's men brought out the others from one section and bound them all roughly. Most of them were splattered with the blood of their mates, and all were pale and terrified.

"What happened in there?" whispered Grimes.

A white-faced boy of no more than eighteen turned to him and said, "Lieutenant Kellard went mad, Sar'nt. He killed four of our boys before—"

"Silence. Gag that man," Hitler said conversationally while pointing at the boy who spoke. He walked amongst the kneeling men, looking at badges of rank and insignia.

"This one, this one, and..." he looked around and struck upon particularly stupid looking young private. "This one."

Immediately, three men pulled their sidearms and executed Hitler's selection so that the men kneeling with them were left covered in blood, brain, and skull fragments.

"Handbuch, come here," he beckoned Gleeson over. "Is the one who mutilated your hand among these men?"

Gleeson nodded, pointing at Grimes who finally realised what was going on.

"You treacherous bastard!" he shouted.

Hitler turned to Gleeson, gesturing toward Grimes. "Consider this… a parting gift," and with a flick of his head, he commanded two men to hook Grimes under the arms and drag him to a hut.

"He buggers us!" shouted one of the younger Tommies, who was joined in a chorus of similar accusations.

"Yeah, he's a fucking bastard!"

"Silence! Bring me the good Leutnant," Hitler said as he strode to his own hut, and then just before he opened the door, he turned back and spoke acidly.

"Just so you know, your officers *were* here. We interrogated them, then we strung them up in Hyde Park. I hope you like pigeon shit."

Afloat – Berlin 1945

When Carla finally stirred from her sleep, Olga decided that she would give her one more chance before ditching the brat. Her conscience was clear, she felt sure there would be no atrocities committed by the Allies, and Berlin was now at least forty kilometres behind them, which by sunset would be over one hundred.

"Rudi, why don't you take a nap? I'll need you wide awake for when we moor up later." Rudi acquiesced reluctantly and lay down on the warm cushions that his sister had just vacated. Carla emerged wearing similar clothes to Olga, a pair of tan cycling trousers and a simple white blouse, she squinted at the sun as she sat down awkwardly by the companionway, as far away as possible from Olga.

"I suppose I should learn to steer this thing, in case you and Rudi have to splice the mainbrace or something," she said. Olga guessed that this was the closest she would get to an apology and decided to accept it.

"Right," she said, moving to create room for Carla, but keeping a hand on both the tiller and the mainsheet. "Slide in behind me and take hold of this, it's called the tiller. Now look up at that little flag, the wind is coming from that way," she pointed south, "and all you need to do is watch ahead for obstacles and keep an eye on the sail for wrinkles, occasionally checking the flag for changes in the wind."

"Okay," she said, "how hard can it be?" Olga let go of the tiller but maintained control of the mainsheet. Carla panicked when the boat began to drift off course and overcorrected, causing the boat to lurch, and the sails to flap in protest.

"Small corrections are all you need, pull it back towards you until the flag is back where it was before, that's it, you're getting it," Olga said patiently.

After half an hour she gave Carla the mainsheet too and ducked below to grab a map. When she'd folded it the way Yael had shown her, what felt like a lifetime ago but was in fact ninety years in the future, she re-joined Carla in the cockpit. Olga worked out that they would soon enter the *Plauer See*, a large lake some fifty kilometres west of Berlin, but first they would need to pass through the town of Brandenburg; a risky, but unavoidable undertaking.

She decided to try to include Carla. Perhaps if she felt important enough to be consulted, she might feel like she had a say in this and become more bearable company.

"Which do you think is safer, passing through Brandenburg in the day or at night?"

"Hmm," Carla mused, still watching water and then the sail, "millions of people are moving west all the time, we are no different. There won't be the maniacal attitude of fighting to the last old man and boy that we saw in Berlin. The people here will probably leave us alone in the day, but at night we might look like spies or black marketeers?"

"Thank you, I think you're right, I think we should push on through the town and spend the night on one of these islands in the Plauer See." Olga recalled the rhond anchors she had seen in the locker, a curved spike with a ring at one end that enabled you to moor up just about anywhere. Then she spotted a symbol she did not recognise on the map. Two chevrons obstructed the waterway, and her heart sank as the realisation hit her. She could see it now, a set of lock gates, manned by watermen and guarded by *Volkssturm*. Brandenburg an der Havel was an industrial powerhouse, the heart of old Prussia's steel production, the gateway to the Elbe and in turn, the port of Hamburg and the open sea.

Olga looked around her. She could not approach the lock, but the map showed an alternative route where the river forked to the south, becoming the Brandenburger *Stadtkanal*. She checked the wind.

"Ready about," and took the helm from Carla, "uncleat the jibsheet and let it fly, that's it, now clap on to the other jibsheet. No, the jibsheet, yes, wrap it around the winch, then as we come about, pull it in."

"Right," Carla nodded uncertainly.

"Lee Ho!"

The bow turned through the wind and the boom swept around onto the opposite tack, Carla hauled on the sheet and the winch rattled as the jib came taut. Olga stood astride the tiller and pulled in the mainsheet until they were close-hauled on a starboard tack.

"Nice work, now make that fast on the cleat there, that's it." Olga beamed at Carla and, for a moment at least, their differences seemed to have melted away.

They hadn't avoided the danger, just swapped it for a different one and bought some thinking time, this smaller canal also had a lock, but not for another mile.

"You know, this isn't the only boat on the Havel," Carla said. Olga looked at her for a moment, unsure of what she meant. Was she back to her old ways or was she onto something?

"You're right, we can ditch this somewhere discreet and walk through Brandenburg, by which time it will be dark, and we can simply help ourselves to another, perhaps even nicer yacht."

"*Natürlich,*" Carla said, smiling.

"Right, wake your brother and gather up our belongings, including the clothes from last night. We'll dump them away from the boat."

"Okay."

Olga spotted a narrow dike and steered for it, deftly trimming the sails as the boat came around. The dike ran in the direction the wind was blowing from, so at the very last moment, she would have to steer upwind, eventually losing control of the boat. In that time, she would have sailed far enough up the dike to hide the boat and be near enough to the bank to step ashore. She sailed as close to the wind as possible, luffing and touching as the sails and rigging complained loudly. At the last moment she turned into the wind, the boat slowed markedly but she was able to ditch it deep into some tall reeds, eventually hitting the bank with a crunch of wood on wet earth. Olga lowered the sails and decided to strike the mast in order to delay discovery for as long as possible. This done, the three of them began the eight-kilometre walk through fields and the sparsely populated outskirts of Brandenburg, with Olga's Galil slung to the rear under her massive coat.

"What vegetables are ripe this time of year?" Olga asked, knowing only that without the high-tech greenhouses of 2036 she would have been restricted to seasonal vegetables because the import and export of perishable goods had been stopped by the Reich. They had branded it a degenerate decadence and Schwarzer fruit, but everyone knew that the top brass had mountains of it on display at their debauched parties only for it to be left to rot in an alley the morning after, stinking of the corruption it so aptly represented. It occurred to Olga that perhaps the real fetish was the hypocrisy, the knowledge that they were in such contrast to the rhetoric they espoused, that it became a depravity in and of itself.

"Let me see, there should be beetroot, carrots, leeks, parsnips, purple sprouting broccoli, radishes, and maybe even rhubarb," Carla said. "Are you suggesting that we steal from these people?"

"Well," she said, "we can take what little we need, or we can starve. I know what I'm going to do."

"Come, Carla, we can take a little from here and a little from there, no one will miss it," Rudi said, for both had spent the last five years rationed to the point of desperation. For the last two years, ration allocations could not be filled anyway. Rudi did not know, but Carla had seen her mother take an SD man into the alley behind their building. All for a parcel of food; it had been a desperate winter. The thing that disturbed her the most was that she had not been shocked, and she had still enjoyed the rich, nutritious food. She imagined the pain her mother would have felt at the slightest hint of ingratitude over that food and wondered how many other times there had been.

It was dark by the time they reached the outskirts of Brandenburg an der Havel and as expected, every garden had been turned to the production of vegetables. Olga approached the task in the way she imagined Yael would have done it. She agreed a signal with her companions and sent Carla up the path to keep a lookout. She watched the other direction and Rudi, the fastest and best rested, was sent to pluck some late winter veg.

The operation went smoothly, Rudi hopped from garden to garden, returning to Olga when his hands were full. Soon, they had a stockpile of nutritious food that should see them through the next week or so, and they walked on, packs bulging and spirits high.

The town itself had been almost completely destroyed by bombing raids over the course of the war, the main target being the Arado aircraft factory. The town stood in stark contrast to the idyllic countryside Olga had enjoyed all day and once again her senses were assaulted by the smells, sights, and sounds of a population suffering under siege.

Women with buckets queued to use the standpipe at the other end of Bauhofstraße, dirty children played in the moonlight amongst the shadowy rubble, waiting for their mothers, and there were certainly dead bodies hidden under there.

Olga could smell them.

They walked casually along the south bank of the canal, trying to appear as though they belonged. The sky was clear, and a bright spring moon danced upon the gently moving water. An enormous red brick building loomed on the north bank, surrounded by barbed wire fences and guard posts. The citizens of Berlin were ignorant to much of what went on in the countryside of Nazi Germany, even as close as this.

They were unknowingly looking at Brandenburg-Görden Prison, a concentration camp and one-time euthanasia centre. This was the testing ground for the use of Zyklon B and other horrific Nazi practices, where tens of thousands of innocent men, women, and children had been systematically murdered. Now the institution operated as a *Zuchthaus*, a prison for inmates with lengthy sentences, many of them political.

The site still had an effect on the mood of the party, and they forged on in reflective silence, unsure why they felt this cloud of solemnity descend. Olga put it down to fatigue. She was used to sleep deprivation since her training with Yael, but the fact remained she had not slept for thirty-six hours. Now she faced the task of stealing another boat and sailing it to an island at the centre of the lake in the dark, and the thought was demoralising. She racked her brains for a solution that involved sleep a lot sooner than that.

Maybe we could sleep somewhere until the early hours and then steal a boat.

But she looked about and remembered that nearly three-quarters of the town was rubble, and most people would be doubling up or sleeping anywhere that offered protection from the elements.

Why is it that the prison remains untouched by Allied bombs?

She accepted that the plan was the plan and she had to follow it through. That resignation gave her a minor boost, so she rummaged for some carrots and handed them out. Crunching replaced the silence as they walked along the towpath towards the marina.

The town was sleeping by the time Olga, Carla, and Rudi reached the twenty or so boats clustered together on the shores of the Plauer See. Olga decided they should hide nearby and watch, noting any potential threats and generally making sure the coast was clear, but after only an hour, Rudi grew restless and Carla had fallen asleep. It was everything Olga could do not to follow her down that warm, comfortable path that beckoned her. It drew her in, gently tugging her eyes closed and her head forward. Her vision began to blur, and she could feel the delicious sensation of sleep begin to wash over her, then Carla would snore or Rudi would fart, making the boy, the twelve-year-old side of him, snicker.

Olga gently shook Carla awake and dragged herself to her feet, leading the group from their hiding place at the edge of a small wood. No one had been by, not a twitched curtain or rattled rubbish bin from the residents of Görden disturbed the night. They approached the marina cautiously in search of a suitable yacht. Olga decided that a gaff, with its short mast and greater stability, was probably the most suitable, but at this point she would take anything with a sail and a bed as long as it swam. She checked several boats that turned out to be unsuitable, either with rotten timbers or frayed rigging, but one seemed a goer until she noted the port shroud was ready to pull free from the deck.

Eventually, they found a white-hulled gaff with deep red sails and the relatively modern luxury of a roller furling jib. This meant that she did not need to painstakingly hank on the sail, but simply pull on the sheet and the sail would come off the forestay ready to use, like a window blind. The wind direction meant that she could do this now and the yacht would sail directly out into the open lake. They loaded and slipped and sailed away under jib alone, to the *Buhnenwerder* or Beautiful Island in English. They found a jetty on the south and moored up for the rest of the night. Olga asked Rudi to stay awake for a few hours, then to wake Carla. She told them that she had not slept for forty hours, then collapsed in the triangular forepeak at the very front of the boat, falling into a deep and restful sleep.

~

"Wake up!" The voice was a man speaking in the unfamiliar accent of the Rhineland, "*Rouse!*"

Olga opened her eyes and stared at the blue sky through the roof hatch, smacking her lips and yawning, she felt as though she'd slept for a month. She propped herself up on her elbows and her heart skipped a beat. Through the crack in the cabin door, she could see two men in the uniform of one of those special SS Police Regiments. They were standing in the main cabin rifling through their things, and beyond them she could see the feet of Carla and Rudi standing in the cockpit, presumably at gunpoint. The items in Rudi's pack were indeed incriminating, and the HJ knife made it clear that he had deserted his post to be here. As for Carla, her papers clearly showed that she was a Luftwaffe *Flakhelferin* and therefore also a deserter. Olga imagined she herself could probably be tried and executed for aiding and abetting.

The *Grüne Polizei* were the uniformed thugs employed to round up resistance fighters, Roma, Jews, or other undesirables, and execute them. This came to be known as Holocaust by bullet and they were responsible for the deaths of over one million human beings.

"What do we have here, Hubert?" The soldier held a tin out for Hubert to inspect, then he tipped the contents onto the saloon table. A dozen or so tiny pieces of gold and silver scattered across the surface. Olga had to think fast. If she did nothing, the worst case was that these were the kind of men that raped their prisoners before murdering them. The best she could hope for was that all three would die painlessly, but either way, she needed to act. There was an automatic weapon under her bed but moving the cushions and lifting the boards was not an option.

"Ach so, the spoils of war, my dear Jürgen," Hubert said, gingerly prodding the jagged pieces with his forefinger. Olga cast about, hardly daring to move, lest she regain their attention. Her eyes fell upon the escape hatch that most boats had fitted in the forepeak, an absurdly small skylight leading out onto the deck. It was ajar to let in the fresh air and she stared at it, willing it to be a quiet sort of hatch.

"But how do these three, who have clearly never been to war, end up with gold pried from the teeth of dead Russians?" one of the soldiers asked.

She rose to her haunches and slowly raised her hands above her head, one eye on the men hypnotised by the disgusting gold.

"You don't think that they stole it, do you, Jürgen?" Hubert said in a voice of mock astonishment. Olga placed the fingers of each hand carefully in the small gap and watched the men. Their guard was down. This wasn't Poland or Russia, and they thought they were dealing with cowardly children, not hardened partisans fighting for their homeland.

"I suppose we can add this to our collection and leave it off the report? We've got more than enough to hang them with as it is," Jürgen agreed.

She sprung upwards, pushing the hatch open with her head as she pulled herself through.

"Shame to waste it."

As he spoke, Hubert turned his head to look at Olga, whose long legs were disappearing through the escape hatch and onto the deck. Jürgen shouted, and his comrade outside looked down into the boat at the noise. His friends protested, gesticulating wildly at the bow. He stood back up to see what they meant, just as Olga slipped over the side and into the icy water.

Olga swam for her life; Yael had once told her that small arms lose enough velocity from a mere two feet of water to become non-lethal. As rounds whizzed past her, this notion spurred her on even as her lungs begged for air. When she finally surfaced, the boat was about one hundred metres away. She was still an easy target, but the soldiers were looking much closer to the boat, firing at fish she supposed, and she was able to slither ashore into the relative safety of the trees.

She crouched, shivering in the undergrowth, watching the men on the boat. She had not thought any further ahead than this point and now she feared for the safety of Carla and Rudi. The soldiers were still looking around the boat for her, firing pot shots into the lake, so she focused her mind and controlled her breathing. These men must have come from the mainland in the flat-bottomed skiff they'd tied off to her boat, but they would likely carry out the flying court-martial on this island, out of the public eye. It was Carla who was in real danger now and once again, inaction would condemn her to death at best.

She gathered an armful of stones and as she moved stealthily towards the boat, she wished she had some pockets or even some shoes. Olga could see their interest in her waning as she drew her arm back and launched a stone into the water on the far side of the boat. The soldiers all looked over the side to investigate and Carla and Rudi's guard fired his MP40 into the water. She moved fast, in an arc to throw another, this time to land it to the stern of the yacht, where all three piled onto the transom and peered over, firing at the ripples. Silently, she slid into the water at the front of the boat, taking the bowline with her. The yacht and the skiff were now free to drift into the lake, so she gave the prow a gentle shove, encouraging the yacht backwards, and held onto the mooring line, barely daring to breathe.

"We are drifting from the shore," Hubert cried.

"That bitch has cut the mooring line!"

"Hubert and I will go ashore in the skiff. Scheiderbauer, you stay and guard the children," Jürgen ordered.

"Natürlich," Odo said, a baby-faced youth with the cold eyes of a mass murderer.

Hubert and Jürgen climbed awkwardly into the motorboat and started the noisy engine. Olga swam to the other side of the yacht out of sight and waited as they sped towards the shore. She carefully climbed aboard, timing the addition of her weight with the wake of the skiff. Then she lowered herself back into the forepeak.

"You," Odo said, pointing his gun at Carla, "get below."

"What for?" she said, the fear evident in her voice.

"Because I fucking said so!" he snapped, a lascivious smile spreading across his pockmarked face.

Rudi was about to cry out when he stopped himself, remembering the Jericho, and he prayed that Olga had put it where she'd said she would. He closed his eyes and breathed in deeply as his sister was shoved down the companionway, landing with a painful thud. He watched the soldier sneering at him as he closed the shutters, he counted to three and carefully opened the locker just enough to slip his arm inside. He could hear Carla struggling as he laid his hand on the cold metal of the pistol.

BANG!

"Oh, God, Carla," he shouted as he threw open the shutters to see the prostrate form of Odo slumped against the companionway ladder and Olga standing in the forepeak with her Galil.

"We have to move. Carla, I know that was awful, but I really need you to put it in a box for another time and take the helm for me." She risked a hug, taking great care not to make skin to skin contact and whispered something inaudible.

"Of course," she sniffed. She had come terrifyingly close to being raped and it was superhuman of her to step up like this. For the first time, Olga saw the strength of a warrior queen shining through that melancholic teenage exterior.

"Thank you." She hugged Carla once more, and turned to Rudi, "Stand with your head out of the escape hatch and use the deck to support this as you fire." She gave him the Galil, picked up Odo's MP40 and followed Carla out on deck just in time to hear the skiff's engine fire up. She gave Carla the correct rope to pull, took up a fire position on one knee and taking careful aim at the two men in the skiff, she fired.

For an experienced marksman with professional training, hitting a moving target from a moving position is close to impossible. Add to that the motion of the water and Carla's erratic steering and you have a feat of human ability reserved for the most dedicated of operators. Olga was none of these things, but she had two factors in her favour. Firstly, the skiff was an ever-increasing target as it outran the yacht with ease. Secondly, she had an automatic weapon.

Yael was speaking to her from memory as she aimed

"*The position must be firm, the sight picture clear and the shot should be followed through without undue movement. Three-round burst, anymore and you might as well put the gun down and throw the bullets at the target!*"

Breathing deep to shut out any distraction, she began to squeeze the trigger, but before she fired Hubert's head whipped back, a spurt of blood followed the unseen bullet and the skiff veered off to port, almost sending Jürgen overboard.

This is good, one man can't fire and steer, not accurately, Olga reassured herself.

"Good shot, Rudi," she called out as a thumb appeared from the hatch, and he rattled off another three-round burst. She took careful aim again and hit the metal hull of the skiff. She looked up at the jib, the only sail they had set, to see it flapping about like a flag. Carla had tied it off and the wind had changed.

"Carla, pull that sheet in. No, the jib sheet, no that's the... never mind. Here, pull this until there are no wrinkles in the sail."

Both she and Rudi kept shooting until she had to search Odo's body for more rounds, but when she emerged, she saw Jürgen slumped over in the skiff as it sped directly for the yacht, the dead man's hand still gripping the throttle. Olga took the helm and pushed it hard to port in an attempt to avoid collision, but the skiff was too fast and it was too late. The sharp corner of the square sided skiff tore a great gash in the hull of the yacht, which began to fill with water alarmingly fast. She looked at the shore where a group of spectators had gathered, including the criminal police.

"Get the bags, Rudi, make sure the Calculations are in there!" Olga shouted as she boarded the skiff, shoving the soldiers overboard with considerable effort and throttling back the engine. She helped Carla aboard and went back to help Rudi, and then they chucked the Galil into the Plauer See; the ammo was gone, and the explanations would be too difficult. Olga decided to keep the Jericho for now and the MP40s with their ample supply of rounds. Within minutes of impact, the yacht was listing dangerously to port, and it was an uphill struggle to disembark and a considerable drop into the skiff. With their paltry rations and few possessions onboard, Olga took the helm and decided to keep running as she wondered in desperation where the Allied advance might be.

Collaboration – 1915

Oberst Reinhardt Freiherr von Schöenfeld was clearly an important man, as the Reich did not assign a permanent car and driver to just anyone. Schöenfeld was SB, *Sicherheitsbehörde*, and his job was to crush the British resistance before it could begin. He had done this successfully in France, in Belgium before that, and he would do it here. The second son of an untitled nobleman, he was a lean man in his early forties with angular features. As a young man, he'd found the officers of 2nd Guard Uhlan Regiment to be full of oversexed, undereducated Junkers with no ambition beyond *Dulce et decorum est pro patria mori*.

He left the lancers to their dreams of a sweet and proper death for the Fatherland, while he studied law in Berlin. Schöenfeld found that among the intellectuals, artists, and degenerates, he missed his regiment. He became isolated from his peers and began drinking and fighting with local men, pugilists, and petty criminals. He would box and gamble with the men and dance with the women. This continued until he met a policeman, a guest lecturer at the university. His name was Klaus Heidrich, a man both intelligent and robust. Heidrich saw that Reinhardt was in a downward spiral and he rescued him, showing him that a man could appreciate art and music, while still knowing how to fence and box and enjoy rigorous exercise. Reinhardt was enamoured and even swore off alcohol to align with Klaus' own preference.

During his time at university, he and Klaus became close friends, despite the age difference. They shared an interest in psychology and human behaviour, often discussing Freud and Wundt well into the early hours. When he graduated, Klaus encouraged him to apply for a Rhodes scholarship at Oxford, where he studied modern languages, fenced, boxed, and explored.

He returned to Berlin a *Doktor* of German law and a master of modern languages. With his Army commission, Heidrich found him a position as a Hauptleute with the Berlin Criminal Polizei or CriPo. At first, he relished the work, hunting murderers, outsmarting jewel thieves, exposing fraudsters, but the initial rush was soon stifled under the avalanche of paperwork, although he plodded on, one eye always looking to pastures new.

He found a beautiful, intelligent woman called Elsa and they fell in love. When they married, he became a Baron or Freiherr. Elsa died giving birth to their first child, Angela, and that was four years ago.

The grief, along with a newly discovered drive to provide for his child, revived his interest in policing and he began to gain notoriety.

At Heidrich's behest, von Falkenhayn approached Schöenfeld to help found the SB.

They discussed patriotism and propaganda as Falkenhayn wanted Schöenfeld to exploit the German national pride, along with a fear of foreign spies, to permit the SB to operate brutally and for them to welcome it. Schöenfeld pioneered the use of propaganda and public relations in Europe, consuming literature on the subject and using what he had learned to shape the way the SB operated. After assisting with the internal security crackdowns, they asked him to begin planning the application of these theories in occupied nations, with the view to preserving a compliant labour force.

He developed a three-stage plan: Deter, Detain, and Distract. The first stage was in two parts, beginning with a simple propaganda campaign. His first act was to circulate the photograph of George V in the uniform of the 8th Rhenish Cuirassiers, a German regiment, with the slogans:

"If your King can do it, why can't you?"

"His Majesty isn't too proud. Are you?"

Propaganda was far more eloquent now since it was his third time using it. He would show them how happy they could be under German Imperial rule, how happy the French and Belgians were and the benefits of compliance.

If the population did not start to comply, he would begin the reprisals, and while he told everyone that he found the whole thing distasteful, he secretly rather enjoyed it. He enjoyed seeing men who thought that they were special, strong, or brave, broken in a damp basement somewhere, writhing as the electricity tossed them about like a rag doll. He relished the screams that came before the fingernail had even been pulled with any force. He had tortured women too, and had found that they often held out longer than the men, which was far more entertaining. Arousing even.

After you had tortured a few, you often acquired the names of the rest, so you were able to detain them, and then you were free to distract the rest of the population with entertainment, comparatively better conditions, and more propaganda. It was basic stuff really, he had read a book on *The Engineering of Consent* by an Austrian called Bernays, a relation of that degenerate Freud, but it was good stuff, and it worked.

One aspect of his work he had to be found crucial, he'd discovered completely by accident, and this was local insight. When he was struggling to gain traction during the early days of the French occupation and torture was not getting him anywhere, he had, out of desperation, tried a friendly approach to one of the prostitutes he'd picked up.

Initially it was more for the fun of seeing her break than any intelligence she might divulge, but the conversation had led him to some very useful conclusions. From then on, he'd always used a local female driver, snapped up early before the resistance could be established, and he'd found their seemingly banal chattering gave him exactly what he needed.

~

Kath Lynch was rushing now because she still had to collect the car and drive it all the way to Belgravia in under forty-five minutes, and she couldn't afford to mess this up. It was the only job she could find, and the landlord was saying that he hadn't had any rent from her dad in weeks. He didn't seem to care what that implied or how it might make her feel to learn that her father might be dead. The slimy bastard just told her that plenty of folks had lost their house but not their job, so pay up or bugger off out of it. She'd spent the whole episode praying that he wasn't going to offer an alternative payment method, and thankfully he'd left it well alone.

Mercifully, the transport depot was a formerly British establishment with English clerks and English forms. Supervised by a couple of uniformed Huns lurking in the back with their beady eyes and that cold, dead stare, like they could grab you and suck out every joyful memory you'd ever had.

The roads were bloody murder, and if it wasn't a bombed-out building or a huge crater, it was a Hun checkpoint. They looked dubiously at her uniform, a hasty design using pre-existing British patterns and German badges. Her official rank was *Fahrerhelferin,* literally driver helper, but so few existed that she was always called *Hilfshelferin* or Auxiliary helper. When they finally asked for her orders after searching every square inch of the car and triple-checking her papers, their eyes widened, and they rushed her through.

Orders first next time, she thought, hands tapping impatiently on the wheel.

The final checkpoint was Westminster Bridge, which she flew through.

These orders are magic, she thought.

As she crossed from Lambeth in the east into the city in the west, she saw the Palace of Westminster, untouched by the bombing and flying the fucking Boche flag. Then she noticed the time on Big Ben and put her foot down, although the twenty-five-horse-power engine did little in response and changing gear in this thing was a faff, so she waited for it to catch up on its own.

The streets of the West End were empty, with only the odd Hun out on horseback. She imagined that all the toffs had packed up their silver spoons and headed for their country estates at the first sign of trouble and she wasn't wrong. Now, the overwhelming majority in west London were the permanent servants in the aristocracy's London houses, and though many had been warned by their employers to leave, that warning had not come with an invitation to go with them. So, with nowhere to go they held out, rightly assuming that the Germans would leave the West End alone. Now they had the run of these houses for the duration, some even impersonating the owners in order to gain favour with the new regime. Others were unlucky enough to be playing host to them, but that too, had its advantages. Collaboration always did.

~

Schöenfeld was late because he had been waiting for his new driver for nearly three minutes. He had never been late, not since Lichterfelde, when he had managed to get his entire class punished for his unpunctuality. The other boys beat him that night, and he was never late again, until now.

"Fräulein Lynch?"

"Hair Ooberst," Kath opened the door of the shining green Vauxhall type D and held it for her new boss. When he did not move, she blinked.

"Right this way, hair Ooberst," she said in the loud voice one used for foreigners and elderly relatives.

"You are late, Fräulein Lynch," he sighed.

"Am I?" she said, looking around for a church clock. "I don't own a watch, hair Ooberst."

"My name," he said, clearly forcing himself to be patient, "is Oberst Reinhardt Freiherr von Schöenfeld, *O. Oberst*," he said, enunciating so that this island monkey could get it right the next time.

"Yes, of course, Hair *O*berst, I do apologise," she said, shutting the door with slightly more force than required.

"Herr Oberst, it may be lovely here in the West End, but where I live it's, well it's a bomb site, Sir. It takes me ages to get anywhere and until your fella at the checkpoint realised I was working for you, they kept me waiting for quite some time," she explained.

"Perhaps it would be more conducive for you to find you accommodations closer to mine?"

"I have my younger brother, Herr Oberst, he's still at school and my mum, she's, well she's gone and," she paused, reluctant to mention her father and brothers in the army. "So is everyone else."

At first, he could hear the panic in her voice, most likely assuming this was some sort of sexual advance. She *was* very attractive but, what was it the Americans said? Don't shit where you eat? Anyway, he didn't want this crude, uneducated woman for a lover.

Then he heard the sadness. She was still grieving, and this was what his people needed to understand: that perceived compassion now, when these wretches needed it most, would go a long way to quelling the resistance later.

As they entered the eastern sector, his own personal dominion, he watched the queues of the newly homeless waiting for food or a housing assignment. For just a moment the disgust was evident on his face, but he hid it almost immediately. Schöenfeld knew these unfortunates were the key, all he had to do was make them think they could be happy or even comfortable. Every one of these miserable souls represented cheap labour for the Reich and these *Dummkopfs* in the army would push them into doing foolish things and force *him* to execute them.

He would make a gesture today and after a few weeks if she seemed like a useful driver, he would give her the mews house. It was built for just that purpose, and he could see the need for a few midnight excursions in the coming months, so having his driver just at hand would be ideal.

"Fräulein Lynch," he said as they pulled up to a junction. "Stop outside this shop here. No need to get out, I'll only be a moment."

They pulled up outside a pawnbroker and Schöenfeld climbed down from the car and walked inside, where he eyed the proprietor with contempt.

"A watch," he demanded. "Accurate, feminine and inexpensive."

"The Herr Oberst asks a great deal," sang the wizened old man behind the counter in his distinctive east London accent, "but I have *just* the thing."

He theatrically produced a watch by the chain, dangling it for a moment before lowering it into his palm, allowing the sprung clasp to open and reveal the face, all the while oblivious to the look of disdain on Schöenfeld's face. Schöenfeld produced a pen and used it to hook the object from the man's gnarled hands.

"How much?" he demanded, lifting it to his face on the tip of the pen while the man looked on nervously lest he should drop the merchandise.

"For you, Herr Oberst," he licked his finger, apparently calculating, then he wrote the figure on a scrap of receipt paper and handed it to him.

"Acceptable," he said, tossing some coins onto the counter and turning to leave.

"Tell your friends, Herr Oberst," the old man called after him. Schöenfeld stopped at the door.

"What shall I tell them? Oh, there is a wrinkled old Jew with a flair for the theatrical selling overpriced…" he waggled his finger, struggling for the English word, then he smiled wickedly, "*schlock*."

The pawnbroker was taken aback by his use of Yiddish and now looked confused, so Schöenfeld left him wondering. He slipped the watch into his pocket and climbed back into the car.

"Where to, Sir?" Kath asked. "Do you mind plain old *sir*?"

"Yes, that is fine, Fräulein Lynch. Do you know the way to Smithfield market?"

"I certainly do, Sir."

"Good, take me to Saint John's Lane, it is just behind it."

"Right away, Sir." She decided that it would be quicker to cross back into the west where the streets were clear.

Kath couldn't make her mind up about this fellow. She snatched a glance every now and then, there was something about him that seemed off, like he was playing a part. Playing it very well, but still acting. It was as though he knew exactly how

137

a person should behave and he was choosing to do that rather than being his natural self.

She couldn't shake the jarring perfection this side of the river because it was like there had been no invasion. The only clues, despite the emptiness of the streets, which only felt like any normal Sunday, were the odd uniformed person or the even less frequent staff car like hers. Most of the high-ranking officers, she had heard at the depot, had opted for London cabbies.

Smart, she thought, then she'd just assumed the old man must be a bit of a pervert. Who wasn't? Most men liked to sneak a look or a sly feel, it wasn't right but that's just how it was. That led her mind to thoughts of old Pankhurst and her mob of Suffragettes. Now, she'd love a vote, but the way she saw it, there were more important things to get sorted first.

Look at them, all ladies of leisure with nothing better to do with their time, while mugs like me and me old mum have to work our whole lives for half of what blokes get. Probably only would've got votes for posh women anyway. Still, that's all over and I've got a job driving a motor car so who's progressive now?

"What's that?" Schöenfeld asked, shaking her from her reverie.

"Sorry, Sir?"

"You chuckled, I wondered why."

"Honestly Sir, do you want to know what made me chuckle?" She hadn't realised that she even had.

"Of course."

"Well, Sir," she said adjusting the mirror so that she could see his reaction as well as the empty road behind. "I was thinking about women's suffrage and how all them posh birds Like Pankhurst, are nowhere to be seen and I'm the one driving for a living, and how progressive that makes me."

"You are progressive, there are only five other female drivers in the entire zone," he said kindly.

"There you go then, Sir."

"What do you think about the suffragette movement, Fräulein Lynch?" he said, sounding genuinely interested.

"It's all well and good if you have the time, but most of us have to work for a living and I reckon that even if we did get the vote, it would only be for posh women, women who owned a house or was married to someone what did."

"How insightful, Fräulein. I imagine that is exactly what would happen too."

"Thank you, Sir, here we are then, Saint John's Lane, back of Smithfield Market," she said, ratcheting on the handbrake. "Should I keep the engine running?"

"Here," he said, dropping the watch into the front passenger seat. "I want you to leave the engine running and if I'm not back in five minutes, drive to the end of Charterhouse Street and fetch some men from the checkpoint. The watch is yours now, maybe you won't be late tomorrow?"

"Oh, thank you, Sir. Wait for five minutes, then fetch help," she repeated back to him.

"Very good."

Schöenfeld climbed from the car and stepped into Passing Alley, a narrow passage off Saint John's Lane. The partially covered alley led all the way through to Saint John's Road, and was the ideal spot for such an assignation. He instinctively felt for his Walther in its holster as he entered the alley, this sort of thing was way below his paygrade, but he *lived* for it, and it was also the reason he went alone. He could feel it now, the rush of adrenaline, that feeling of extreme focus and near euphoria, this was the nearest thing to fear he had ever felt. Schöenfeld found it difficult to empathise with cowardly men, although in his line of work a coward was a far more welcome sight than a man who imagined himself to be brave.

He could see him now leaning against the wall, a silhouetted figure, homburg pulled low, standing with one foot on the cobbles and one the against the wall, he was smoking and clearly not nervous about this encounter either.

"Mister Sampson?"

The man simply nodded and without speaking, threw his cigarette down. Turning bodily to meet Schöenfeld, he stood now with feet apart, his arms hanging loosely at his side.

"Colonel," he said with a nod. His face was drawn and deeply lined, with a pronounced droop to his left eyelid.

"Do you have it?"

Sampson opened his coat and reached in, causing Schöenfeld's trigger finger to twitch, but he controlled it as Sampson held out a thick package.

When Schöenfeld reached for it, Sampson pulled back.

"Don't you have something for me?" Sampson spoke in the cultured drawl of the educated Englishman, but something about him said, *I work for my money.*

Schöenfeld wondered if there had been money for the education but no estate or allowance for the younger son. He produced an envelope bulging with banknotes.

"I own you now, you know that don't you, Sampson?"

Sampson said nothing and as they exchanged packets he quickly turned to leave, tucking the money into his pocket as he walked away towards Saint John's Road.

Schöenfeld checked his watch and quickened his pace back to the car. He didn't want to watch Lynch driving away while he waited to explain to a bunch of meatheads that it was a false alarm.

"Four-forty-five, Sir, I was about to send for the cavalry," Kath chuckled. "Get what you needed?"

"Yes, thank you. Whitehall, when you're ready."

He fingered the paper protruding from the top of the packet, randomly selected and carefully removed a single sheet with a photograph attached. The document was a police report pertaining to one Paul Clement. A bearded man stared back at him, brow furrowed, and lip curled in contempt. The report described Clement as a radical anarchist with links to extremist groups and knowledge of explosive manufacture. The rap sheet showed previous convictions for assault and affray, with his last known whereabouts listed as Whitechapel.

Let's hope the bombs got this one.

Resistance – 1915

When Lieutenant Kellard and his men failed to return, Gerald sent out a search party. They appeared the following day, minus their officer, hanging from the trees and lampposts that surrounded the Keep. The fear that gripped Sir Gerald on the realisation that the Germans had been right outside their walls stringing up bodies for what must have been hours, was paralysing.

He had no orders for his battalion. Once again, he felt like an imposter. He *was* an imposter.

What was he doing toying with these men's lives? What right had he to do that? He stayed in his room in the mess for days, taking meals there, refusing invitations and passing his duties onto subordinates.

On the evening of the second day he stood at his window and watched the wretched figure of Private Savage being led from the gun by an oddly sympathetic looking provost. Despite the proscribed times, Gerald had ordered that he be tied to the gun wheel for three hours every morning and three in the afternoon, six days out of seven. Around his neck hung a sign which read 'deviant.' The poor boy was in the second month of his sentence by now and the change in his physical appearance astounded Gerald. His shoulders had become rounded, and his arms hung forward, he looked defeated and broken beyond repair. Gerald resolved to commute his sentence first thing tomorrow.

He awoke to the sound of banging against his door.

"Clive!" the voice that accompanied it was loud and devoid of respect. "Open this bloody door!"

He answered it in his dressing gown, bleary-eyed and somewhat stupid.

"Yes, what, oh, Marjoribanks, what is it?"

"Sorry to wake you," he said sarcastically, "but I was going through your desk for some papers. You know how it is, running a battalion and a company at the same time?"

"Err…"

"It was a rhetorical question. While I was carrying out a perfectly legitimate search, I found this." Marjoribanks held a dispatch tightly in his hand, crumpling it slightly, his anger tangible.

"Oh."

"Oh, indeed." he unfolded the paper, stepping back in order to hold it in front of him and read it aloud.

"Captain Clive, we understand that in the absence of any officers of field rank, you have taken command of the First Battalion Norfolk & Suffolk Infantry. If this is in fact the case, you must hand over command to a more experienced officer, as you are not qualified to hold this appointment nor any field command. Please report to HQ south in Cheltenham for reassignment immediately."

He shoved the letter angrily into the inside pocket of his greatcoat and eyed Sir Gerald.

"This is dated weeks ago, when you granted us all brevet rank and promoted half the battalion, including yourself! Twice!" he shouted, bright red in the face now, but master of the emotion that raged below the surface. Still Gerald said nothing, so he continued.

"You promote yourself to Colonel, an unqualified reserve captain, who decided to insinuate himself into the command of a battalion of infantrymen. Then if that wasn't enough, you send the best of them off to die on some ridiculous raid, all on the word of some silver-tongued mick you found wandering around the occupied zone!"

"Lieutenant Colonel."

"What?"

"I promoted myself to Lieutenant Colonel, not Colonel."

"Oh, that's fine then, forget I came."

"What now?"

"I'll tell you what now, you're going to pack your things and when you're ready to leave, you can tell the entire battalion what you bally well did, you can explain to the other company commanders that they are captains again. Then I'll have *Lieutenant* Stanhope make a list of the other promotions you gave out with no authority."

"Where will I go?" He knew that he sounded pathetic, he felt it, but he really did not know where to go.

"I don't care where you go, Clive."

"Sir Gerald."

"What!" Marjoribanks demanded.

"I am still a baronet, and you will afford me the proper form of address," he said, stiffening and staring over his interlocutor's left ear.

"My God, you jumped up little prick! You realise that you are the only man here that calls me Marjoribanks?"

"What?" Clive said in confusion.

"Everyone else in the mess calls me Douglas, or if they're being polite or perhaps facetious it's Viscount Bosham. You see, my dear boy, I am the heir apparent to the Earl of Tweedmouth, so you may call me Lord Bosham or Sir, no need to use my first name at all."

Gerald's mouth moved as if to form words, but when none came he had the good grace to stare at the ground.

"If you're waiting for me to tell you what to do now, then you are even more deplorable that had first imaged," Marjoribanks said, shaking his head and sighing deeply.

"You're a waste of uniform, rations and oxygen, and I want you gone before first light."

~

Beneath the streets of London, beneath the subways of the tube, beneath the Victorian sewerage system and even Hampstead station, there lies a network of tunnels. A national secret, until a quick-thinking politician made either an extremely clever or an extremely foolish decision. When the naval cryptanalysis in Room Forty learned of the imminent threat of invasion, naturally, the first man in government to know was the First Sea Lord.

When Asquith dismissed the danger, Churchill began acting on his own initiative, forming a plan to aid in the establishment and subsequent success of a London-based resistance movement.

Together with a close friend and chief inspector with London's Special Branch, Churchill compiled a list of rough men who would stand ready to do violence, resist, defy and eventually help defeat Britain's enemies.

The men were approached, vetted, given a small retainer and instructions to follow in the event of an invasion. These men now stood in a cavernous convergence of the four main tunnels, some seventy feet below London. Suitably clothed, armed, and fed, they listened intently to their self-appointed leader, one Harry Tench.

He was a shorter man, about five-seven, with a thick red beard and a matching mop of hair. His face was careworn, and like most old seamen he bore a great many tattoos. Some were works of art and others less so.

"We're all here for a reason, perhaps for a particular skill or a past deed, but mainly because we have something special about us that stands out," he called out in a strong East London accent that carried with it the echoes of his time at sea, as well as the hundreds of books he'd devoured during those long voyages.

He surveyed the men before him, nodding to those who made eye contact.

"Something that sets us apart from the men what ran, from the men what collaborated, and from the men who will join the resistance only when things get really fucking desperate. We are the men what stood for something before the world was on fire. We're men of conviction, men of decision, men of action!"

Tench had to shout the last words over the roar of the hundred or so men who stood now, invigorated, and inspired to act.

"Okay, mate, but what are we actually gonna do?" came a voice from the crowd.

"First order of business, we go out amongst the chaos as unarmed civilians and we sabotage. We cut phone lines, we tear down street signs, deny the enemy all that once was ours. This could be trucks, food, power, gas and most importantly, public records!"

"Why burn a load of paper?"

"Because, fellas, those records show the Boche who's who and what's what. I don't want Fritz knowing that I've got form because he might come looking for me. We can't be the only useful men in London, and if these other men are found out from some pig's paperwork, they would be lost to us; dead or interred. Now, go where you know, where you're known, where your own people might be willing to hide you if the Huns come quicker than we thought. Stay out as long as you can but don't get pinched."

The men filed out, collecting wire cutters and matches from a table on their way past.

"Well said, Harry." The voice came from behind, rounded and refined.

"Thanks, what's your name anyway, friend?"

"You can call me Jones if it makes you feel better," he said flatly.

"Suit yourself, Jones."

"I'll be off then, Harry."

"Yeah, bye!"

Harry Tench had been invited to leave the navy some years ago when his political views became misaligned with those of the senior service. After that he'd tried socialism on for size, finding it to contain too many intellectuals incapable of action. He'd looked at nationalism, which was a bit too much like being back in the mob.

Communism seemed a lot like socialism, but then he'd found anarchism and he fell in love. It spoke to him on a metaphysical level. He had never felt so at home, so amongst his own kind. People had always liked him, listened to him, and been willing to follow him, but he secretly hated it. He wanted to be left alone, and he despised the people that felt drawn to him. Internally he called them sheep, externally he would subtly abuse them until he was completely alienated, then he'd move on.

This was different though. He'd done the anarchy thing for years now, been imprisoned for it and at one point, he felt like he was making some progress. But he found that people were just so disappointing, following their emotions wherever they went and shaming others for doing the same, they were just so phoney.

Now that the Germans had decided to invade, his outlook had changed. At first, he felt like another pretender dropping his beliefs the second something else more interesting popped up, but then he thought about it, and knew that this was serious business because the Hun was literally at the gate.

Now people were looking to him, and he understood why. He knew stuff about bombs, about disruption and guns, he could hold a crowd and he'd planned a few things in his time. He was feeling like this was what he had been born for; this moment and the coming war.

But then this Jones character was telling him what to do. It had been his idea in the first place, for Tench to take charge, telling him that his country needed him. To Harry Tench that was obvious, he had seen the guns in the estuary on his way down here, but this chap calling himself Jones would soon out-live his usefulness and Harry looked forward to putting him firmly back in his box.

~

Sir Gerald Clive, formerly of the First Battalion the Norfolk's, was on his last reserves of strength when they found him. Marjoribanks had decided that it would be bad for morale to publicly denounce him, so they packed him a haversack with water, rations and a blanket and they had thought it all very charitable when they let him keep his Webley perhaps hoping his would do the decent thing and turn it on himself. He wrote an apology addressed to the entire mess and they shoved him out of the back door.

"Sorry it had to be like this, old chap, but you brought it all on yourself, you know."

He walked alone along the empty lanes of the Cambridgeshire countryside, eating blackberries, and drinking from rivers and streams.

He contemplated the events that led up to his third downfall in as many years. The shame of losing the family seat in Hampshire had all but finished him. From the sale he'd managed to scrape together enough for a passage to South Africa and seed money for a mining concern, and he'd truly believed it could work, but mining was expensive and the men he'd hired turned out to know more about cards and drink than they ever did about gold.

The miner's strike finished him off and he suffered the humiliation of a trip back to Southampton in second class. He travelled under the pseudonym of Carl Geraldton and spent the entire passage hiding in his cabin, lest he be recognised by someone from the London set travelling in first.

Upon returning to England, he opened the London house and was extended a line of credit by convincing the bank that his concerns in the Transvaal were profitable and lasting. He had some skill at cards and was beginning to feel like he might claw back control over his finances, when his friends at the club grew tired of losing and stopped inviting him to games.

This drove him from polite society and into the gambling dens of the East End, where he found the stakes far lower but the number of willing participants far higher. Most importantly to Gerald, an accusation of cheating there did not mean the same as it did in his world. There was no formal calling out, no threat of pistols at dawn, or any of that tiresome nonsense. He thought himself superior in every way to these men and he took no trouble hiding that fact.

Eventually, the men who had grown tired of losing their hard-earned money to the arrogant aristocrat simply waited outside Sankey's one night and dragged him into an alley. The beating was merciless, because Gerald represented every humiliation, every degradation, every time they had been made to feel like an insect throughout their long, hard lives.

He found himself face down in a puddle while three men kicked him in the torso, although they were careful to avoid his head as the police would be forced to care about the likes of him turning up dead, and they didn't need that kind of bother. Children and ladies of the night stood by and laughed as he drifted in and out of consciousness, their painted faces and high-pitched laughter dancing through his dreams.

By the time he had recovered, the Christmas Day naval attacks were all over the news and war was imminent. He decided that this was his chance, he could gamble with other bored officers where there would be pay, and he could close the London house and live cheaply in the mess. Wars were about the only time that men without means or influence could win lucrative promotions. He undertook to win a medal or some such bravery accolade and rise through the ranks, buying back Broadlands and rejuvenating the family fortune.

When England stayed out of the war, the army didn't want an untrained officer that cost the pay of a captain, and they told him to wait for the call-up. He'd spent the last of his cash retrieving his uniform and mess dress from the pawnbrokers and he had arranged to stay at his club while the London house was let, the advanced rent long since frittered away. That was when he started looking up old friends, inviting himself for one last weekend of fun before marching off to war. This worked for far longer than he imagined it could, and it used up every last ounce of goodwill that the landed gentry of Great Britain had left for the cad Sir Gerald had become. He rode the wave right up until his weekend with Henry in Norfolk.

Now he was disgraced, homeless and incorrectly dressed, driven out of his mind with hunger and contemplating the use of one of his six rounds to shoot a partridge.

"Hello, Sir, are you alright? You don't look alright. In fact…"

"Let him answer then, Jim."

"What's that then? Looks like he's a Colonel if I'm not mistook."

"Jim, will you leave it?"

"Hello," Gerald whispered. "Do you like partridge?"

"You what, why you whisperin'?"

"I'm stalking a partridge," he whispered again. "If you're quiet, I'll share it with you."

"He's lost the plot, Margie."

"Jim," she hissed.

"What? He's not shootin' no partridge, not with that Bulldog, certainly not in the state he's in. Come on, Sir, we've got some food you can eat."

"You have food, well why are we out here trying to shoot game with a bally pistol then? Come on, lead the way."

"Right you are, Sir, why don't you put that away for now?" Jim said.

Margie and Jim took Gerald about two miles away to a small farm where a large group of refugees were living in the outbuildings. The farmer and his extended family were in the cottage and Margie and Jim lived in an empty stable. Gerald saw the comparative squalor these people were living in and thought of the comfortable conditions that his forward planning had provided to the men of the Keep.

"Come on, we'll take you inside to meet Tom," Margie said.

"Tom's the Farmer," Jim said.

"Indeed," Gerald replied.

The farm was a picturesque, red-brick idyll, from the inglenook fireplace to the ivy-covered barn, to the troop of geese patrolling the yard. The farmer was a sturdy, quiet man in his late forties, his wife Jane being equally sturdy and equally stoic. Their muted kindness was typical of some country folk and Gerald welcomed it. Tom's son Michael sat by the fire reading *The Ragged-Trousered Philanthropists*. He'd been in the artillery until the breach of his Howitzer had accidentally closed on his hand during the Doomsday invasion and they sent him home. He waggled a raw looking mutilated hand at Gerald, who ate soup in the tiny parlour.

"Doomsday?" Gerald asked.

"Yeah, the day of the invasion."

"Oh, we were calling it Day Zero," he said with a shrug.

"What happened, Sir, how come you're here? I mean, you're more than welcome, but don't you have a battalion to command?"

Gerald had been racking his brains about this ever since he saw Jim and Margie, and he'd hoped the partridge stunt might buy him some time, but he couldn't keep it up. The truth was obviously a duff, why hadn't he had his sleeves tailored before he left? He knew why, that batman knew what was going on, knew what he was up to and there was no way he'd have sewn his old captain's pips back on anyway.

Better say something soon or he'll get suspicious.

"That bad was it, Sir?" Michael asked.

153

"Sorry, what?"

"You looked rather pensive just then, Sir, I thought that maybe you were thinking about what brought you here? Maybe the loss of your unit to the Boche is a little too raw to talk about just yet?"

"It wasn't my whole unit, but the rest of us sort of, went our separate ways," he said with finality.

"What will you do now, Sir?"

"Do you happen to have a map?" Clive asked.

Tom cleared the table, unrolled a map and weighed down the edges.

"That's Cambridge, Newmarket, that there's the old London Road and that's us. Woodend Farm in between Bottisham and Stow Cum Quy."

Gerald studied the map for a while, every so often glancing furtively at his audience. When he was satisfied, he grunted.

"What you thinking, Sir?" Michael asked.

"I heard that Cambridge was holding. Who is there?"

"From what I can gather, it's just a bunch of students, OTC types, backed up by the townspeople and quite a few refugees from closer to London," Michael said, Tom nodding in agreement.

"Indeed, no regular army presence of any kind?"

"No, Sir, there just aren't the numbers. Two thirds of the BEF were stationed in the southeast, now they're either POWs or toast. Apart from a few scattered units, like them lot in Bury, the rest are desperately trying to train the reserves. Apparently, there's a few months until the Boche can afford to fight again and try to occupy the rest of the country. My advice, Sir, if you're looking for the Army, is to head for the Midlands."

"To tell you the truth, Michael," Gerald said wearily, "I don't want to run from the fight, I think there's plenty to be done right here." He pointed to their location on the map.

"We are so close to the enemy, is there any resistance activity in the area?"

He eyed at Michael now with a look of genuine interest, a look he imagined that the lad had never received from an officer before and from that moment on, Michael was his man.

"I was hoping you'd say that Sir. Now, give me five minutes and I'll come and fetch you." Michael rushed from the room, pulling on a coat with his good hand.

Ten minutes later Sir Gerald Clive, apparent Colonel of infantry, stood before about twenty bedraggled men and women in the big barn. Very few had what Gerald would have called a soldierly bearing, in fact most had ripped or darned clothes, but all at least were here and willing, and most importantly, they were armed. Some with shotguns, others with Lee Enfield rifles and one or two even had German MP40s.

Gerald surveyed them as Michael talked. They were mostly young and fit, farmworkers most likely and the best bit was that they had no clue. They would hang on his every word, and if it went wrong, it would be their lack of experience that the others would blame, not Gerald's incompetence.

"Lads, this is Colonel Clive of the Norfolk Regiment. He's sick and tired of the inaction of the so-called government in hiding and he wants to take the fight to the Boche!"

He turned to Clive.

"Sir, I give you the East Cambridge Militia."

"Good evening, ladies and gentlemen. Words cannot express how pleased I am to have found you. I was separated from my men during the invasion, and I have been eager to do everything I can to play old harry with these Huns ever since. Now, I have been able to do a few things on my own, sneaking into the occupied zone and disrupting what little I can, but together we could do so much more."

He felt no remorse as he lied to these people about his rank or his actions since the invasion, he only thought about how desperately he wanted that feeling back; the god-like power, the respect, the absolute authority to play with men's lives.

"Does anyone, apart from young Michael here, have any military experience, however limited?"

All eyes fell on an older man carrying a German Mauser. A dark green, cable-knit jumper hung loosely about his solidly built frame. It bore the marks of darning over years of heavy use. His lined face was slightly obscured by grey stubble and a livid scar, his hair thick and streaked with flecks of grey. Alf Grant scratched his nose and sniffed before squaring his shoulders and taking a step forward in a pseudo-military manner.

"This is Corporal Alfred Grant, he fought in the Second Boer War with the King's Own Yorkshire Light Infantry," Michael said as they shook hands.

"Sir, once upon a time I was Corporal Grant, but I've gone by Alf these many years and I'd prefer to keep it that way," Alf said in a thick Yorkshire accent.

"A pleasure, Alf, I see you've already bagged yourself a Boche rifle," Gerald chuckled, turning to both men and leaning towards them conspiratorially, he said, "I think that we three should have a little chat later on, make sure that we're singing from the same hymn sheet, what?"

He turned back to the rest.

"I think the thing to do here is for us to have a bit of a training day tomorrow, getting to know each other and getting a feel for the level we're all working at, then perhaps we can start to plan a few sorties into the occupied zone."

He raised his eyebrows and smiled at the group, he was back from the wilderness and in charge once more.

~

"Now, how have you been managing the planning and command stuff thus far?" Gerald asked, sitting around the kitchen table with Tom, Michael, and Alf.

"Michael has taken on more of a training and administrative role on account of his mangled hand, Sir," Alf said, slouched and smoking a rolled-up cigarette with his armpits hooked over the back of the chair.

"That's right sir, I'm not much use with a rifle these days, but I do know quite a bit about how the army likes to do things and more importantly how the Boche like to do things. Alf has been leading on the ground and between us, we have done some worthwhile work."

He made a gesture that included his father in *us*.

157

"What sort of things have you been up to?" Gerald asked Tom.

"Well, Sir, we started off just taking folk in, then we realised that a few of us had guns and we understood that it was a common desire to have a pop at the Hun. Alf here…" he pointed with his pipe and Alf took over.

"I had a few tricks up my sleeve from my time in the cape."

"Do tell, old chap!"

Gerald saw this as a chance to glean some information and add to his fictional experience. He was leaning forward now, animated in anticipation of a good story.

"Well, my number one rule is you don't shit on your own doorstep, and that goes for all parts of life, not just scrappin'."

He winked at Michael, who laughed. Alf continued.

"Now, that means everything we do is a long way from Woodend and well inside the Occupied Zone. I started by taking three of our best lads out to recce the area, work out what was what, where the Germans were living, where they patrolled and what sort of weapons and vehicles they'd brought with them."

"What did you find?" Gerald asked, inviting Alf to show him on the map.

"Well, after five days of watching from high ground we built up a pretty good picture of what's going on over in Essex and Suffolk. The answer was, not a lot, the Boche were nowhere to be seen. So, we begged some food and water, and we pushed a little further in towards London. That's where we found them,

158

thousands of 'em. We kept off the roads, only moving at night, you know."

He winked knowingly at Gerald.

"And we reckon the nearest Hun garrison to us has got to be Bishop's Stortford, then east to Braintree and Colchester and to Stevenage. The border basically follows Stane Street, you know, the old Roman road?"

"Indeed, so the ground between here and there is a sort of dead zone, a no-man's-land if you will?" Gerald asked.

"Aye, *no-man's-land,* that's a good term for it. Of course, there are a few holdouts, but most came north and west to escape the Boche. See, they're rounding folk up and putting them into concentration camps. Got them digging a canal between London and Portsmouth, according to a farmer we met. His eldest was taken, no reason given, just grabbed off the street."

Alf looked away and out of the window.

"Gosh, that's not cricket, not at all," Gerald said sadly.

"Kitchener did it in Africa, that's how we won in the end, the Boers wanted to stop their women and children starving to death in the camps," Alf admitted.

It was Gerald's turn to look away as he did not like to hear the British compared with the Hun like this, but it certainly would explain his less than warm reception in the Transvaal.

"Perhaps. Now look here, are any of our men local to this area?" Gerald asked, indicating an area about ten miles to the south of Woodend Farm.

"Aye, Fred is, he came with us on the recce," Alf said.

"Michael, do you think you could fetch him for me? There's a good chap."

159

He went unquestioningly, and Gerald knew that he was in. This was his militia now, and his farm if he wanted it.

"Now, what's this place here? Audley End?" Gerald asked, knowing perfectly well what it was and that his old friend Thomas leased it and hardly ever stayed there. He intended to take the residents of Woodend Farm into the occupied zone and onto the Audley End Estate where it would become a stronghold much like the Keep at Bury. This was his vision, and he would be patient in realising it, allowing the others to think it was their idea, then he would have them begging him to lead them and he was going to love every second.

Lock - Berlin 1945

The little boat planed eastwards over the Plauer See offering a contrasting experience to sailing at five knots in near silence, and soon they were wet and weary from the spray and the noise.

Olga's chest tightened when she spotted uniformed men on the bridge at Kirchmöser, knowing that she had to make a choice: hope that they wouldn't fire upon children and try to head west to the Allied line, or head northeast up the Havel and hope the advance hurried up. She gritted her teeth, kicked a tarp to hide her MP40 and opened the throttle right up. The force jerked all three of them back, reminding Olga of the mag-lev train she'd taken to Bristol all those months ago, ninety years in the future.

Rudi was quiet now the adrenaline of earlier had gone. He was wet, cold, scared, and the noise from the boat was horrid. On top of that he had just killed two of his countrymen. He was only twelve years old and should be playing or at school, not defending himself from the soldiers of his own country.

He decided at that moment that he was finished with Hitler, finished with National Socialism and with Germany. He was going to learn English and leave this broken and haunted place because he hated it. All the adults were crazy; they'd followed Hitler into a war against the entire world believing they could just keep winning. He had believed too, but he was a child, an indoctrinated member of the Hitler Youth and the *Volkssturm*.

Not anymore though. Now he was defecting.

Olga said he would be a physicist, so in that case he would be a British physicist and eat deep fried fish with chips and drink tea with milk and sugar.

The men on the bridge ordered them to stop. Olga studied them, realising that they were old men in CriPo uniforms, not young bullies in Nazi costumes. She pointed the boat at the centre of the bridge, and as they passed beneath they all closed their eyes while Rudi groped for the gun just to feel the comforting ridges on the pistol grip. The spray continued to shower them, the engine continued to deafen them, and fear continued to grip their hearts. Olga dared to open her eyes, flinching slightly to find that they had reached the other side unscathed.

"We made it," Rudi cried, hugging Carla and then Olga, which they both found quite awkward so he stopped.

They had stolen a Nazi police boat and gotten away with it. Olga felt capable of anything, and in that moment she felt invincible. She believed that they really could see this thing through to the end, build the time machine and fix whatever needed to be fixed. She thought of finding a school for Rudi and Carla, a little cottage, maybe she could take some classes too. Then when he was ready, they would find him a university with an excellent physics program, and finally he would be able to build his time machine and she would fulfil her destiny.

"Olga?" Rudi cried.

"What?"

"Look!"

"Shit!"

"I know," Carla said. Just ahead they were faced with the concrete edifice of the Wusterwitz lock, twelve metres wide and two hundred long, and every cold grey concrete inch of it was covered with uniformed policemen of every description.

Black-clad Algermeine SS men, Green Ordnungspolizei, grey Waffen SS, and civil policemen in leather trench coats. These were not kindly old men as before at the bridge, not combat veterans, but dead-eyed dealers of death. These were the various mechanisms of Adolf Eichmann's holocaust, that for the last seven years had dedicated themselves to the systematic murder of men, women, and children in the name of racial superiority. These men would happily kill them and anyone else they thought they could get away with killing before their near decade-long orgy of depravity would finally be over.

~

A few miles northwest of Kiev, Ukraine, there lies a steep-sided ravine called Babi Yar. On a cold day in late September of 1941 the local Jewish population was ordered to report to a street near the rail flats. Here, the Jews of Kiev assumed that they were to be deported to farms in east, so they arrived with their worldly goods and most carried food for the journey.

Even when they were marched past the trains and out of the city, they trusted their Ukrainian guides, their countrymen, to treat them well.

After two miles they reached Babi Yar, but they could not see the ravine, for it was hidden from view by masses of troops. A macabre production line ensued, surprising the victims who due to their own great number, could not see what was going on ahead until it was actually happening to them. Their luggage was taken, then their shoes and coats, before they were systematically stripped of every possession, every garment, every dignity, each item piled high with its cousins. Photographs of beloved family members, the delicate shoes of little girls and boys, spectacles and most interesting to the soldiers, the money and jewellery of their wretched victims were piled high for the clerks to inventory.

This atrocity was made possible not only by the depravity of the Ordnungspolizei – the SS, SD and SiPo – but the countrymen of the victims recruited specially to garner the trust of these people, making it easier to lure them to their unimaginable fate.

When they were stripped naked, huddling together cold and afraid, their undergarments piled high, they were channelled into a tunnel formed of club-wielding Aryans. These men loomed, threatening to beat any who ran or tried to warn those behind still oblivious to their fate. At the end of the tunnel was Babi Yar, the ravine. Forced to walk over the soft, warm bodies of their now-dead family members, neighbours, and friends, they too stood in the ravine, shivering and terrified. While forty at a time, they were made to lie down on the naked body of that friend, that child, that fellow human being and wait for another fellow human being to join them in the fifteen-metre-deep ravine, but this man was clothed, clothed in the *feldgrau* of the *Einsatzgruppen* or the faded green *Ordnungspolizei*. He moved among his prey efficiently, inhumanly, and fired a single round into the back of the head of each of the crying, naked and humiliated humans until everyone that was different to him was dead. Then forty more and forty more all day for two whole days until nearly thirty thousand sons, daughters, mothers, fathers, sisters, brothers, and grandparents had been systematically exterminated.

It was these same men who returned from the war in the east with bags of gold teeth and the treasured heirlooms of families who no longer existed, crying that they were only following orders, that they were not evil, just that disobedience was not something that was ever entertained. However, some men did refuse to participate, and these men were moved to fighting units whereby they could kill Russians, safe in the knowledge that the playing field was level.

These men, these ghouls, dead but for a beating heart, numb but for the rush of power that came from control – the ultimate control being the denial of the existence of another human – stood now on the lock waiting for one last chance to kill.

Each pair of sunken, soulless eyes watched Olga, Rudi and Carla baying for more blood, more violence, more death; desperate to slake an unquenchable thirst – gratified at any cost. The boat grew closer but slowed, and Olga did not know what to do. She did not know about Babi Yar, but she knew the look of pure evil in the eyes of the men she was approaching, and she knew she did not have a plan. They would be played with like a cat might play with a mouse until the cat grew bored, then they would be dead. The boat was idling now and a new noise replaced that of the motor; the orchestral droning of aircraft, growing louder as the boat slowly drifted towards its fate.

Olga tried to breathe and filled her lungs with water as the shockwave from the four-thousand-pound Blockbuster, a gift from one of the hundreds of B-17 Flying Fortresses now overhead, flipped the little boat and obliterated the lock, vaporising the despicable men occupying it. Olga clawed desperately at the shards of light above her, willing herself up, up, up to the surface where she coughed and inhaled smoke instead of water. Debris littered the surface and she scanned it desperately for Rudi and Carla, calling only to find that no sound came from her. She thrashed about with no energy to call upon, she longed to go back to sleep, back to the cold caress of the dark water that called to her, pulled her down and she gave herself over to it.

He slammed his open palm on the cheap wooden table, but Olga did not flinch, she just stared directly ahead at the spot on the wall she was beginning to know better than her own face.

The room was cold and uninviting, the walls a painted brick that in parts revealed layers of different colours beneath, likely the whim of some Nazi psychologist who had decided which colour would be most conducive to interrogation. The British who now occupied it seemed less concerned with the decor than they were with completing the denazification process that would allow them to finally return home after six long years of war.

166

"If you would just admit what you are we can move on. We can get you processed and sort something out for your young companions."

"I am not what you say I am. I am an British citizen. My father is Frank Felsen, Warrant Officer Class 1 in the Queen's Royal Regiment."

"Yes, Olga, you've told us this and there's no record of a WO1 Frank Felsen in any regiment, arm, or branch of service, there's no record of you, and your friends out there are most *definitely* German citizens."

"I was born in Clapham on the first of June 1926, my address in twenty-four Load Lane and my mother is Nadine Felsen nee Lyn—"

"Yes, yes, okay, I have it all written down here. Tell me again how you came to be on the outskirts of Berlin on the twenty-seventh of April of this year."

"I don't remember, I told you that already too!"

The man lit a cigarette, closing his eyes as he inhaled, and he threw his head back to blow smoke at the ceiling of the grey, featureless interrogation room. When he had first introduced himself last week, he wore the collar dogs and mudguards of the British Army's Intelligence Corps, along with the three gold pips denoting the rank of captain. Now his jacket hung, crumpled on the back of a chair and the sleeves of his uniform shirt were rolled up. His braces hung about his legs and he appeared to have aged in the short time she had known him.

"You understand my untenable situation here, Olga? As long as you claim British citizenship, we can't simply ship you off to a camp, because if it turned out you *are* telling the truth there would be scandal," implored the intelligence officer.

"So let me go home to England, to my mother and brothers," Olga replied coolly.

"And what of these German children you claim responsibility for? Children who by all accounts pulled you out of the Havel last week. We are not keen on shipping them off either, not without possession of all the facts first."

"And then the bomb went off and we were thrown into the water. Rudi clung to a piece of debris, a tyre perhaps? Then I saw Olga disappear beneath the surface, so I swam towards her and dragged her back up, but she was unconscious."

Carla stopped and became distant, which the interrogator put down to the excitement of the experience, something akin to shellshock, she'd live.

But she had seen something in the water that day, the first time her skin had touched Olga's, and now she saw it again. Russians, so many of them, and her mother and the little, stuffed *Kuschelbär*. She began to cry and tears ran down her impassive face, because this wasn't the past and it couldn't be the future. *Kuschelbär* was lost and so was *Mutti*. Another vision, hazier, Germans, a scaffold in the Gendarmenmarkt...

"Fräulein Kessler?" Are you alright?" The woman stood, reached over the table and tapped Carla's shoulder with the very tips of her fingers in a sort of unwilling gesture of condolence or perhaps comfort.

"Tea?"

The heavy wooden door opened at the same time as the intruder knocked.

"Good morning. Major Henry Clive," the intruder announced, offering a hand to the captain, who took it in the way that a drowning man might accept that of a rescuer.

"Der Engländer?" Olga said under her breath. Clive raised his eyebrows.

"Well, I can take it from here, old chap," he said, removing his jacket.

"Very good, Sir," the captain replied, grabbing his belongings and rushing from the room, almost looking forward to interrogating the truckload of brainwashed kids found hiding in the forest and calling themselves *Der Werwolf*.

"I am a British subject!" she said, while Clive rolled up his sleeves in a decidedly unsoldierly fashion.

"That remains to be seen," he said, lighting a cigarette from a monogrammed case.

"Oh," he looked from her back to the case, "it says in your file that you have repeatedly refused the offer to smoke."

Although Henry Clive wore the uniform of a major in the intelligence corps, he was in fact an intelligence officer with the Special Operations Executive. Orders from on high had demanded all personnel to don a uniform of some kind, and this seemed the most appropriate and least conspicuous of the near god-like field officer ranks.

169

He drew deeply on the French Gauloise and stared out of the high window at the clouds, he was tired, tired of lying and being lied to, tired of Germans and tired of Germany.

Clive had not seen England since he was landed on a beach in Brittany in 1942 and looking in the mirror that morning, he'd seen a man he did not recognise. Years of malnourishment had left his face drawn and appearing far older than his twenty-three years. His only visible scar, a drooping eyelid, upset him more than he would ever admit, but he cried almost every time he was alone, which was often.

He had been in Hamburg for some months relaying messages across battle lines and sabotaging the remnants of the first *Fall-schirm-Armee,* when the Allied advance washed over the city and transformed a fiercely resistant and brave *Volkssturm* into droves of dejected, starving, and homeless wretches. Every last one had to be fed, housed, and processed, and the real Nazi fanatics needed to be identified and removed from the general population. This denazification process of determining who was a scared civilian and who was a fully paid-up Horst-Wessel-Lied-whistling party member with blood on their hands, however indirectly, fell to the intelligence services.

Clive was now seconded for this task and resented it immensely, he deserved a break and he deserved to go home to his family. His interest was piqued, however, when a girl of unconfirmed nationality wearing German clothes and ostensibly travelling with German children, claimed to be a British citizen speaking perfect English with a middle-class London accent. He read the file and told the local commander he was taking over, so now here he was. The report was accurate so far, but new intelligence had come to light about an incident prior to the bomb and the lock where she had nearly drowned.

"What were you doing stealing a yacht and fighting with German soldiers?"

"My duty."

She stuck out her chin in defiance.

"It's your duty to steal yachts from German civilians? I say yachts because it was more than one, wasn't it, Fräulein Felsen?" the Fräulein was a deliberate ruse.

"*Miss* Felsen, I'm not a bloody Jerry," she said, repeating an insult she herself had received only that morning.

"Forgive me, but you have no papers. In fact, the only thing you have is that commendable accent, but you couldn't even say who the king was…"

"I could," she cut him off indignantly, because her fascist brainwashing school had made them memorise the kings and queens of the Houses of Hohenzollern and Saxe-Coburg and Gotha.

"You said that our king was called Edward VIII of Saxe-Coburg and Gotha."

"I did."

"Edward VIII of the House of Windsor was only king for a few months in 1936, our king since then has been George VI of Windsor," he said incredulously.

"That's not what I learned at school."

"Where did you go to school?"

"Clapham."

"Which school?"

"Clapham School for Girls."

She lied with such conviction that she thought he was going to buy it.

"Doesn't exist."

"You smoke too much."

"I hardly think that's any of your business."

"It's bad for you. It can cause cancer, lung disease, emphysema, and erectile dysfunction."

"Now see here, that's quite enough of that, young lady." He pulled hard on his cigarette, but she'd stolen the joy from it, so he stubbed it out and, leaning forwards with both hands on the table, he looked her directly in the eye.

"Who the hell are you?"

"My name is Olga Fels–"

"Enough! I don't need that again, I've read all that, and it's a bally German name anyway. Why pick a German name for an alias?"

"We don't pick our names, Major Clive, our parents do!" she said, with an expression of puzzlement, "isn't Felsen the German word for cliff?"

"Yes," he said affecting disinterest in that quintessentially British way. "I suppose it is. Where are you going with this?"

"Clive means cliff!" she intoned.

"What…what do you think you know?" He seemed bored now, pulling the chair up and sitting directly opposite her, as Olga recalled the words of Ruth, her Mossad rescuer:

You are the only person who can survive the jump.

She instinctively grabbed his bare forearm, but he pulled it away reflexively and frowned at her. His face became a mask of confusion, contorting through myriad emotions until eventually, tears began to run silently down his cheeks.

"You have jumped…through time I mean?" Olga ventured.

"Oh God, the things I…"

"Shh," she touched his arm gently, "you haven't done anything, not yet."

"Oh, but I have, I've done so many terrible things."

A shadow fell across his face and his eyes seemed to focus upon something very far away.

"Hey," she whispered, "I've done things too, things I *had* to do. It's people like us who do what needs to be done, regardless of the personal cost, which keep the rest of the world from harm."

Olga was confused, for in him she saw no evil, certainly not on the scale he appeared to mourn. She saw a scared boy forced into manhood by war, nearly broken by it, but not quite. She caught glimpses of a beating in a Parisian alley, a sword fight in an Alsace Châteaux, and torture in a Rouen basement. She could feel his heart harden and the boy he'd been melt away.

"People like us who fight wars in the shadows, without recognition or parades, we need to stick together," she whispered.

Clive placed a hand in each of hers and took a deep breath.

"What now?"

"Well, now I've got two terrified kids that need somewhere safe and warm to sleep."

"Yes, of course, I'll have papers drawn up this morning and British passports by the end of the week. I'll be here in Hamburg for some time, so perhaps the best thing is for me to acquire a comfortable house and set you three up there?"

173

"I assume you mean to get us to England eventually."

"Unless you had a better idea?"

"No, it's just that I want time to get their English up to scratch. Imagine school for them with those accents?"

"Gosh, that would be frightful…hmm, perhaps a private tutor to begin with?"

"Slow down, Henry, talk me through your plan, I'm lost."

"Yes, I tend to get rather ahead of myself…a house here in Hamburg for a few months while I tie up loose ends and pave the way with my father?"

An image of a much younger Sir Gerald Clive came to him, although it wasn't a photograph he'd seen at Broadlands but an actual memory of his father. He was dressed like a French Maquisard minus the beret, the pips and crown of a colonel on one of the wide epaulettes of his brown leather jacket. He carried an MP40 and German stick grenades, with a Luger stuffed into his wide leather belt. The MP40 took him to a laboratory in 1962 and further into the unexplored rabbit warren that was now his mind.

"Henry?"

"What? Sorry, I was miles away."

"The plan?"

"Oh, yes, indeed, err…" he lit another Gauloise for something to do and when he had blown a lungful of smoke at the ceiling, he continued.

"Broadlands is my family's estate in Hampshire. We can go there and live quietly until Rudolph is old enough. I'm sorry, I felt like I knew what we were supposed to be doing but it eludes me."

"We have to keep Rudi safe until he can build us a time machine, but in the meantime you and I need to work out what exactly we need to fix and how to do it," she smiled. "We could encourage Carla to study modern history, she will have graduated long before Rudi will know enough to build a time machine."

"I see," he responded as he rubbed his temples. "So we go to Broadlands and get them a tutor. I think it best if I stay on with this lot, it'll give me access to all kinds of useful stuff."

He looked at Olga for a moment.

"I have to make this right, Olga," he said, putting his jacket on.

"I know," she said quietly.

Spy – 1915

Kath's brother James did not want to leave his familiar school in Mile End, nor did he want to move into the Hun's mews house, but when the other children discovered that his sister was working for the Boche he soon reconsidered.

Children could be cruel, and these children were angry, homeless, hungry, and many of them orphaned. It started with crude graffiti of his sister on her knees to a German, complete with spiked helmet, and he'd broken a boy's nose for that. When someone called her a Boxhead whore to his face, he really lost his cool.

James could fight as well as any other eleven-year-old, better than most, even. His father was a talented boxer who had taught all his children how to fight, including Kath, and that it was okay to fight dirty when the odds were against you. However, three on one were the slightest odds that he would accept, and after that it was time to scarper. So he did, all the way to the servants' quarters of Schöenfeld's swanky West End drum, where he found himself at a smaller school, one for the children of servants to the great and good of Belgravia. If he was hard before, now he was untouchable. The lessons were tougher, but he was king of that playground and he loved it.

"When you have dropped me at Whitehall I want you to take the afternoon off, Fräulein Lynch."

176

"Yes, Sir," she said, eyeing him in the rear-view mirror as they sped through the empty streets of Westminster.

"I will need you this evening and possibly well into the night, so make sure that the car is refuelled and you get a hot meal from the cook before we leave," he instructed, smiling at her reflection.

"Yes, Sir."

It was only quarter past twelve when she dropped Schöenfeld off and she had filled the car up that morning. There was little Kath loved more in this world than a nap, so she raced back to Belgravia to the most comfortable bed any Lynch had ever slept in. She parked in a garage beneath the small mews that she and James lived in. James was never at home these days. He and his band of local children roamed the streets of the deserted West End looking for empty houses to loot or bombed-out houses to occupy for a few hours. She stuck her head into the kitchen and grabbed a soft white roll from a stack cooling on the scrubbed oak table.

"You need more than that, Kath, my dear, you're a growing girl. Stay and have some of this soup?" the rotund cook said, motherly and kind *now*, but cross her and your life would not be worth living.

Kath flashed her winning smile.

"Could you put it in a mug for me, please, Mrs Higgins? I'm rushed off my feet here and I need to get a couple of hours sleep because old snowflake wants me out driving all night."

"You mind how you talk, you know better than anyone what that man is capable of. Here, enjoy your nap," she winked and smiled, revealing a very few teeth, none of which were white.

177

"Thank you kindly."

Kath walked out across the cobbled courtyard to her little house. Stairs inside the garage led up to a two-bedroom apartment, with one other large room serving as parlour, kitchen and everything else. Servants from the house kept the place clean, emptied the chamber pots and replenished the coal.

On cold winter mornings, when she woke early to start the car, Kath would find that the fire had already been lit and her heavy boots placed to warm in front of the grate. She loved it here, the design meant that on those bitter mornings, she didn't have to go out into the cold air or scrape ice from the windscreen.

When she reached the top of the stairs, she kicked off her boots, putting her now empty mug into the sink and proceeded to undress, hanging her uniform up in her room and wrapping herself in a thick dressing gown. Kath filled a large, long-handled brass pan with coals from the fire, replaced the lid and carried it carefully into her bedroom where she placed it between the covers and began to move it slowly around, warming the bed. After tipping the coals into her bedroom fireplace she let her robe fall to the floor and climbed into her nicely warmed bed.

She lay still for a while and thought of the dream she often had, always the same but never any less exciting. He would come into her room at night and slide into bed beside her, kissing her neck and whispering the things he knew she loved to hear. Afterwards, they would lie for a long while in each other's arms before he whispered a reluctant goodbye and left her.

Kath shook her head, it could never happen it would be far too dangerous, and she enjoyed her comfortable position here too much to jeopardise it for a cheap thrill. Kath thought about the day they had met, Schöenfeld had sent her into Spitalfields while he met a confidential informant. She wandered through the market, browsing the many stalls, touching the rich fabrics, inhaling the fragrant spices and flowers and admiring the jewellery.

"You should buy that," came an unfamiliar man's voice over her shoulder.

"Fuck off," she said, turning to face it. "Oh…" He was actually quite handsome and she found herself smiling. She placed her hand on her chest and began to apologise. "Sorry, I thought…"

"Don't worry, I get it all the time. You should, though, it would really bring out your eyes." He held the green costume emerald up level with her face. "Yeah, beautiful, with or without the necklace." And he smiled, delivering her first disappointment. But then, most people's teeth were awful, so what could she do?

"You're a bit forward, aren't you?" she said, tapping him lightly on a rock-hard shoulder. "I'm Kath." She held out her hand.

"Harry Tench. Shall we get a cuppa, maybe a bun?"

"I just met you," she said, placing a hand on a slab-like pectoral through a collarless, soft cotton shirt. "I have got some time to kill, though. Come on." She linked her arm through his and then threaded through the crowd to a small café called Sinbad's.

"What's this?" he said after ordering two iced buns, and two coffees. Kath had developed a taste for it at the Belgravia house and Tench on the HMS *Surprise*.

"You know full well what *this* is," she said, fingering her lapel. "And you know that I don't have a choice if I want a roof over my head."

"You're too bloody right as well, "he sighed. "What do you do for them, for this roof?"

"I'm a driver," she said, playing with the saltshaker.

"Nice," he nodded approvingly. "You don't see many women drivers, do you?"

"No, I'm a pioneer," she said with a wry smile.

"Who do you drive?"

"Some stuffy old Colonel, more like a policeman really. He's okay I s'pose, but you hear things, don't you?"

"What kind of things?"

He seemed genuinely interested, and she found this very attractive. Most men couldn't care less what she had to say about anything, unless it was juicy gossip about someone they didn't like, or you were talking about them.

"He's supposed to be a right wrong 'un, rounding up those poor boys from the resistance and doing all sorts to them in the basement under Cannon Row. Nasty stuff. Stuff I don't want to know about."

"Are you comfortable working for a man like that?" he asked flatly.

"Like I said, I ain't got much choice. It's that or the poor house, and my local one of them got bombed."

"Okay, I didn't mean nothing by it," he raised his hands in a conciliatory gesture and the coffees came, an Arabic man with a great bushy moustache brought them with two iced buns.

"Thanks," they said in unison and chuckled.

There was something between them. She could feel it, and if she was honest, it had been months since she had felt anything. She wouldn't touch any of the Germans on principle and the servants that were young enough were so soft and far too interested in their own appearance to attract girls like Kath. She looked at Tench. He was a lot older than her, but he wasn't old, and he was muscular and rugged. He seemed dangerous, but not in a threatening way.

"What's going on in there?" he asked, nodding at her head. "What are you thinking?"

"I'm thinking that I'm bored."

She stuffed the iced bun into her face and smiled to reveal a mouth filled with food. Pulling out the watch Schöenfeld had given her and looking at it, she said, "I have to be back at my car in ten minutes."

She took a long drink of coffee and stood up with a wink and a jerk of the head, indicating that he should follow.

He took her by the hand and led her through the market quickly. They weaved through the crowd in a blur of colours, smells, sounds, and an electric, heady excitement over what she was about to do.

Tench opened a service door for her and led her down some steps to a storeroom. As soon as the door closed, they began kissing and pawing at each other. She ran her hands over the muscles of his back and his broad shoulders. He slid his hands under the hem of her uniform skirt and brought it up around her waist, revealing the tops of her stockings and a suspender belt. He picked her up with ease and she wrapped her legs around him while he struggled with his fly. Kath gasped with pleasure, giving herself over completely to the sensation.

"Oi, you're not allowed back here! Fuck off out of it, now!"

Light flooded the room as a man dressed in the grey dustcoat of the market officials stepped over the threshold.

"Alright mate, keep your shirt on," Tench sighed, fastening his fly.

"It's you what ought to keep his shirt on you dirty bugger, and you, does your commanding officer know that you're out cavorting instead of performing your duty?"

"Seriously mate, fuck off now, you've made your point and we're goin'."

"I'm obliged to re—"

"Let me stop you there," Kath interjected dangerously. "The man I work for would not appreciate the indiscretions of his personal driver being made public knowledge. It would embarrass him, and those what embarrass him wind up in the basement under Cannon Row."

Kath fixed the old man with her piercing green eyes and he withered visibly at the thought of that place at the horrors associated with it.

"Why are you still here?" she snapped, and the old man backed through the door, his face mask of terror.

182

Her watch fell from her uniform pocket and swung back and forth between them from the chain fixed to a button on her tunic, Kath snatched it up and glanced at the time.

"Bollocks, I'm going to be late," she whispered breathlessly, while tucking her watch away and pulling down her skirt.

"I'm here at this time every Tuesday," he told her breathlessly. "Or Thursday evenings from six?"

"I'll see you on Thursday," she said, smiling as she walked to the door, then she turned and looked him in the eye. "Next time, I won't let you off so easily."

She smiled again, stepped out into the passage and realised she had no idea where she was.

"Can you, er…" she said, sticking her head back into the room, "show me out please?"

They kissed once more before re-entering the market and parting ways. Kath checked her watch and noticed that she was a few minutes late. She picked up the pace, turning her shoulders left and right to cut a path through the throng and out along Brushfield street to where she had left Schöenfeld. Checking her watch again before entering his field of vision, she realised she was about ten minutes late.

She'd been late before, and he had shown his displeasure in such a subtle way that Kath was oblivious. Now though, she could see that his meeting had lasted longer than anticipated, so she hung back waiting for the man whose face she was not supposed to see conclude his business with Schöenfeld.

The man eventually climbed out of the car. He looked British and well-off, one eye was half closed and as he looked around, he looked directly at her. Kath froze, but he made no sign of this to Schöenfeld, simply closing the car door and walking away. She waited another minute before approaching the car herself.

"I saw you was busy sir, so I left and came back."

"Yes, thank you. You didn't happen to see my contact's face, by any chance?"

"Oh, no, Sir."

She didn't know why she'd lied, but it was the first truly rebellious act of many to come.

~

Months passed since her first meeting with Harry Tench, and she had met with him most Thursday evenings. At first it was all about the sex, but they began talking and she had so many questions. He told her about the navy and about politics, but he never talked about his life since the invasion. She didn't know where he lived or what he did for work. He always had money for drinks, but his clothes were old and wearing out.

One evening over a cup of coffee at Sinbad's this changed.

"Do you remember when we first met?" he asked her.

"Course I do," she giggled.

"Not that, I mean before, when we sat in here and I asked you how you felt about working for the Boche?"

"Yeah, you nearly blew it," she said in mock anger.

"I know, that's why I left off, but does it bother you that they are slowly breaking us? The camps full of dissidents, the fucking royals and ruling elite all fucking collaborating and getting back their lands? Except now they're Graf von Kent or Freiherr von Westminster and I'll bet there's plenty in the free zone that'd love to collaborate, but it's the reprisals that get me. Those bastards are vicious, and all the resistance want is to get their country back. I swear…the things that have been done to them…" he paused, waiting to gauge her response to his dangerous words.

"It is," she said, "and it does…"

She had been making circles in the salt with her finger but now she looked up at him.

"…*bother* me, I mean. I wish there was something I could do, but…"

She had said the magic words and Tench fought the compulsion to smile widely.

"What if I told you there was? Just a small thing here and there?"

He hated this part, the look they gave him as they realised that this, right now, this conversation was what it had all been about, information. They never said It though, they just looked sad and hurt and either agreed to do it or left. Kath Lynch was the first mark Tench not been sure of since he'd started recruiting after the invasion.

"Are you having a fucking bath, Harry Tench?"

Her voice was quiet but the malice was evident.

"All this time, you fucking piece of shit. Come on then, what would you have me do? Spy on the old man? Blow up his car? I'd be driving it, you fucking idiot, and I've got James to think about. What happens to him if I end up in the basement under Cannon Row?"

"Keep your voice down," He hissed, grabbing her wrists tightly. "I liked you, I *like* you, but you're right, I saw the uniform and I thought you might be a good person to have onside.

I'm sorry if that seems like a betrayal, but this is bigger than some weekly fuck in a storeroom. This is the future of Britain! Our capital is under fucking German occupation! Do you understand? I need all the help I can get, and you need to know that when the time comes, if you didn't help, you'll be strung up with the rest of the collaborators, then where will that little brother of yours be?"

"Jesus fucking Christ," she said, her lip curled in disgust. "You're a right piece of work, you cold fucking bastard, but yeah, you're right. I do think about it and I *am* going to help, but not 'cause you threatened my family, or to string me up, but because I want to, and I'll pick and choose. If I think it's too dangerous, I ain't fucking doing it, alright?"

Her reaction was novel, but still, she was onboard, fight or no fight and that pair of balls she had would come in handy.

It was small stuff at first, just like he'd said. Schöenfeld's routine, his likes and dislikes, who he met and how often, just talking with no actual cloak and dagger stuff. Then he wanted her to find things out about troop transport, weapons storage, and rations. She didn't know how to get that kind of information, so he walked her through it and slowly she gathered it, a snatch of conversation here and a glimpse of a file there and soon she was able to build up a pretty grim picture of the state of the *Deutsches Heer*.

They were underfed, undersupplied and undermanned, the war in the east had been a costly one and the lack of vital imports of cotton, camphor, pyrites and saltpetre was slowing arms production to below half of pre-war levels.

Kath was torn. It was terrifying when she was doing the spy stuff, but the buzz was better than anything she'd known before and when they met up, they would shag and she would tell him all about it. She was living on the very edge of the knife, and it felt amazing.

Now she lay in bed thinking about Harry and waiting to get up and drive Schöenfeld. She washed and dressed and made her way across the freezing courtyard to the kitchens for a hot meal.

Audley End – 1915

Gerald watched through a pair of field glasses as a glorious orange sun set behind the house at Audley End and cast an imposing shadow on the expansive lawns. He and Alf were in a hide they had occupied for the last few hours. Alf and two others had been there a few days, just watching the place from different vantage points. The militia were now forty able-bodied men and women, each with a military weapon of some description from one side or the other. They now lay in hiding, twenty in the woods behind Gerald and twenty in a forestry block to the north waiting for the signal to attack.

"This is what it's been like for the last five days, Sir, a couple of staff that stuck around and nowt else. I sent Fred down to speak with them, he knows one or two, just to say hello, like. They seem terrified but they stayed because they say it's their duty to look after it for Lord Howard de Walden. Who is God knows where with the Tenth Hussars, but you never know, he could be napoo."

"Do you think they'll be any trouble?" Gerald asked.

"Nah, I think they're terrified, they'll be glad to feel protected. Fred says that they've been busy growing vegetables and raising livestock on the grounds. I think this place is going to work nicely, we'll just have to be careful not to shit on own doorstep."

"Indeed. Let's bring the troops to the edge of the treeline while Fred and I walk down and have a chat with the staff, then I'll give you the nod to come down in twos and threes. We don't want to spook the staff and in the unlikely event that the Germans are in the area, we won't show our hand until the last possible moment."

He surveyed it now, the palatial seventeenth-century home with its crenelated rooves and light limestone façade. The fastidiously landscaped grounds bordered on three sides by water and the stoutly built stable block that would house his newly acquired personal army.

As he and Fred took a leisurely stroll through the fields to the house, he could not help the wide grin beginning to spread across his jowly face. He'd done it. He'd got himself a command again, albeit a small one, and now he had his castle back; a far grander one this time. He instructed Fred to find the gardener or the stable hand and bring them to the kitchens while he went to see what household staff were about.

"Good evening," he said to a matronly woman whom he took to be the cook. "My name is Colonel…"

In for a penny in for a pound, he thought.

"Sir Gerald Clive, late of the First Battalion the Norfolk regiment."

He watched with delight as she curtsied.

"M'lord. Mrs Cowperthwaite, head cook, what can I do for you? Are you a friend of his Lordship?" she asked deferentially but with the keen eye of a suspicious old crone.

"Indeed, Howard de Walden and I do know one another, though it is merely a passing acquaintance," he said, although in truth he had beaten the man one too many times at piquet and now they barely spoke.

"I was hoping we could sit down and have a chat about this bally occupation. Oh, and Sir Gerald is fine. Alas, I am not afforded the title of Lord."

"Tea, Sir Gerald?"

"Lovely," he said as he sat down at the scrubbed oak table.

The huge kitchen with its immense stove and endless worktops took him back to his youth at Broadlands, sneaking in and stealing cakes or biscuits from under Cook's nose.

"It'll be a minute, Sir Gerald," she said taking a seat with a sigh. "What did you want a chat about? These bloody Boche? To be fair they've left us alone since the invasion... we never see them these days."

"That's what I wanted to talk to you about. We come from a farm north of here, near Cambridge, and we've been doing our very best to make as much trouble for the Hun as we can but the problem is that we're just too far away, you see, we don't like to sh—"

Mrs Cowperthwaite shot him a reproachful glance, reminding him so much of nanny that Gerald took a slightly different tack.

"We don't like to do anything too close to home, lest there be...Reprisals. So we'd like to use this estate as a base of operations to be able to push further south and really give the Boche a jolly good drubbing, what?"

"You want to turn Audley End into a Barracks?" she asked, disgusted.

"Think of the protection my men and I could offer, and we would bring some civilians to help you in the kitchen and on the grounds."

"I might as well walk around with a big target on my back!" she protested.

"Now, Mrs Cowperthwaite, one day this will all be over, and there will only be two categories of person. There will be those of us who fought to save Britain and those of us," he paused, fixing her with a cold grey eye, "who collaborated."

"Oh, Sir Gerald, I am no collaborator, I have never even spoken to a German," she said indignantly as she rose from her seat to take the whistling kettle from the stove.

"Excellent, I'll fetch my men. Ah, Fred, and you've made some friends, I see?" Fred stood at the door with a decrepit gardener in wellington boots and a motheaten tank top, and a stable boy of about twelve; his limbs too long for his torso and ears far too big for his head.

"Sir, this is Peter the gardener and Andrew the stable boy. I've brought them up to speed and they say they'll be glad of the help and the protection."

The four staff of Audley End, the other being a scullery maid of nineteen called Gracie, now stood with most of the militia in the great hall. A fire blazed in the hearth and hot soup gurgled in the eager bellies of the congregation. Sir Gerald, self-appointed Lord of the manor, addressed his dominion.

"Ladies and gentlemen, brave warriors of the resistance, and loyal supporters of the cause, tonight marks a new chapter for Audley End and for the fight against our oppressors. Tonight, we have gained back hallowed English soil in the name of Great Britain and His Majesty. Tonight, we have won a bloodless victory against the vile Hun and their cruel regime. Tomorrow, we begin fortifying the palace and turning it into a defensible stronghold against the Boche."

"Three cheers for Sir Gerald!" Michael shouted.

"Hip, Hip, Huzzah!"

"Three cheers for the resistance!"

"Hip, Hip, Huzzah!"

"And one for luck!" Michael cried eagerly, smiling as the assembled voices rang out. When the excitement died down, he stepped forward to cover some administrative points.

"Shortly, Tom and Jim will arrive from Woodend with our baggage and the supplies we've amassed in the last months. We will need to get the whole lot unloaded into the stable courtyard so that they can return while it is still dark and fetch the last of the supplies and the rest of our people. I'd ask that everyone lend a hand with the task, so that our comrades aren't travelling in broad daylight."

Michael had taken to his role of adjutant admirably, although he never wore a uniform, everyone treated him with the respect afforded to someone of a far higher rank than Bombardier. Some of the militiamen had taken to calling him Sir, which gave Alf a good laugh.

The next day they began the task of fortifying Audley End. Gerald wanted to avoid drawing any eyes, be they German or local, and so to that end he invited, insisted, and coerced the residents of Saffron Waldon to take up residence in the palace, stable block, or surrounding farms. The site was either walled or protected by one of three rivers, the Cam being the largest and most visible both from the front of the palace and the main road. To avoid overt defences on this side, the field on either bank was flooded by partially damming the Cam at the southbridge making a full-frontal assault very unlikely from the west, while the three gatehouses were manned and fitted with telephones.

"If we're going to defend this place against more than the local WI we're going to need machine guns. At least five to do it right," Alf said as he, Gerald, and Michael toured the grounds inspecting the defences. They had flooded more fields to the north, forcing any enemy attack to come from the east where they had dug a series of ditches fed from the Cam and filled them with barbed wire and spikes.

"The whole thing looks quite innocent, I must say," Gerald opined.

He hoped to remain inconspicuous here for as long as possible, but he understood that they needed the machine guns to take advantage of the defences which, in truth, would only ever slow down a determined enemy.

"Where do you suppose we *get* five machine guns?" Gerald added.

"I'd hoped that *you'd* have had some leads on that one, Sir." Alf said, eying him sceptically.

"Yes, well the way I see it, we have two options: steal from our own or steal from the Hun," he said, as if the matter was closed.

"Alright, Sir, but do you know where we might start looking?"

"You tell me Alf, haven't you lived in this area for years?"

"Aye, but I left the army nine years ago, and all I can think of is the OTC in Cambridge, but I don't think they'd have one Vickers even for training."

"Agreed, and I hardly think that pinching a Hun gun would be possible, given our numbers. What we might concentrate on in the immediate term then, is gathering intelligence and we may find that what we seek comes to us."

"That does sound sensible, Sir," Michael said, "but if we are to make do without machine guns then I'd like to get the men practising their shooting. It's said that a couple of good Tommies firing fast enough can fool the Boche into thinking that there's a machine where there's not one."

"There you have it," Gerald said.

~

The newly named Audley Liberation Front spent the next few months stockpiling supplies for the winter and tentatively pushing further and further out from the palace. They brought in anyone willing, and after a period of screening, they were allowed to join the main residence. Gerald had allocated himself a suite of rooms overlooking the ornate gardens, and the mahogany four-poster bed he shared with Gracie was fit for royalty, which was to be expected from arguably the most magnificent estate in Great Britain.

They left the Germans alone to begin with, opting instead to build relationships with other groups and to build up a picture of the ground around them. This tactic of caution finally paid off when they were very cagily approached by another resistance group about a potential joint operation. The group called themselves Liberty, and had received a tip-off about a consignment of Caldwell machine guns that had arrived from Australia right before the invasion. They were now sitting in a warehouse just outside Ipswich where they had been waiting for onward transportation to the training school at Belton Park.

"Listen, George, I don't know you from Adam, and I've had bad intelligence before," Gerald said to the small, stocky man in military boots and putties, with a leather jacket and a knitted cap. Slung at his back he wore the coveted German MP40, though nobody knew that he only had ten rounds for it and those he kept in his Luger: a trophy of the same kill.

"I guess you'll have to trust us, Sir Gerald."

Beyond his military attire, everything else about this man was Essex, including his nasal accent.

"No, that's just it, old chap, I don't, but you need our numbers just as much as we need your intelligence. Now, I've come up with a plan that should keep us both happy. Michael?"

He invited Michael to speak to the small group, comprising Alf, George, and George's Lieutenant, Nigel.

A large-scale map had been mounted on the wall of what had been the nursery but was now their operations room, and which overlooked the flooded lawns to the west of the house. Michael had affected the use of a riding crop since arriving at Audley and suited the position of ununiformed adjutant well, discovering that he fitted into the clothes left by the land steward and now wore the shooting tweeds every day.

"It's simple enough, chaps. The assaulting team will consist of George's men and the fire support team will be men from our outfit. We undertake to cover you if anything goes wrong and, more importantly since you don't have the means, we will handle the extraction and insertion logistics. Your increased risk will be acknowledged by way of a forty/sixty split in your favour."

He smiled at George and Nigel, who seemed to have reservations.

"Hang on a minute, we take all the risk, and you get near 'arf the swag? Nah, I'm not having that; I don't care if you're the Duke of Bleedin' York."

"You can't do it without us, and we simply don't trust you yet," responded Michael firmly.

"Seventy/thirty," George demanded.

"Are you a gambling man, George?" Gerald asked, a glint in his eye.

"It's been known."

"I'll make a different deal. We only need six guns, so if you agree to give us that amount, we'll let you keep the rest, and we split any other *swag,* as you call it, seventy/thirty?"

"What if there are only six guns?"

"Then Lady Luck is not smiling on you and therein lies the gamble. However, if there are twenty guns, you will get fourteen, and I cannot imagine that the British Army would ship such a trifling amount as ten or even fifteen," Gerald said, with palms turned up in a conciliatory gesture. He had sworn off gambling since leaving the Keep, and his position was far too precarious to make enemies over worthless money.

Besides, the real currency in this new world was power, and he had that in spades.

Rat – 1916

"Surely, Sir," Gleeson said, more deferential than ever before, "that's my obligations fulfilled, and I can be on my way back to Ireland?"

"But you were so effective on your last mission… so reliable and you really delivered the goods."

Hitler's English was better every day, he was using all the funny little idioms and really enjoying the language. He raised a limp hand for silence. This man was his dog now and there was no way he would lose someone so useful.

"We simply cannot entertain the idea of your leaving. You should have got out when we were winning, right after the invasion, but now is a bad time. Anyway, this next one is very juicy. London… *undercover.*"

He raised his eyebrows, letting the sentiment hang in the air like bait.

"We've circulated some police reports about you to give you the appearance of… well, exactly who you are, actually. A thug, a rabble-rouser, and a terrorist."

He sat back in the chair of his commandeered office, luxuriating in the soft leather, and watched Gleeson turn a deeper shade of red.

"I want you to infiltrate the resistance in London. Your contact is a man called von Schöenfeld, a colonel in SB intelligence, code name *Havelok*," he said, tossing a dossier across the desk and motioning for Gleeson to pick it up.

"Undercover work can take months. Years even," Gleeson complained.

"If you take that long, I'll assume you've defected and have you expunged."

Hitler tried the word out on his lips, using it in a sentence for the first time.

"*Expunged*," he repeated, satisfied with his choice.

"Can I at least have a few days at home before I go in?" Gleeson pleaded.

"I'm afraid not."

Hitler pondered this piece of English. *What a strange expression*, he was not afraid to give this man bad news. This English habit of dressing things up and not saying what they meant had its uses, but not here. He would speak to his teacher about more direct language. Then he considered the ambiguity of the word *expunged* and realised that he still had a great deal to learn about this language that was apparently so similar to German.

"Right you are," Gleeson said through gritted teeth, before snatching up the dossier and leaving.

"Oh, and Gleeson," he waited for him to turn around, "don't think that we won't pay a visit to Saoirse and"—He read from a note on his desk—"Aoife, if you don't check in with *Havelok* regularly."

He butchered the pronunciation of both names, but Gleeson was no fool. He knew he was over a barrel and did his utmost to remain calm.

"Probably get me own boys to do your dirty work too, no doubt?"

"German resources in that part of Ireland are limited, so it would be more economical to have local assets handle work of that nature."

Gleeson left, closing the door behind him with slightly more force than was necessary.

Gleeson had arranged to be transported to Limehouse police station in East London where he would be released, apparently after a night in the drunk tank. No British officers saw him arrive, and the morning shift had all the paperwork to believe his story. Now he was on his own, he thought back to the ride down from Suffolk with Schöenfeld and of that little firebrand of a driver.

He knew his stuff, clearly an ex-cop and a good one if a bit of an oddball, but then the best intelligence officers were. He had made it very easy to stay in touch without risking discovery and given him a code word to use if he was picked up by any one of the police forces patrolling London these days. They had discussed the key players in the London resistance movement and Gleeson felt confident that he could make short work of the whole thing.

"This is Sampson," Schöenfeld explained as he handed over pictures. "You'll know him from his drooping left eye. He's a puppet master of sorts, ostensibly bankrolled by the government in hiding and other wealthy men in the free zone. Do not approach him or acknowledge him as an authority figure because he is an agent of mine."

"Who then?"

The car bumped along the dark road and Gleeson looked out of the window to find a fog had descended, shrouding the car and causing his driver to slow.

"It's a real pea-souper tonight, Sir," she said.

"Yes," Schöenfeld replied, impatient of the interruption, which had not been the first. He continued to brief Gleeson. "Who the leader is remains unclear, and his identity is a key objective in this operation."

"Thank you, Sir. I have to ask, what's the actual mission here? And when can I go home and see my family?"

Schöenfeld began to roll his silver pen between the thumb and forefinger of each hand, staring at it lazily, he sighed and turned his head, fixing Gleeson with his cold, grey eyes.

"You are here for as long as you want your family in Ireland to remain unharmed. I was informed that this had already been made clear to you. When a resistance no longer exists in London, then you may go home to the snake-infested bog that you crawled from all those years ago. Now," he said, brightening unnervingly and smiling at Gleeson, "do we have an accord?"

"Aye, understood."

He sat staring out of the window at the darkness for a long time, studying his reflection; his face, broad with a bulbous nose sitting between warm green eyes, bore the lines and ruddy complexion of a hard life lived outdoors. His ears seemed to have grown. He was sure that they hadn't always been this big, had they? He floated a course of action to Schöenfeld.

"I wonder if the best way to go about it is to try to usurp whoever is in charge. A series of botched operations should do it. I'll publicly argue for a different course of action every time and you can ensure its failure. When the mob grows tired of the constant fuck-ups, I'll be the obvious choice. Then, when they're mine to control…"

He shrugged unwilling to say out loud what would happen next.

"Perhaps, but you will need to get a feel for the dynamic and discipline levels first and you cannot do that without infiltrating them and winning their trust. One step at a time, as they say," Schöenfeld said jovially, striking Gleeson's chest with the back of his hand.

And so, James Jack Gleeson stood outside Limehouse police station at nine o'clock on a Friday morning in January, wearing a donkey jacket and scuffed army boots, the kind issued to Tommies. He wanted it to be clear to anyone that was looking hard enough, that he was ex-British army and he'd taken these from a dead soldier back in Suffolk. It was well known that the Irish rebels had facilitated the German invasion and that they now operated as spies. He had considered putting on an English accent, but as Schöenfeld said, he could be here for years, and the best cover was as close to the truth as possible.

He was Sean McNairy for the foreseeable future but besides that, everything was the same. Boer war, hometown, even living in Suffolk for the last three years, except instead of spying for the SB, he really had been an artist. He even had some half-finished paintings and materials with him.

Included in the intelligence received from Schöenfeld were the favoured haunts of a couple of the resistance's straight men.

These were men who had no connection with resistance activities, enabling them to move freely through the occupied zone, and often they were business owners or even worked for the occupation in some way. The Landlord of The Grapes was said to be such a man, and his role was that of vetting officer or go-between for those looking to meet with, or join the resistance.

The Grapes was a narrow Thameside pub consisting of a bar and three tables, the type of place where patrons pissed in the alley during the day or directly into the river after dark. The clientele were rough men, dockers and sailors on shore leave, and Gleeson felt their hard-eyed stares as he entered. It was clear they were making sure that he was exactly like them, a working man with a hard job, and satisfied, they resumed their sullen consumptions.

"Pint of best, please," he said to the barman. "You the landlord?"

"Who's asking?" he said in a tar-thickened local accent.

"Name's Sean McNairy," Gleeson said, placing some coins on the sticky bar, at which the man jerked his head to indicate the sign above the door that read *Albert Strang, Licensee and Landlord*.

"I'm Albert," he said.

"In years gone by, I hear there were an uncommon number of sandpipers?" Gleeson said.

"Yes, alas, no more, the waterfowl are scarce on the estuary these days," Albert said in the wooden voice of the nervous actor.

"What now?" Gleeson asked, wiping foam from his mouth with the back of his sleeve.

"Now you wait, make yourself comfortable over there. You hungry?"

"Starving."

"I'll get her indoors to rustle something up while I fetch your man."

Before his pint was gone, he was tucking into a full English minus the meat, which was impossible to get these days, but he had toast, fried bread, beans, mushrooms, bubble and squeak, and two fried eggs. He had one more pint and left off until the sun came into view through the south-facing windows of the pub, reflecting off the scummy surface of the Thames. As he took this in, enjoying the welcome heat of the low winter sun, two men blocked it.

"McNairy?"

"Aye?"

"Come on." The man jerked his head towards the door.

Gleeson rose, picked up his bag and followed the men out onto Narrow Street. They were both dressed in the practical clothing of stevedores, and they would have looked authentic but for the bulges at the small of each man's back.

A van bearing the signage of a bakery was waiting, and he was helped into the back and left alone to get comfortable on some flour sacks. He closed his eyes, concentrating on the direction of every turn and the time elapsed between each one. He imagined that they had gone west for a couple of miles then north and were maybe in Shoreditch, but he wouldn't have bet his life on it.

The van began to snake through alleys and side streets making him lose track, perhaps he didn't know London as well as he'd once thought. They stopped with the engine still running, and he heard a large door slide open as the van lurched forward. This time the engine was cut and when the light from outside faded, the van door swung open.

"Come on, out you get, Paddy."

"Less of that, you know my name," Gleeson growled.

He decided that he was going to stick to tough, because tough was what he knew and with men like this tough worked.

"Alright, mate, keep your hair on."

This man, the taller of the two, had done all the talking so far and if forced to guess, Gleeson would have said they were brothers. Both were teenagers, and to him they didn't look old enough to be driving.

"I don't know *your* names though."

He didn't want to be in the position of asking them questions but made it sound like one anyway.

"And you won't, not until we've finished up here. Take a seat, mate."

The taller of the two nodded at a wooden chair in the corner of the garage. To its left sat a battery charger complete with crocodile clamps, and innocuous or not, they made Gleeson wince inwardly all the same.

"Okay, just trying to be friendly, brother."

"Yeah, well don't. And you don't need to talk unless we ask you a question, an' all," the shorter brother said, speaking for the first time.

Gleeson sat and looked at the men with a close-mouthed smile, drumming his fingers on his knees. The tall one had the planted dossier and Gleeson had to admit he was impressed,

205

both with the security and with their ability to get hold of things so fast.

"Says here that you was a sergeant in the army, you fought in Africa and then you left. Why's that then?"

"My time was up. I didn't want to do it anymore," he said with a shrug.

"Funny place to come knocking then, mate, you do know what we do here, right?"

"It's different now," he gestured, seemingly to the whole of London, or even Britain.

"That's fair, what was you doing in Suffolk?"

"When I left the army, I took up painting. I actually made enough to live on for a while there."

Both brothers fell about laughing.

"Oh, excus-ay mwar, *mon-sewer*," the short one said while making a theatrical bow.

"Yes, monsieur 'as really captured zee light when reflected off my arse," the tall one roared in a French accent to yet more laughter.

"I didn't say that when I left the army I became French," Gleeson said coolly, although he wanted to laugh. The pair were funny, but that was not the character he was playing; he was a tough guy and tough guys didn't laugh when two clowns he'd never met started taking the piss out of his artistic outlet.

"Alright china, keep your shirt on," Shorty said, still recovering.

"Look, you've seen my file, I sat in your damn pub all morning, but now I'm getting bored."

"And what?"

"Make your mind up, am I legitimate or am I not? I came here to help keep the fuckin' Boche outta London, and so far the only thing I have that gives me any confidence is that file, and how quickly you got hold of it."

"Listen, mate, you can't just waltz into The Grapes one morning and start demanding to see Harry fucking Tench, it don't work like that. We've got protocols, security measures, understand?"

"So, you put me in the back of a van and drive directly to Spitalfields Market, then you tell me the name of your leader. Is that your security protocol?"

The location was an educated guess, but by the look on their faces Gleeson knew that he was dead-on.

"How d'you know where we are?" the taller one said.

"This is not my first time at the fair trying to finger Nancy Donnelley, fellas, I know a thing or two about a thing or two."

"Well," he replied, somewhat deflated. "We're supposed to ask you how you heard about us."

"Fair enough. I found myself in the drunk tank last night and I started making discrete enquiries about a resistance movement in London and my cellmates were most obliging."

"What have you been doing since the start of the occupation?" the short one asked monotonously, reading directly from a notebook.

"I was lying low. You know that they've got lists of men like us and they spent months trying to round us up, so I was faced with a choice. Make a run for the free zone or try and get to London and make a real difference. So here I am."

"Okay, you ain't gonna like this bit, but now we have to take you to another safe house where you'll wait for Harry to come and vet you himself. If he's happy, then you're in and we'll take you to the—"

"We'll bring you home with us," cut in the taller brother.

"Don't worry, we'll put in a good word with Harry, tell him not to keep you waiting," the short one said.

"Can I get your names now, boys?"

"I'm Dave and the lanky prick is Andy."

"Nice to meet you both," Gleeson said, rising to shake their hands.

The safe house was filthy and it smelled like fried food and rat shit. Andy apologised and vainly attempted to make the place less of a shit hole, while Dave went to get Harry. Gleeson perched himself on the very edge of a soiled armchair and looked around, hoping to God that the rest of the next year or so was not going to be with people like him in pigsties like this.

He knew he was a terrorist. He'd killed innocents in the name of home rule, and he knew that he probably deserved everything he got, but this was awful. He got up and walked around, hoping to find refuge in another room but it was all the same. Stained walls, bare floorboards and grime-smeared windows.

"How did you end up here?" he asked out of sheer boredom.

"In the resistance?"

Gleeson nodded.

"A bomb fell on our house and killed mum. Our dad couldn't handle it and went mad. Got tooled up and went looking for Huns. Found some too... they say he got six before they killed him. Harry and the old man go way back, so he took us in, showed us a thing or two and now we handle recruiting, among other things."

"Is Harry the main man?"

"There's another, Jones he calls himself, funny eye, but he only ever speaks to Harry. Harry says that he's just a bean counter, a money man, but if you watch them—"

Gleeson held up a hand for quiet and jerked his head at the door as the footsteps grew louder and the door flew open.

Harry Tench stepped through the door and stood for a moment taking in the room, effortlessly confident and physically intimidating. Gleeson could see how this man had wound up leader of the infamous Hoxton Jacks.

"You must be McNairy," Tench said, holding out a hand.

"Aye," Gleeson took the hand and shook it firmly.

"Harry Tench. Please, sit down, we're just gonna have a little chat and after that, as long as I don't think you're a Boche spy, we'll take you home with us. Sound alright?"

"Aye, fine."

"A man of few words, eh?"

"I'm more a man of action."

"So, I've heard."

Tench produced the dossier which Gleeson reckoned these men used as a prop. A demonstration of their reach.

Sloppy, thought Gleeson.

"Says here that you was with the anarchists up north for a bit?"

"That's right."

"Know much about bombs?"

"I can cook, rig, and place, but I'd rather leave the cooking to younger men," he replied, holding out an artificially trembling hand.

"Okay, maybe you can teach a cooking course. Maybe we can exchange recipes?" he said with a smile.

"Very good," Gleeson laughed dutifully, "I'd be happy to help the cause in any way I can."

"That's what we like to hear, innit, Andy?"

"Err, yeah, yes, Harry."

Harry frowned.

"Painting?"

"Ah, yes, I'm not bad and even men like us have to make a living, Harry."

"Yeah, when I was ever short on scratch I'd take a turn in the ring. A couple nights prize fighting would sort me out for a few months."

"Each to his own. I'm ugly enough and honestly, I'm a little past my prime," Gleeson said conspiratorially.

"Come now, Sean, I'll bet you can still scrap."

"Aye, but there's scrappin' and there's pugilism, with all the rules and such, and I'm not that kind of fighter."

"*Wen versuchst du zu täuschen, McNairy?*" Tench challenged him with a pitch perfect Berlin accent, as he sprung to his feet pointing at Gleeson.

"We know you are a spy. Confess now and we'll give you a quick death." Spittle flew from his mouth as he shouted and gesticulated.

The brothers looked on, unmoved by Tench's habitual eruption.

Gleeson remained sitting casually as he looked at Tench and smiled.

"I don't speak that filth, brother," he said, which he didn't. He felt that learning German would be accepting that this was a long-term commitment, and he had never wanted that. "What is it you said?"

"Sorry. I asked you who you were trying to fool. Believe it or not, that has actually worked, more than once. You shoulda' seen the last poor cunt, just melted right there on the settee, begging for a clean death. Tell him what we did, Andy."

"We sparked him out, then we strung him up outside White-hall with a rope under the armpits and a sign that said *Dirty German Rat*, in German o'course, then you elvis...elvis..."

"I *eviscerated* him, Andy. If you can't say it, son, just say gutted," Tench said with a paternal smile.

"Jesus," Gleeson said, "remind me not to be a German spy."

Tench held out his hand a second time and Gleeson rose to shake it.

"Welcome to the Hoxton Jacquerie, Sean McNairy."

"Jacquerie?"

"It's French, means uprising."

"Gotcha."

Gleeson rode up front this time minus blindfold or restraints. He noted the exact location as they pulled up in a yard off the Kentish Town Road at the back of an abandoned tube station. Tench didn't bother to check if anyone was looking when he threw open the service door.

"The drivers gave up stopping here over seven years ago," Tench said as he felt around for the electric light switch. "Then some bright spark had the idea to board up the doors on each and every station on the line just before the invasion. Boche don't even know it's here."

The station was typically painted brick, peeling in places, with posters on the walls, an office in one corner, and the ticket booth contained a sentry who greeted them unenthusiastically.

"That's my gaff, I'll show you where everyone else sleeps now."

They descended a set of steep concrete stairs past more posters advertising London Life Cigarettes and Kavanagh's British Workman's Boots. By decking out the track, the platform had been transformed into a large, useful space. At both ends, access tunnels provided space for bunks and an army tent in one corner appeared to contain a field kitchen. A rifle range pointed down the track to a set of targets.

Gleeson was impressed by the set-up but not by the number of men, and those who were up and about seemed sullen and tired.

"Where are all your men?"

"Some are sleeping, but I reckon this is about it, mate." Tench gave him a pat on the shoulder. "Was you expecting a few more?"

"To be honest, I was. What can you hope to achieve with so few?"

"Now listen here, me old china," Harry rounded on him, "these here are London's finest, the only men who, in the face of total annihilation, stood up and said no, NO, not in my fucking city!"

He was shouting by the end, his voice echoing around the walls, and judging by the reaction of the men down here, or lack of one, he did this sort of thing often.

"I don't doubt it," Gleeson said, thinking how easy this was going to be and soon he could be home with Saoirse and Aoife.

"Now I'm going to be out of town for a while, so Dave here will look after you and show you where to sleep. I thought you might start by giving some training to the rest of the boys, make use of what's in that loaf of yours?" Harry actually tapped the side of Gleeson's head with his finger.

"Sure," he said with all the patience he could muster.

⁓

"Come on, boys, we ain't got long until this treacherous cunt is gonna turn up expecting to see a really shit resistance hideout where we've been living for six months."

Harry surveyed the space his men had completed in the short time since he'd received the tip-off about the spy. He'd picked his best men to come and build it, and he arranged for about twenty new recruits who had never seen the real base to come and appear to be the whole movement.

He felt a bit guilty about keeping them there for weeks, but that was always the protocol for new men. Two weeks in the cooler on the outskirts of London on half rations, then they could come to the main base in Hoxton. Unless of course, you got an opportunity like this one, and Harry was going to milk this clown McNairy for everything he was worth before executing the dramatic climax he had planned.

The men arrived unwashed and unfed, and as soon as he'd received the warning, he'd ordered for them to be woken up and drilled for the rest of the night and all morning, so now they looked terrible, and their collective attitude was exactly what he had hoped for. He didn't speak to them or make eye contact, he simply watched them file in, looking around, disappointed at their new home and ripe to swallow McNairy's poison.

"There's a lot of guns here, boss and a lot of pissed off blokes who don't owe you nothing. Is it wise to leave them here alone with that snake?" Andy asked. Harry liked it when his lieutenants asked him questions like this, as long as it wasn't in front of the men, because it showed they were thinking.

"Firstly, my old son, they won't be alone, as well as ten or so solid blokes from Hoxton, your brother will be here with Paul and Si and what's his face from Kent."

"Stiff Mickey?"

"Stiff Mickey, that's right, and secondly, yes, they have got guns, but they're rusty pieces of shit from the second Boer War."

"Still a bit risky, boss?"

"I'm glad you persevered there, Andy. Now the practice ammunition is in a box under the platform by the shooting range. It's only half filled, though, the operational ammo is in the tin over there and it's all dud, but there is a small stash for Dave and Si and Stiff Mickey in case things get lairy."

"Looks like you've thought of everything, Harry."

"I fucking hope so, Andy, cos this slag's supposed to be a right piece of work."

Raid – 1916

When Jack Spade joined the resistance, he knew it could mean death or torture, even reprisals against his family, but he also knew it was the right thing and he trusted that Sir Gerald and Alf Grant would see him right.

What he hadn't counted on was the waiting.

"Hurry up and wait," was what Michael always said, so Jack guessed it was the same in the regulars too. Like any nineteen-year-old he admired himself in the unofficial uniform, posing with his German submachinegun and practising his war face. He had a mental list of things he would say if he met a Hun, lines from books and comics he'd read like, "The only thing he'll be occupying is the obituaries column."

He wasn't sure if the Boche did obituaries and he didn't think that every dead Hun could get a mention, but it sounded witty and that was what young Jack thought was important. He had been a deckhand on a small fishing vessel when the invasion happened. Fortunately, they were taking shelter in The Wash and missed the whole thing, at least that's how the old man had seen it.

"Want to know how I've made old bones, Jacky boy?" he would say some evenings after a tot. "I doesn't go looking for trouble. Mark my words, boy, trouble will find you often enough without you go seeking it out."

The old man been in the Royal Navy at one point, and he liked to say that he'd never been in the sea.

"Which was just as well, Jackie Boy, 'cos I can't swim."

It got him laughing every time, so hard that it set off his lungs and he'd cough so hard his eyes watered. Jack knew it was bluster because other men, men who had known, told Jack that he'd been a hero of sorts, saving untold lives from a wreck in boiling seas off Makapu'u Point. Modesty was not a trait that Jack considered an attribute.

Why do anything brave if no one knew about it? He knew he was in the minority and brave men often kept quiet about their exploits, but Jack wouldn't. Jack longed for a story to tell and a captive audience to hear it, and if he was honest with himself, it was probably why he was here and not collaborating.

"That's them," Alf whispered. "See that lamppost? It goes dark and then light… that's them passing in front of it."

Jack had volunteered for the raiding party, but Sir Gerald had flatly refused. He looked at the warehouse, one of the dozens in this part of town and he knew it well. The familiar smell of the sea brought a wave of nostalgia over him as he lay watching from his vantage point on top of the hill. The building was surrounded by a high brick wall topped with broken glass, and Jack imagined running to assist in the raid and planned a route around to the front in his mind.

"That wasn't the deal, old boy, and I'm not willing to risk your life unnecessarily. Besides, a chap never knows how he'll react when the lead starts flying, and trust me," Gerald placed a hand on the boy's shoulder, "you'll want to be among friends."

And that was it, all he could think was, "*There's no glory in hiding on a hill shooting an enemy that can't see you.*"

The muffled rattle of a submachine gun made its way up to their position, where Jack was desperately hoping to be sent down to help if it went wrong. It did not occur to him that if things went wrong, that would mean his fellow countrymen were dead or dying. He, like many other ignorant young men thought that the greatest, most noble thing he could do was to kill Germans and die in the process. Perhaps not fully die, but a neat facial scar or a flesh wound from a Boche bullet; something to show off down the pub when he was old.

More small arms, a steady drumbeat, to and fro.

"Not as easy as we all thought," Alf observed.

"We should go and help them," urged Jack, shifting his position restlessly.

"Absolutely not, boy, you understand? This is not important enough for you to go risking your life over it."

Alf's word was law, he'd made sure they all understood that from the start. Sir Gerald had a rule: no one leaves, so if you join us, learn our secrets, and eat at our table, you're here for the duration.

"That's all well and good," he'd heard Alf say, "but if we can't banish folk, then the discipline has got to be tighter than... well, tight."

Alf was a hard man and strict on certain things, like following orders and weapon safety. He couldn't give a damn for dress and bearing, nor did he care if they shaved, but orders were orders.

One day early on, a big lad called Martin had refused to do something, maybe it was filling sandbags, Jack couldn't remember. The lad towered over Alf and demanded that he be allowed to rest a while longer. Alf replied that it was his turn and if he didn't like it, they could step outside.

Outside, the lad stood, again looming over the much smaller Alf, smiling stupidly. Maybe he thought that when he beat Alf in a fight, Sir Gerald would make him the top boy, who knows?

Alf approached him and offered him the chance to obey the order and Martin laughed, so Alf moved one of his feet back and before anyone knew what was happening, he'd sucker-punched Martin, causing him to bend double, then as his head came forward Alf gave him two mean lefts and a jaw-shattering right. He was like a tree, he stumbled back and upright, then slowly and rigidly hit the cobbles of the stable yard.

Martin was now one of Alf's favourites, trusted and given all sorts of perquisites, although he didn't say much.

Jack knew that Alf wouldn't hesitate to crack his jaw if he disobeyed orders, and this would not be his only chance at glory. After all, the Germans *had* invaded. He knew it was the wrong thing to do and he knew the consequences, but it consumed him. As he lay on the cold December ground, the idea that he couldn't be a spectator anymore warmed him.

"Alf, it's my life. If I want to risk it, surely that's my decision?"

Alf grabbed him by the hair and jerked him around so that the two prone men were face-to-face, and Jack could smell the man's breath.

219

"Fucking listen in, you selfish little prick, there's a lot you don't know about, and this," he jerked his head towards the raid and the gunfire, "*this* is one. I brought you to do a job, so you will wait here until I need you to do it. If you run down that hill," he gave Jack's head a wobble, "I'll shoot you in the fucking back and if you don't believe me, just you fucking try it."

Alf shoved Jack's head away and resumed his observations.

Jack could feel tears welling up. Everyone would have heard that arse chewing, and it was so shameful that he wanted to bury himself in the ground. If Alf really did shoot him then at least he wouldn't have to face the music and all the eyes on him back at the End. If he went down there and helped Liberty, maybe George would want him to join them. The route he had planned didn't involve running down the hill anyway, even if Alf did mean what he said.

This was it, he looked down the hill at the unseen firefight and his chance of glory, his chance to be the man Jack and not Jackie Boy. He was nineteen and people still called him Jackie Boy.

Fuck this, I'm gone, he thought as he folded his arms across his chest, hugging his MP40. He rolled to the right and away from Alf, springing to his feet and running as fast as he could down the reverse of the hill.

As he expected, no one called out. He listened for footsteps and heard none, so he slowed to a jog, catching his breath which misted on the cold night air. He got his bearings and took a roundabout route to the warehouse where the fog was thick, and the pool of light from the lampposts showed ethereal yellow in a sea of greys and blacks. The only sound over the distant gunfire was the gentle padding of his boots on the cobbles.

If he approached from the south in daylight, he would be able to see Alf and the rest of his team. As it was, he could barely see his hand in front of his face. He could see the muzzle flash now, and the noise was louder here and far more real. The adrenaline began to flow, and he became nervous and excited. This was it; this was make or break, his moment to be a man, a warrior, a hero of the resistance.

He ran towards the sound of the shooting, unsure which side was which. *Were the Germans guarding the warehouse or had they discovered George and his men already inside?* He moved in for a closer look, heart racing, head rushing, hands sweating. The fact that both sides had the same guns was not helpful. Peering through the mist at one group of muzzle flashes, he thought he could make out the distinctive coal-scuttle helmets of the German Army, but he couldn't be sure. Closer still, he could smell it now, cordite and the iron scent of blood. Fishermen had strong stomachs and Jack was no exception.

He stood at the post of the open gate, exposed and still unsure of the direction of the enemy threat, lost in the fog and out of his depth. A barely trained, inexperienced boy with no clue, he dashed for cover behind some packing cases and still couldn't tell who was who. Now in between the two sides, ensconced in the crates, he sat flaccid and useless as the fight raged on, desperately looking at each party for a sign, any indication of identity at all.

The group inside the warehouse slowed their rate of fire and a shadow appeared at the door. There in a pool of yellow light he saw one of the Australian Caldwell machine guns and the men operating it looked decidedly German to him.

They would make mincemeat of George and his men with that thing.

This is it, he thought, *this is my chance to prove myself, to show my mettle and be a man.*

He imagined that the Liberty men could not see far enough through the fog to know their fate. He could go and warn them or he could try to flank the Hun, believing that his MP40 would make light work of four men clustered around a gun. He moved back through the boxes and towards the warehouse until he was parallel with their position. These men had probably used machine guns in every European theatre of war, but they were struggling to get the unfamiliar Australian gun working.

Jack watched the shadowy figures, psyching himself up for what he had to do. He made to move and checked himself. He had not chambered a round, he would have pulled the trigger and nothing, not even a click. His heart was in his mouth. What the hell was he doing? The truth was that he didn't know, but it was too late now so he cocked the MP40 and drew a deep breath, eyes closed.

He exhaled, rolled his shoulders, and ran for the open ground. He sprayed the men in front of him with 9mm rounds. The weapon vibrated and kicked in his hands and he realised he was screaming. He watched the fall of his shots, saw the lead tearing holes in the men. As soon the magazines were empty, he dived for cover and fitted new ones. Peering around the crate, he saw no movement in the fog and the firing had stopped completely.

"Sie sind alle tot, Herr Feldwebel," called the voice of an approaching soldier.

Sickening realisation hit Jack like a boot to his guts and he vomited, barely able to comprehend the gravity of his mistake. All thoughts of heroism and glory slid out of view as he committed every muscle and sinew to maintaining a grip on his new situation.

If the Germans were alive, then who had he killed?

They had been George's Liberty men, his comrades in the resistance, brave soldiers fighting the same desperate fight he was. He risked a look around the side of the crate where the Germans stood confused, their guard lowered with their perception of the threat.

Jack pulled back the cocking handle as quietly as he could. He would try to take as many of them down with him as possible, because either way, he couldn't go back having done this.

As long as he wasn't captured, he realised that he didn't care, he wanted this. He had asked for it and when wiser men said no, he took it for himself. Now he was a killer, a taker of life, and his victims were four British resistance fighters. Brave men fighting for the same cause he was.

A second MP40 lay on the ground, ostensibly dropped by one of George's men. He took hold of it and silently checked it was loaded. He lit a cigarette and drew on it, leaving it in his mouth as he gripped a weapon in each hand. Choking back tears, he stepped out from behind the packing cases, firing from the hip into the gaggle of confused Germans crowded around his murdered comrades.

Round after round ripped through his leather jacket and into the flesh of his arms and torso. Still he stood, spraying indiscriminately at the group of soldiers. He was sure he'd killed five before they brought their arms to bear. Eventually, as Jackie Boy dropped the empty gun to favour his other, a bullet found something vital and he fell to his knees. He died with his finger curled around the trigger, spraying rounds in an arc as his limp body fell backwards to the ground.

Alf stood over the bodies of the dozen or so men who lay dead or dying and shook his head. He'd been against it from the start, but men like Clive always got their way and the German uniforms had been easy enough to steal. He knew which lads would be open to this kind of dirty dealing and the ones that weren't – like poor Jackie. He counted twelve brave men, fierce freedom fighters, who had died for Clive's greed. Still, he had gone along with it and now he would have to live with what he had done.

"Forty?" Clive exclaimed as the trucks and farm trailers carrying the machine guns rolled into the driveway at Audley End. "This *is* a coup. Just think, we can change the course of the war with this kind of firepower."

He moved closer to Alf, adopting a conspiratorial tone. "Is, err, everything…? Are all the loose ends, are they tied up?"

"Aye, Sir, dead men tell no tales." Clive's face lost all colour, it had been his idea to kill George's men and take all the spoils for himself, but he was a planner, the sordid details were Alf's purview.

"All of them, even our six? Good God, man! Still, if the means justify the end…" he gestured towards the crates of heavy weaponry.

"There's something else, Sir. We've captured a Hun."

As the residents of Audley End lay awake in their beds listening to the screams of the German soldier echo around the stone walls of the great house, Alf and Clive were listening intently to everything the young Gefreiter had to say. To begin with, all they got was the party line: morale is high, supplies are plentiful, a big push any day now, but when the thumbscrews came out and the scalpel went in, they got the real story.

"We hate this *verdammt* war as much as you do," he bawled.

"Oh, I doubt that, old boy, but do go on."

"We are starving, we have no winter clothes and last week, the bulk of our personal ammunition was handed back in for redistribution in other areas."

Salty sweat dripped from his face and into his eyes, causing him to wince. It hadn't taken much to get the man talking and the wounds inflicted were superficial, much to Clive's chagrin.

"Really Fritz, you'll have to do better *that,* perhaps another round with the thumb screws with render you more… amenable?"

Where is Sergeant Grimes when I need him?

Cannon Row – 1916

Kath paced the small sitting room of the mews house in her uniform as the dawn crept over the rooftops of Belgravia. She needed to speak with Harry but it was Saturday, and she only knew when and where he would be on Tuesdays and Thursdays. There was an emergency drop box, but she didn't dare leave the house yet. If Schöenfeld found out that she had crept out in the night, he would demand an explanation, and what would she say?

Whatever it was, it would look suspicious. Tonight had been a step-change in the level of trust that Schöenfeld placed in her, using her could even be a test. Had McNairy been playing a role?

These thoughts had occupied her mind for hours.

The best thing I can do is to play it cool. Worst case, I get a message to him, and he has to kill McNairy after bringing him in. Maybe he could turn him double? Now that would be a result, what word did Harry use? A Coo? Never mind. So, play it cool. I've got today off, maybe I can visit the market at Spitalfields to buy something nice for myself, and if I see Harry, I can say something and if not, I can try to get away Tuesday. But will this information wait until Thursday evening? No, it probably won't.

The phone rang and she jumped out of her skin. It still scared the life out of her, she'd never had one before and this was only an internal line to Schöenfeld's office in the main house.

"Hello, Sir?"

"Fräulein Lynch, I hope I did not wake you?"

"No, Sir."

"Excellent. Now, I know that it was assumed that you would take the day off after driving last night, but I have a matter of the utmost importance that cannot wait. Please be ready to leave in ten minutes."

He hung up without waiting for a response. He was very British like that, manners for the sake of manners, but an order was still an order, and she preferred it this way. She splashed water on her face and drank some left-over cold coffee while pulling her boots on before trudging down the stairs into the garage to warm the car. She opened the door a crack to let out the fumes and paced about in her greatcoat, blowing on her cold hands until the engine was warm. She pushed open the flimsy wooden doors and eased the car onto the road before stopping and climbing out again, closing and locking the garage, then drove around to the front of the house to collect Colonel Schöenfeld.

"Good morning, Fräulein Lynch," he said cheerfully. "I have a surprise for you today."

"Sir?"

"Drive us to Cannon Row and you'll find out."

The words were like a punch in the gut, and she struggled to control herself as she drove east on Birdcage Walk with Saint James's Park on her left. Cannon Row was the late headquarters of the British Secret Service Bureau. Always the first to know, the former occupants had informed the government of the invasion and together with Special Branch, escorted a handful of ministers, aides and generals into hiding in Birmingham. The basement of Cannon Row was rumoured to be Schöenfeld's playroom, filled with all manner of horrific instruments for the extraction of information and the infliction of pain.

It was a short journey and Kath's first time inside the building. Schöenfeld led her to his office where they had coffee.

"Do you enjoy the work you do for me, Fräulein Lynch?" he asked, delicately sipping espresso from a tiny cup.

"Yes, Sir."

"And I suppose that you and your younger brother enjoy your warm and comfortable home and the safety of living in west London?"

"Yes, Sir."

Where was he going with this?

"Then it would be fair to say that you would never do anything to jeopardise your position of privilege and comfort with me?"

"No, Sir, I mean, yes, Sir."

Oh God, she thought, the knot in her stomach growing and churning, so that she could feel the watery precursor to bile collecting in her mouth.

"Good."

He knocked back the coffee and rose, smiling. Picking up his homburg, he said, "Please, come with me."

She put down her untouched coffee and followed him from the office in a trance. Her head spun and she could not focus, she tried to convince herself that that was it and now they would go home, but they went straight past the lobby, down a corridor to a spiral staircase which to Kath's horror, they descended. The only light down here came from bare electric bulbs, and in this place it would be impossible to know the time of day. The corridor seemed to stretch on for far longer than the building's length, and it occurred to her that perhaps tunnels connected the various government buildings in this part of London.

"Just in here," Schöenfeld said, smiling warmly.

Am I worrying over nothing, is this a pleasant surprise?

The heavy iron door juddered and scraped along the concrete floor.

No, the answer to that question was no, and that was what she realised she was saying out loud, over, and over: "No!"

This was the room, Schöenfeld's playroom, the stuff of nightmares, the torture chamber. Contraptions, machinations and instruments for which Kath could not begin to imagine the purpose, lay dormant around the edges of the room, waiting to inflict terrible pain. In the centre, beneath a single, unshaded bulb, sat a wooden chair complete with ankle and wrist restraints, and in the chair sat a boy. His brow was split, blood mingled with snot, tears and saliva were smeared all over his face. The boy was James and Kath vomited.

Only one wrist was bound, the other hung limp at his side, and he was conscious but barely. He did not recognise his sister when she called his name and when she ran to him, no one stopped her. She produced a handkerchief but only made it worse, smearing the fluids around his face. Although he began to come around and when she wiped his eyes, he spoke.

"Kath?"

"James." No more words came as she started to cry. "Why?" she implored, turning to Schöenfeld. "Tell me why!"

"Your brother bit the hand that feeds, my dear."

229

He was still jovial, still smiling. She looked around the room to see three other men, two in uniform and the other wearing a leather apron over his issued shirt and trousers.

"What the fuck do you mean?" she demanded.

"Now, Fräulein Lynch, there is no need for that kind of language. Young James has made some new friends in the resistance, and we simply want him to tell us about them. Perhaps you can persuade him before we are forced to… *increase the pressure*. You should see this as a courtesy to you. Normally we would have started breaking his fingers some time ago. Now please, talk with your brother."

"What," she choked back more tears, "what do you want him to tell you?"

"Everything he knows," Schöenfeld said slowly, still somehow smiling. This wasn't a menacing smile, however. It seemed real, an expression of genuine, heartfelt joy. This apparent sincerity made it all the more disturbing, and Kath couldn't help looking back to him, hoping he would stop.

"James, you have to tell them, you have to tell them or they'll really hurt you. This," she cradled his face in both hands and found eye contact.

"This is nothing, they're bad men, James and they'll do things like cut off your fingers…Or electrocute you or, or…" she looked around the room at the apparatus and tried to imagine what it could be for.

"Why are you here?" James screamed in her face. "It's true what they said, you are just a Boche whore!"

"That's an idea," one of the men said, half sitting, half standing against a countertop cleaning his nails with a large knife. "If

230

you don't start talking, we're going to rape her. We will rape your sister!"

Kath looked at Schöenfeld in alarm, if he found the notion disagreeable, showed no sign at all in his unreadable expression.

The soldier said something in German to his colleague and together they positioned a workbench directly in front of James. He said something else, and the second man made for Kath. She fought, scraping his shins with her heavy boots, and throwing her head back hard enough to break his nose.

"No," screamed James. "Stop, I'll tell you. I'll tell you everything," he sobbed.

Angry, the second man picked Kath up and set her down hard her on the workbench, pawing at her and trying to kiss her. When she fought back, he punched her in the stomach with such violence that she doubled over and stepping back to let her fall. He allowed her head to strike the hard floor with a sickening sound. She lay sobbing quietly, too afraid to move.

"Please, I'll tell you," James cried through the snot and tears. "Where, where do you want me to start?"

"What is the name of your contact?" Schöenfeld said, stepping over Kath's prostrate form.

"He calls himself Walter, but I've heard people call him Andy."

That was it, once you started spilling your guts, you had to spill the lot, especially if you were an eleven-year-old boy.

"Now that wasn't so hard, was it? Where did you first meet?"

Schöenfeld pointed at a low stool without taking his eye from James and clicked his fingers. The stool was brought to him, and he sat, his face level with James'.

"I was playing in the road with me friends and he just came over and we started chatting," he said, still breathing heavily from the ordeal.

"What road?"

"Lyall Street."

"Good, and what did you do for them?"

"Just, breaking things and putting posters up, stealing street signs and…"

"And?"

"And he wanted me to burn down a records office but that was ages ago and I didn't do it," he blurted.

"Why not?"

"When I got there, it was already on fire."

"One last question, did they know who your sister was and who she worked for?"

"God, no, I ain't stupid, if they did know they never said anything."

Schöenfeld rose from the stool and stepped back, placing his notebook away inside his jacket and glancing at Kath.

"Now, I assume that you want to continue living…pick her up, make sure she pays attention."

The two soldiers stood her up and leant her against the workbench. One gave her face a few light slaps to bring her round and the other threw a cup of cold coffee in her face. Sausage-like fingers grasped her curly hair and pointed her head in Schöenfeld's direction.

"As I was saying, I assume that you want to continue living in comfort and for your sister to remain unmolested and in my generous employ?" he continued without waiting for an answer.

"Then, James, you now work for me, it's all really rather convenient. Continue as you are with your petty crimes, and if my men see you, they will arrest you as the ringleader and let you go later the same day. No more basements, no more threats against your sister."

He looked into Kath's eyes now that she had come around and was beginning to realise what was happening.

"All I want is for you to come and visit me every day at six o'clock in the evening for a chat. That is not so bad, is it?"

That's how it starts, Kath thought, bitterly. *That's how it starts.*

"Take your brother home in my car and enjoy the rest of your day off," Schöenfeld instructed her as he walked through the door.

No one showed them out, they just let them hobble from the room supporting one another, the sound of Schöenfeld's footsteps fading ahead of them.

"Be careful what you say in the car," Kath whispered, before attempting the spiral staircase.

She was clearly recovering her wits by that point and found that her physical injuries were minimal, so at the top of the stairs she turned to James and asked, "What did they do to your arm, why was it hanging limp like that?"

"Oh, I thought they might ease up if I looked a bit more pathetic, so I just let it hang there."

"Clever," she said as they walked through the lobby and out to Schöenfeld's car. Kath and James drove home in silence and went straight out for a walk.

"What are you fucking playing at?" she hissed as they strolled along Wilton Crescent.

"I'm trying to do my bit, trying to stop the Hun from getting his claws in so deep that he never lets go," he replied. Kath sighed because he sounded just like Harry.

"What you sighing for? It's more than you've ever done, swanning around in that big car with your SB Colonel, and don't think I haven't noticed that you're never around on a Thursday evening. Is that when you go to him?" he sneered, disgust twisting his face.

"It ain't like that and as for doing my bit, you don't know the half of it, and I'll never tell, because Schöenfeld will just wheedle it out of you in one of your chats. Just know that you've got me all wrong, little brother, okay?"

"Really, have I *really* got it all wrong?"

He stopped and turned to look her in the eye.

"Yes, James, really, you have."

"Well, I won't ask because I clearly don't do well under interrogation, but do you think that they'll come after me?"

"Who?"

"The Hoxton Jacks for spilling my guts like that? I've seen what they do, Kath, with the traitors. They string you up and gut you, hang a sign around your neck so everyone knows you had it coming."

He looked at her, pleading to be told that everything would be okay.

"Oh, James, everybody talks, I mean everybody, and you're still just a kid, but don't worry, okay? It'll be fine. Shall we get home, see if Mrs Higgins has any of that broccoli and stilton soup?"

James did not reply, staying silent the whole way home while Kath's mind raced. She now had two important pieces of information for Harry and something else, she was going to ask him to get her and James out. Maybe they would help with one last big job, and he would hide them for a while until they could be smuggled into the free zone.

Against her better judgement and any maternal instincts she might have, she wrote a quick note to Harry which said simply, "*McNairy, EN agent, keep alive, compromised, JACKFLASH.*"

Jack Flash was Kath's code name with the resistance. She gave the note to James and sent him to meet with Walter.

Broadlands – 1945

The journey from Hamburg was long, and even with Clive's status at the foreign office greasing the wheels of bureaucracy at the border, Olga and the children found it difficult to enter Great Britain. Finally, the car bumped and shook along the drive of Broadlands, only to be met with further resistance from within.

"What are you playing at, man, bringing a pair of bally Jerries to Broadlands?" demanded an aged Sir Gerald Clive, standing in the drawing-room of his Palladian mansion on the South Downs and staring out of the window at the River Test.

"Father, these children are important, and if you would just meet them, you would see," Clive implored.

"What, and have the whole village know that I've been cavorting with the enemy?"

"They aren't the enemy, they are children, they never *were* the enemy. Please, Father, they are already here. Just meet them and then, if you wish, I shall take them away."

He knew saying their German-sounding names would only exacerbate his father's aversion.

"Oh, very well, if only to tell them to bally well… Just bring them in," he said petulantly.

Henry walked calmly from the room and returned moments later with the children and Olga to soften the blow.

"Father this is Olga, she is from London, her parents were killed during the war."

Gerald pulled a face at the non-British name until she spoke.

"Sir Gerald, how do you do?" A vision of the English rose, with a cultured accent that was music to his pretentious ears.

"How do you do, Olga?"

He pronounced the name as if it were a complicated foreign word. She offered a hand which he took after a momentary hesitation, because women did not shake hands. His face darkened, his pupils contracted and he gasped, releasing Olga's hand and taking a step backwards.

"Forgive me," he said, flustered and embarrassed. "An...an old war wound, I should sit down."

Henry led him to an upholstered chair and fetched him a glass of water.

"Father," he said, feigning ignorance, "what happened?"

"I, the war, it, it wasn't. I wasn't, you were?"

He looked from Henry to Olga, to the floor and back to Henry.

"It's alright, Father, there's plenty of time to explain, stay seated while you meet Carla and Rudolph."

He beckoned them over.

"Ha, a right pair of little Jerries with those names, aren't you?"

"Father, they speak English," Henry said reproachfully.

"Oh, err, how do you do?"

"Sir Gerald, how do you do?"

"Sir Gerald."

They had both been practising their English and their accents were improving. Henry made a hand gesture with splayed fingers, indicating that they shouldn't shake hands.

"Sit down, children, tea will be here soon. Olga, join us, please? Father," he took his father's hand. "Father, what did you see?"

Gerald tore his gaze from the window to look at his son with glassy eyes.

"I saw," he placed his other hand on top of Henry's, more physical affection than he had ever been shown before. "I was great…then I was lost, and I wandered…then I was found, and I…I became great again," and with every few words he would look somewhere else; at Olga, the window, a beach scene by Constable, at the floor. He looked around frowning as if this wasn't real anymore.

"Father, none of those things actually happened, they are what *might* have been. Do you understand?" Gerald rose from his seat.

"I was a God, I had thousands of men under my command, a bloody palace, Henry, Audley Bloody End, my boy," he shouted before deflating.

"Where's it all gone? This morning I was a retired infantry officer, and not a very good one, but now I can remember a completely different war; a war in England, a war during which I distinguished myself. I was ruthless, but I had such power."

He went on comparing the two lives for some time, his voice growing loud and excited when he spoke of the resistance, then sad and quiet when he spoke of the trenches.

Tea arrived and Henry tried to steer the conversation away, but Gerald was deep inside himself comparing two realities.

It could send a man insane, thought Henry, *at least he only has two.*

238

"Olga," Henry said quietly, ushering her away from his father. "I want to show Rudi and Carla to their rooms, get them settled, that sort of thing. Will you sit with Father?" Olga nodded with a sombre smile.

The nursery wing at Broadlands was larger than the entire floor of the apartment building they had left behind in Prenzlauer Berg. The children had their own rooms as well as a playroom and schoolroom, the décor bright and colourful. Henry rang a bell and a servant appeared.

"Ah, Lucy, could you run baths for these two? Carla can use the guest bathroom. And could you help them with anything else they might need? They're going to be staying with us for the foreseeable."

"Yes, Sir."

Her tone was cool as she eyed the children with contempt.

"Lucy, may I speak with you outside?"

"Certainly, Sir."

"I should like to speak with the entire staff in, say…" he checked his battered Judex wristwatch, "fifteen minutes. Four-thirty?"

"Beg your pardon, Sir, but the *entire* staff is now just me and Mrs Stevenson, oh and Jed in the gardens."

"I see,"

The old man's finally economising.

"I suppose, what with the war on… Listen to me then, Lucy dear, these children are war orphans, do you understand what that means?"

"Yes, Sir."

239

"Really? Because I'm not convinced that you do," he said through gritted teeth.

"It means that they are children who have been traumatised by six years of war and brainwashed by thirteen years of Nazi totalitarianism. It means that their home was destroyed, their parents are dead, and their city is a huge pile of smouldering rubble! And despite what you and the others might believe, they were not in fact members of 1st SS Panzer Division *Leibstandarte* Adolf Hitler!"

"Yes, Sir," Lucy said, whose voice had jumped an octave and cheeks flushed red, and when Henry motioned for her to leave, she practically ran from the scene.

He came back to the drawing-room to find Olga deep in conversation with Sir Gerald and he lingered at the door out of sight.

"So, after I gave them what for, I realised we'd have to run. I knew there'd be Nazis searching high and low for us, so, we did, all the way to the Wannsee, that's a lake in West Berlin, and I'm afraid that when I was there, I did something rather naughty."

"What?" Sir Gerald asked hoarsely. "What did you do?"

"I stole a yacht," she said demurely, looking up from a down-turned head, like a child confessing to taking an extra scone.

"Gosh, that was a bit naughty, what kind of yacht?" Gerald asked excitedly.

"A twenty-six-foot gaff-rigged sloop. Do you sail?"

"Let's just say that I have a club membership that I don't use often enough," he laughed, gently tapping her knee.

Henry moved away from the door and back up the corridor, then began talking loudly, as if starting the conversation before he entered the room.

"Father, we really need…Sorry am I interrupting?"

"No, no we were just talking about yachts and Nazis," Sir Gerald said with a conspiratorial wink at Olga.

The problem with being a spy, Henry thought, is that people can't just have a conversation. Everything sounds like something else, words or inflexions that sound innocuous to some set his alarm bells ringing and that, that secretive little, "no, no we were just," is exactly the kind of nonsense that mother could not stand.

"I wondered, Olga, since you're still so young, would you like to spend some time with a tutor as well? Maybe brush up a bit and try for university?"

"Ha, Henry went to Oxford, cost me an arm and a leg. Then he up and packed it in, just like that, couldn't hack it, what?"

"Father, I left to fight in World War Two. My marks were good, I loved university and I plan to return as soon as I'm de-mobbed."

"Fight! sculking about in the French countryside and photo-graphing airfields? Not what I'd call fighting, but what would I know?"

"About what I got up to in occupied France, Holland and finally Germany? Very little, I'd imagine."

"Now, listen here, if you wanted to come home to fanfares and parades, you should have joined a proper regiment and fought like a man. You should've looked your enemy in the eye before taking his life."

"You know, Father, I really thought that seeing what you saw earlier would have changed your point of view, that maybe you would understand."

"What does my having a funny turn have to do with any of that?"

"Funny turn? Father, what you saw at teatime was real, insomuch as an alternate reality can be real. You did those things. You *were* that man."

"What the bloody hell would you know about it?" he demanded, his mottled cheeks glowing red while his moustache bristled.

"I was there. I was Jones, the man behind Tench and the Iceni, I…"

"What are you talking about, you weren't even born. Have you been knocked on the head in one of your clandestine rendezvous?"

"You said it yourself, Father, I was there," he hissed through set teeth.

"I was confused, I…" he stopped, as if seeing it again, an older version of his son in a Homberg and trench coat, lurking, meeting with men on all sides, no one completely sure where his loyalties lay. "You were a rotten, dirty spy then too, you double-dealing…"

"*I won us the bloody war!*" Henry snarled, rising to his feet and raising his voice. "I spent the better part of a year risking my life as I led Schöenfeld a merry dance and fed Tench and his army of cockneys everything I could to help them get the upper hand."

Olga decided to take control of the situation by placing a hand on Sir Gerald's, and again as she did so, he glazed over and stared off into space. Perhaps he saw things more clearly than the first time, because he seemed to accept something and turned to Olga, looking down at her hand as she removed it.

"Perhaps I was...what I mean is, I don't believe that you could ever be disloyal to your king or your country, Henry."

Henry only nodded, then padded silently to the drinks trolley to pour them all a livener.

~

Henry had his friends at MI6 expedite naturalised citizenship for all three of his new charges. Olga not technically existing in this time meant she took the identity of one of the many dead during the confusion that followed the war. If she'd wanted to do anything official, her name was Theodora Bormann, originally from Leipzig, where she'd served in the SOE and was killed in action in 1944. That page of her file was lost and a few months later she received an invitation to join the special forces club in Clivesbridge, London.

During the general election of 1946, Henry placed all of his savings and some of his fathers on a Labour win. The odds were high and the pay-out substantial. It was normal, however, for men like Henry Clive, heir apparent to the Baronetcy of Cholmondeley Chase, to place outlandish bets in this fashion. He continued to do so whenever an unlikely outcome occurred to him. Thus, he was able to replenish the estate's coffers while still maintaining the illusion that financial ruin was only one lavish party away. This helped to curb Sir Gerald's spending and gave the children the security they needed.

He found a tutor in a former nurse with the British Red Cross. Felicity Goudhurst had already come to terms with the fact that Germans were people too. She had treated their wounds and cared for them indiscriminately during the war in France and then Holland and finally Germany. She also understood that children who had experienced what Rudi and Carla had would need to be treated with kid gloves, and traditional schoolroom discipline would need to go by the board in favour of something a little more empathetic.

Miss Goudhurst was a brisk woman with a heart of gold, and she gave young Master Rudolph and Miss Carla the perfect blend of care and education. As expected, Rudi excelled in science and maths, struggling somewhat with foreign languages, and foregoing German as a subject after Carla brought him up to her level. Conversely, Carla found she had a talent for languages and before long she required a tutor for French and Latin beyond Miss Goudhurst's abilities, but her real passion lay with history.

The importance of understanding the mistakes of the past, why they happened, who people were and how they lived, their motivations and beliefs. She wanted to understand what gave men like Adolf Hitler and Joseph Stalin a platform, why the Kaiser was desperate for war and what drew the rest of Europe and eventually the world into wars that ostensibly, nobody wanted.

Both Rudi and Carla woke in the night, drenched in sweat, and searching their surroundings desperately for a sign of safety. A sign they were not where they had been. Rudi dreamt of torture at the hands of the Stasi, of dark rooms and deep water, blood-gurgling Russians and the ominous words of dying priests. Carla relived that night on Sonnenallee, the disbelief at what her liberators were doing, the smell of their breath and the sound of jeering, the pain inside and the feeling afterwards, the inability to wash herself clean, or to forget or to ever feel safe again. She found herself thanking God that these feelings were only echoes of another life and not the traumatic memories they could have been. Then she realised what Olga had done for her and for her mother, and when this sunk in, the resentment washed away, replaced by gratitude.

Sir Gerald finally began taking his yacht out again, of course he would let Olga do all the work and instruction while he reclined in the stern sheets with a drink and a cigar. The makeshift family created many happy memories messing about on the Solent aboard *Freyja*, a forty-foot Bermudan-rigged cutter.

Henry joined them whenever he had leave and he and Carla would always converse in Latin or French while Rudi was afforded the time and resources for all kinds of scientific pursuits. Being on the right side of the iron curtain he had access to so much more scientific literature, and the library at Broadlands now had a dedicated section for academic journals and textbooks. One Saturday in November 1945, Henry returned from London with a gift for Rudi, a copy of 'The Time Machine' by H. G. Wells.

He must have read it a dozen times by the New Year.

When the SOE was disbanded in 1946, Henry, who in the last iteration of time had been given a position on the Berlin desk, was not taken on at MI6 at all. Instead, he was offered a choice between a major's commission in the Royal Hampshire's or something vague in the foreign office. This might have been due to the rumours of the three German children he had smuggled out of Hamburg, but he could never truly know. He took instead the opportunity to resume his studies at Oxford, switching from Greats to political history, and living there full-time, visiting Broadlands once a month.

Olga, who had wrapped Gerald around her finger on day one, arranged for other German children in the surrounding areas to come for tea parties and dancing every month or so. Outside of Broadlands, Rudi and Carla hid their accents to avoid understandable hostility from the local population still reeling from six years of war.

Olga studied privately with Felicity, explaining her strange mix of education with a lie about religious fanatic parents and the war. When she had learned everything Felicity had to teach her, she asked for medical instruction and revelled in the privilege afforded by the library at Broadlands, consuming knowledge like a sponge.

Olga took the children individually for martial arts lessons a few times a week, and when the practice brought back memories of Yael and Ibrahim, of the desert and their journey together, her feelings of loss and regret developed into a dullness. There was some pride and love in there, but she had learned that not feeling was far easier. She repressed the grief and the sadness, and often a song or a line of text in a book would trigger a wave of inexplicable melancholy, followed by tears.

She hated to be seen like this, dreading the questions and refused to contemplate what it meant. Both children loved to spend one-to-one time with Olga and worked hard to learn Yael's Krav Maga and smatterings of other disciplines.

When Carla celebrated her seventeenth birthday, she announced that she would like to attend university to study modern history and politics. Henry suggested Saint Hugh's College at Oxford, but she preferred Somerville.

"Okay," Henry said, "but you can walk on the grass at Saint Hugh's."

Carla wasn't sure what that meant and applied to Somerville later that year. News of her departure in 1949 hit Rudi hard, and he was becoming dissatisfied with successive tutors who simply were not up to the task. At sixteen he was frustrated by what he described as the woefully mediocre physicists he was surrounded by, declaring that no self-respecting scientist would be tutoring teenagers when they could be furthering the course of physics.

In four years his somewhat abstract love for Olga had grown into an adolescent obsession. This infatuation was backed up by an unknown number of decades of real, physical love between two adults. Every year on his birthday he would ask Olga if he was old enough and every year a pained expression would befall her, and she would let him down as gently as she could.

Olga would never love another, but at twenty-two she couldn't see this pompous teenager as *her* Rudi. She knew he was in there, or at least his memories were, and she knew that his love for her was as real and as deeply felt as ever it was. She resolved to wait until he was eighteen and she twenty-four and every day it seemed that a small part of the Rudi that he would one day be shone through brighter, both thrilling and saddening her.

Because of this, she decided to distance herself from him, as much for herself as for Rudi. She didn't want to ruin what they had once had and lost so many times. With that in mind, she thought about joining Carla at Oxford, until she discovered that she had to learn Latin for the entrance exam. She did, however, accompany Carla on a familiarisation visit to Oxford and while Carla took care of some necessary paperwork while Olga took the opportunity to wander the city.

Oxford didn't have a campus, its colleges, libraries, and theatres being scattered about the city connected by a charming labyrinth of alleys and streets flanked by walls of the same Cotswold limestone that had built the Altstötter's Gloucestershire home.

As Olga reflected on how far she had come since then and the woman she had grown into, she stumbled upon a meeting hall. The fire exit, open against the heat of the June day, allowed her to listen to the speaker.

"*…and it has been only four years since we were all in it together, in uniform, manning antiaircraft guns, working the land, building bombs, sewing up soldiers at the front and driving trucks and tanks back here. And had we only been given the chance like our sisters in* *the Soviet Union, we would have fought alongside the men, at El Alamein, at Monte Cassino and on the beaches of Normandy..."*

"Hey," a whispered voice came from inside jerking Olga back to reality, "come inside, this is open to all of our sisters."

The whisperer wore a light grey trouser suit that Olga decided she simply had to own.

Inside the hall were fifty well-dressed women of university age who were all vocal during the speech, and Olga found the whole thing exhilarating. She basked in this new feeling of collective strength and soaked up the revolutionary notions of these feminists.

When she re-joined Carla, she told her what she had seen and insisted that Carla should take a look at the FemSoc when she started in the autumn. On the train home, Olga thought hard about the women and the speeches and she made a decision. If she had to wait for Rudi to finish his education, she would wait for him in Oxford, she would join the movement and stay there with Carla, and she knew that if she asked in the right way, Sir Gerald would probably finance it all for her.

In Oxford, Olga was delighted to find a Karate club. She found out when classes were and waited impatiently for the day she could attend. She found a uniform and carefully pressed it the night before and hung it from a hook in the flat she shared with Carla. It would catch her eye every so often and she would smile at it in anticipation.

Olga arrived early and found the space empty but for one middle-aged man reading a newspaper.

"Excuse me, I'm here for the eight o'clock class," she said, confident yet respectful in her tone.

"No, you're not," the man said without looking up from his newspaper.

"Is it cancelled?" she asked.

He sighed theatrically, closing his eyes and pinching the bridge of his nose.

"No, but you will not be taking part, young lady. Now kindly leave."

"I don't understand," she said, though she thought that she did, but this arsehole wasn't getting rid of her that easily.

"Listen, I don't know what you expected to happen, but this is a serious dojo."

He placed his thumb and forefinger together to emphasise his point.

"A place for men to learn the ancient martial arts. What it is *not*, is some sort of a calisthenics studio or women's exercise centre."

He was standing in front of Olga now, arms folded. He wore a Gi tied at the waist with a faded black belt.

Olga smiled.

"I came to practise martial arts and I'm not leaving until I do."

She let her bag fall to the floor at her side and continued to smile at the reddening man.

"I won't ask again, get out of my dojo."

"Let her stay, Sensei."

Olga turned to find that she was flanked by two men already dressed for their class. The one who was speaking wore a brown belt and his taciturn friend wore a green one.

"You never know, we might have some fun."

The man smiled salaciously at his classmate and then the sensei. He spoke *about* her, not *to* her, as if she wasn't there.

"Great," she said. "I'll get changed."

She kicked off her shoes and bowed as Yael had shown her, marching into the centre of the room and casting about, but this was it.

"There isn't a changing room," chuckled the brown belt, "you'll have to change here, in front of us."

He still wore that disgusting expression, looking to each of his friends for approval.

"Fine," she said, allowing her simple cotton dress to fall to the floor. The underwear she had chosen was practical and in no way provocative, but she could still feel their leering eyes roaming over her body. The idea that she should be an object of sexual desire when she only wanted to train infuriated her as she pulled on her crisp, white Gi and tied it with a white belt without acknowledging her unwanted audience.

"I already told you that you will not be participating, young lady."

The sensei's tone was sharper and Olga could hear his rising anger. She knew that these revered men were supposed to be masters of their emotions and paragons of self-control.

"Well, I'm here now, and you allowed me to change. Surely that wasn't just to see me undress, Sensei?" she asked, smiling at him as he refused to make eye contact.

251

"As you wish," he said finally, apparently resolving some internal conflict. "I assume you know what to do here and how to behave?"

"No, I was trained in the field, in North Africa and then Europe," she said flatly.

"Trained in the field?" brown belt said incredulously. "Do you mean the battlefield? You expect us to believe that you learned karate when you were fighting the Germans during the war?"

He scoffed, and as he walked towards Olga, he lowered his voice to a whisper.

"Listen girly, I fought at The Kasserine Pass, Salerno and on Gold Beach. Friends of mine never came back from those, those...you listen, I don't know what you're trying to imply but you..." he trailed off, too angry to continue, the demons of his past clouding his mind as he fought his own personal war, the war that no one could see, the war that for many, never ended.

"I...I was there, right until the end," she placed a hand on his arm, "I know."

He recoiled at her touch and rounded on her.

"What do you mean, right until the end, are you saying that because I didn't march into Berlin my service isn't as good?"

"No, not all..."

"You don't even look old enough and besides, you're a *girl*. What were you, a FANY or something?"

"Or something. I reported to Baker Street," she lied, knowing that her cryptic reference would either go over his head and he would continue to disbelieve her, or that he would shut up,

252

content that she was one of the three thousand women who worked in British intelligence during the war.

"What on earth do you mean, Baker Street? In fact, just shut up, you stupid little girl, you know nothing of war, and you shouldn't act as though you do."

He turned away and lined up with the other students on the mats.

Olga was torn because her assumed identity was that of an SOE agent. While her line about Berlin and North Africa was technically true and she *had* killed plenty of Nazi's, but she wasn't who she was implying she was and this man knew nothing of the Baker Street Irregulars anyway. She decided to leave it, because she didn't want to cause trouble for herself with further half-truths.

Olga took a place next to another white belt and the class began. The sensei made no reference to her as he took the class through the drills, so she mimicked her classmates and kept up, enjoying the ritual atmosphere. After fifteen minutes of group work, they were instructed to pair off, the odd number leaving her without a partner and looking forlornly at the sensei, who smiled wickedly at her, until she smiled back and he flushed again.

She stood opposite him as he spoke to the class.

"Okay, I want you to try to hurt me."

He beckoned her with both hands and adopted a well-practised fighting stance.

"Sure," she said inclining her head slightly and adopting her own, well-practised fighting stance.

This is it. He's never going to let you come back here, so just mess him up while you've got the chance.

They both bowed and made eye contact, the ghost of a smile crossing his face, and she was on him, two hands from above her head to the either side of his neck. He stumbled back and she closed the gap, to hit his nose with her left palm and with her right she punched his exposed throat. Olga stepped around him and grabbed him by the jaw and face, applying pressure to his septum and pulling him on to the mat face first. Taking his wrist, she brought it around his back and controlled him easily before letting his arm drop the ground and stepping away.

He got to his feet and without speaking, offered her his hand, which she took, reconsidering.

Maybe he isn't such a misogynistic arsehole after...

He jabbed her with a left out of nowhere, maintaining the grip with his right and ignoring the student's murmurs disapproval, he continued delivering expert blows to her face and torso. Dazed, Olga tried to gather her thoughts to maintain an effective guard against the onslaught, to breathe with the blows she couldn't block. He tried for a kick and she backed out of range, which was all the opportunity she needed.

Seizing his ankle, she shifted her hips to change body position and force him onto his back, falling upon him and raining expertly placed blows to his eyes, nose, throat, and temples, stifling the urge to scream with rage as she did.

Olga rolled away and jumped to her feet, her nose streaming with blood as another cut ran red into her eyes. She circled him, watching for signs of his next move, but he wearily rolled onto his front and raised himself onto his hands and knees.

Kick him, Yael whispered in her mind. *This man is without honour, he cannot be trusted.*

No, I will not let his dishonour guide my hand.

With the sole of her foot Olga nudged him on to his back where he lay forlornly, unable to make eye contact with her or any of his students.

She could see he was beaten, and she didn't want to hurt him anymore than she already had, but she also couldn't trust him. Unsure of what to do Olga remained still, looking at the other students who were equally confused. She made eye contact with brown belt, and he stepped forward.

"I get it now, at least I think I do."

He kept a respectful distance and maintained a neutral stance.

"Go, I'll see that he doesn't do anything else to dishonour this dojo."

Olga stepped away, her eye's never leaving the prostrate form of the disgraced sensei as she walked to her bag. She discarded her blood-stained Gi and mopped her face with a towel before slipping into her dress. Nobody ogled her this time, and she strode confidently from the dojo in silence, stepping out into the crisp night air.

The following day after some stretches and a hot bath, Olga started the Oxford FemSoc martial arts club. Like the suffragettes, these women also learned to defend themselves against the foot soldiers of the patriarchy, and her life became one of training and campaigning. She attended marches and rallies, wrote letters, and produced pamphlets. She found dojos in other cities that accepted female students and visited them, learning, and exchanging different techniques all over Britain.

The women she spent her time with made her feel strong. It wasn't a physical strength but a sense of belonging, of being an integral piece of something greater than the sum of its parts. The confidence that Yael's mentoring had given her paled into insignificance next to how she felt now, but with it came a hyperawareness of the injustices faced by the women of 1950s Britain. She worked hard and often in vain to remedy them, writing letters and organising protests. The women who didn't seem to realise the oppression they lived through were the most frustrating, some even berated her, hurling vile abuse, angry that women like Olga would upset their status quo.

~

When Rudi was allowed to attend university in 1951, he was looking a lot more like the man she remembered, but she decided to let it happen organically. Resuming their training was the first step, and after a few weeks they kissed.

Olga had waited for this man. All around her the women of post-war Britain were discovering a new attitude to respectability. Their parents had lived through six years of war and learned what it was to lose the one you loved, be it temporary or permanent, and the urgency that war had placed on love still existed. Her generation had come to terms with their mortality at such a young age that it was hard to value the stuffy ideals of the 1930s.

This was by no means the sexual revolution that was to come in a decade's time, but Olga was aware of many of her friends enjoying a more liberal approach to love. She had echoes; feelings linked to distant memories of nights spent with Rudi and hot summer days by a lake, but her only *real* experience was that night six years before when Altstötter had tried to rape her. All of these factors added to her anxiety, as though now this long anticipated *first time* had something to live up to.

At the end of Michaelmas term, just before the three of them were due to spend Christmas at Broadlands, Olga snuck into his college and, naked, slid into bed beside him. They kissed for a long time, exploring one another with the urgency of youth. Afterwards, Olga snuck out, and was waiting for him with Carla when he arrived at the train station.

Revelations – 1916

The Hoxton Jacks had grown considerably since the original members summoned on the day of the invasion. Now there were nearly two thousand men and women living in the network of tunnels underneath London, not to mention the countless agents living among the occupying Boche. Supplied by farms and factories in the free zone, they ate better than anyone else in the city and their intelligence assisted factions all over the south-east, with reports of German discontent becoming commonplace. No one up there on the surface had enough food, the soldiers were demoralised and all either side wanted was for the Germans to go home.

"Listen, Jones, you and I need to have a little chat."

"Of course, Harry old boy, I have time right now."

They both stepped into Harry's sanctum sanctorum, a former maintenance-store-turned bedroom, office, and sitting room, it was one of a handful of truly private spaces in the entire complex. Jones noticed that recently the room had acquired a feminine touch, one of the walls even had a fake window complete with curtains, behind which hung an oil painting of Chichester Canal by Turner which Jones could swear was the original.

"Now, don't get me wrong," Harry said, pouring them both a generous measure of a ghastly blended scotch. "I can appreciate what you do for the resistance and for the country, but I've had enough of the vagaries, the sudden reappearances and disappearances… In short, Jones, me old china, I need you to level with me and I need you to do it now."

"To candour," Jones said, raising his glass and quaffing the lot, because old habits died hard.

He dabbed at his face with an impossibly clean handkerchief and exhaled.

"Before the war I worked as a spy almost exclusively in Germany, and during my tenure I made a great many connections. Among them were some SB men and one of those men, who believes me to be loyal to Germany, is Colonel von Schöenfeld."

He let that sink in while he helped himself to another scotch.

"What d'you do?" Harry said accusingly. He eyed him intensely, searching Jones' inscrutable face, his drooping eyelid and a tiny drop of whisky that was running down his chin. "Must have done something, something post-invasion, to convince Schöenfeld that you're on his side, so what was it?"

"Ah, yes, there was something, you're quite right."

He inhaled deeply and looked down to his left and back to Harry, rubbed his impeccably clean-shaven jawline as he spoke.

"In the early days of the occupation, while you were busy burning all the records…"

"I remember."

"Well," he continued, "I was stealing them. I compiled rather an extensive dossier of likely resistance members."

"I don't like where this is going!"

"But there's something else you should know."

There was a barely perceptible increase in tempo as Harry's face darkened and he put down his drink with a little too much force.

"I doctored some of them."

"Keep talking," Harry growled.

It wasn't that Jones was scared of Tench, although there was no questioning the man's ferocity, but it was the hundreds who would stand between him and the surface if it came to blows.

"A select few, including yours, were altered in order to down-play your strengths and allow you to fade into the background somewhat."

Behind his mask of serenity, Jones was praying that this man, this violent, much-beloved leader of resistance would see the enormous favour he had performed, not only for the cause but for Tench personally.

"Haven't you wondered how you have been able to move freely around London for the last six months?"

Tench's face went from snarling beast to minor confusion and then to satisfying realisation.

"You crafty bugger, you are a dark horse, in't ya and I 'spose our burning all the real records helped seal the story tight?"

"Something like that," he said, unable to mask the relief he now felt, "and after that apparently unforgivable betrayal to my country, that vainglorious bastard was putty in my hand. Every-thing else I fed him was lies. I told him you didn't trust me; he thinks you're stupid and because he's such a snob he has no re-spect for you or your abilities."

"Good job I ain't a vainglorious bastard, 'ey?" Harry said with a wry smile.

"Quite," chuckled Jones. "Now, since I've only just come back from the free zone, you'll have to bring me up to speed, old chap."

"Where to start?" Harry mused.

"With a drink," Jones said, pouring two more generous drams.

"Cheers," they said in unison.

"First off, I should tell you that I had a very well-placed informant," he let that sink in for a moment. "Schöenfeld's driver."

"Yes, she made me once, it had actually been playing on my mind," Jones admitted.

"Well, she gave me a cracking description and it's the main reason we're sitting here now having this conversation, because I was ready to have you bagged and strung up in the U-boat."

The U-boat was a plant room full of valves and gauges, prompting an old submariner to comment on the likeness to an iron coffin.

"I'm glad you decided to have a chat first, old boy."

"That reminds me," Harry stood and walked over to the door, barely opened it, said something inaudible and sat back down, "where were we?"

"My narrowly avoided trip to the U-boat?"

"Right, so she had more than that to say when I saw her last."

"Am I correct in assuming that she's living down here now?" Jones asked, looking at the subtle additions to the decor.

"I'll say it again, Jones, you really don't miss a trick," he smiled and took a sip of whisky. "The other reason you're not screaming bloody murder in a cupboard right now is when she told me about your meetings with Schöenfeld, I had her lay several traps for you and I'm pleased to say that the verdict is… not guilty."

"Celebratory cigarette?"

He proffered a handmade French cigarette from a case monogrammed 'HC' and lit it for him.

"Thanks."

"Now, I heard a rumour of some sort of explosion at Lots Road Power Station," Jones said.

"Aren't you curious about our deceptions, Mr Jones?"

"Let me see," he said, looking at the ceiling and blowing out smoke. "Mr McNairy's apparent absence. His real name is Gleeson, by the way, an Irish rebel instrumental in the invasion of Suffolk by all accounts. I suppose the sudden appearance of a dozen Australian machine guns would have come back via Schöenfeld if I'd blabbed and… and I'm not completely sure on this, but could it be the fact that Schöenfeld's driver is still breathing?"

"Who's HC?" Harry fired at him.

"The unfortunate bugger to whom my cigarette case used to belong." Henry was quick, but had he been cool enough?

"Whatever you say, mate, but if you think I'm stupid enough to believe you're called Jones, then I guess you ain't the master of espionage I'd pegged you for."

He stared at Jones for some time before continuing.

"The other one," Tench sniffed, "was that you don't seem to have been confirming McNairy's clearly inaccurate intelligence, but I'm still impressed."

The pair sat in silence for some moments, surmising one another's motives, allegiances, and possible next moves.

"That reminds me, old boy, what did you do with our Irish friend?"

He stubbed out the cigarette and lit a second for him and for Harry, who chuckled through the half of his mouth that was not dedicated to clamping down on it.

"That's the best bit," Tench smiled revealing his uneven, nicotine-stained teeth. "He's in a completely different set of tunnels teaching forty or so of our new recruits everything he knows, thinking they're the whole bloody outfit. I'd love to know what he says to Schöenfeld about the state of the whole thing."

"Why don't you ask the driver?"

"She's blown, hence the flowers and that," he nodded at the room in general.

"Oh, I do hope she made it out in one piece?"

~

A few weeks earlier

Kath went to meet Harry, against her better judgement, and told him everything and when she was finished, he was silent for a long time.

"You gonna fucking say something?" she said finally.

"I'm thinking."

"Think faster."

He blew air through his closed lips and rubbed the back of his neck.

"Is James alright? Where is he now?"

"Out with his friends. Schöenfeld expects him to carry on as normal, reporting back every evening."

"And where does he think you are?"

"The same place he thinks I've been every Thursday since we met, I should imagine."

"You did the right thing coming. If you suddenly changed your behaviour, he'd know something was up."

He looked at her and took both her hands in his.

"Listen, I'm going to get you both somewhere safe, but there's one thing we have to do first."

"What?" the anger evident in her voice.

"It's nothing really, Schöenfeld just needs to hear one scrap of information from James, and I'll have you out of there before you can say..."

"You're a cold fucking bastard, Harry Tench."

"Yeah, but you love me all the same."

He tried to grab her arse, but she spun around quickly, landing a small, powerful fist just below his right eye.

"Fair enough, I deserved that. Now, what is it we usually do on Thursdays?"

"I'm not in the mood," she said, at which Harry shrugged.

"Tell James to say that..."

"Did you know?"

"Know what?"

"That Andy was running James?"

"No," he said flatly. "I do know that most of my Lieutenants have a few boys working for them, but I can't know every single one, in fact not one name springs to mind of any particular boy."

"Even when you're fucking their sister?"

"Look, James clearly has some nous and cleverly, he left out the part where his sister is a driver for the most hated man in London."

"The fact is, Harry," she said, brushing a lock of red hair from his eye and dragging her fingers through his thick beard. "I don't have much choice. I either believe you and you get me out or, I risk it with Schöenfeld and the Boche."

"I know what I'd do, but I *know* you'll be safe with me," he drew her in for a kiss and scooped her up into his arms.

Kath was dozing on the settee under a mountain of blankets when James walked through the door, tears in his blue eyes and a face whiter than the snow that currently engulfed much of England. She opened the cocoon and motioned for him to join her, but he shook his head.

"I spilt my guts again. I sang like a canary. I'm nothing but a coward and a collaborator," he sniffed.

"Oh, James," she chuckled as she walked over to the gramophone and restarted the record already on the turntable before getting very close and whispering to him.

"You are funny, you were supposed to blab. I told my contact in the resistance that we were in trouble and he put this together, but you can see why you couldn't know, can't you?"

"Because for him to believe that he'd weaselled it out of me, it had to be real?" he sobbed.

"He's an expert, maybe not quite as clever as he likes to think, but bloody clever all the same. Now come here."

They hugged warmly for a whole minute, but James was still trembling.

"Go and pack a bag, we'll leave around midnight."

Her bag already was packed and hidden in the garage downstairs, so she snuggled back down into her pile of blankets and dozed off again.

"Kath, Kath, it's nearly midnight," James was gently, shaking her awake. "Come on, you said we were going at midnight?"

"Alright, alright, I'm getting up, it's freezing, why'd you let the fire go out?"

"I didn't see the point."

"You didn't see the point in me freezing my fucking tits off in the frozen wasteland that is our house?"

"It's not our house," he said, "never was."

They both looked around at the warm, comfortable home they had been given by their enemy.

"They stole this place from Englishmen," Kath said, answering the unasked question.

"Englishmen that fled at the first sign of trouble and will expect to waltz right back in when it's all over."

Whether we win or not, she thought.

Kath pulled on her uniform for one last time. Checkpoints were easier to navigate for collaborators. In the garage she started the car and retrieved the bag she'd packed days earlier and hidden in a cupboard behind some old tins of paint. While the engine coughed and spluttered, she put their bags on the back seat and closed the door. She was about to tell James to open the wooden garage doors when something stopped her, a feeling, or perhaps just paranoia. She went to the point where the doors met and peered through the crack. There must have been two dozen armed men of *Vergeltungskraft* out there.

She moved silently to the workbench and stood on it to reach the high window, seeing a similar sight in the courtyard. She felt sick, her neck burned, and her head swam. They were going back to the basement of Cannon Row and this time they weren't walking out.

"Get in the car, no, the back seat, lie down on the floor. Don't argue, just do it," she hissed. This was crazy but what else could she do? She'd rather be shot than end up in that nightmare again. She climbed into the driver's side and adjusted the seat so that she could crouch in the footwell. Then perching on the edge of the seat, she disengaged the clutch and selected first gear. She inhaled, she exhaled, gritted her teeth and she stamped on the gas.

The engine roared and she let in the clutch, spinning the wheels wildly on the smooth floor to fill the garage with smoke as the rubber found traction. Eventually, the car fired forwards, splintering the door like matchwood and filling the street outside with smoke, which provided a small advantage in the confusion buying them a few more vital seconds before the shooting began. Crouched in the footwell as she was, Kath had to remain in first as the engine screamed for the reprieve of a higher gear. Bullets rained down from all directions, and one must have found the radiator because steam billowed from the bonnet as Kath ploughed blindly through the wall of men.

When she felt safe enough, she raised herself up and changed gear, adjusting her seat, and calling to James to "stay down, for fuck's sake."

Sweat soaked the steering wheel and caused her curls to cling to her face as the car limped along at twenty miles an hour on three flat tires with an engine running on little more than willpower. Kath skidded around corners in the snow with one eye permanently on the rear-view mirror, she'd planned this route in her head, gone over it with Harry dozens of times, he'd told her where to avoid and not to worry if she was followed. Albeit slowly, she moved unhindered through the empty streets, leaving pristine tracks in the fresh snow for her pursuers, who were not far behind. She avoided bridges, as she headed north through Mayfair, then east through Holborn towards the pickup point Hoxton. As she crested a hill, the mirror showed her the enormity of the pursuing force, a score of military trucks snaked through the streets behind her and appeared to be gaining. She forged ahead, praying the engine would keep running at this temperature, because the bitterly cold night air rushing over the hot metal of the block was the difference between a long, painful death or a chance at living a while longer. On the way down the other side of the hill, she knocked the gearbox into neutral and coasted, giving the engine a minor respite, but at the bottom of the hill, when Kath let in the clutch, the engine roared plaintively as the thermometer spun around past one hundred. The piece of waste ground in Hoxton was fast approaching on their left and Kath willed the dying machine onwards, praying to a god she didn't believe in to watch over her and James.

"Get ready, James, I'm going to turn a corner hard and when I stop, be ready to run for the nearest hiding place. Do you understand?"

Silence but for the screaming engine.

"James?" she felt around behind her seat and found him. She shook him, *how could he be sleeping through a car chase?*

"James?"

She had to focus, the turning came up and she continued to call his name as she threw the wheel over and pulled the rear brake lever. The car skidded around and into the site, bumping over the debris as she felt in the back, desperately calling her brother's name.

"James?" she pleaded, and tears filled her eyes as she began to fear the worst.

Her hand found something warm and sticky and her heart stopped beating. For the second time that night the hot feeling of dread washed over her as she braked gently, afraid of making it worse, then threw open her door and nearly tore the rear one off its hinges.

"James?"

Cold lifeless eyes stared up at her as footsteps grew louder and men approached.

"*James!*"

Men in the unofficial uniform of the resistance ran past her, one lobbed a satchel onto the front seat without breaking his stride and continued moving away. Another tried to bring her with him, but she fought.

"I won't leave him, he's not dead! He's all I've got left, *get the fuck off me!*"

269

The force with which she pushed her would-be rescuer knocked him to the ground and, shaking his head, he got to his feet and left her. She began to drag James clear of the car as more footsteps approached until Harry picked her up bodily as she screamed.

"No, *no*! I won't leave him!"

Her fists hammered his back and her legs flailed uselessly as Harry moved surprisingly quickly under his burden. He picked through the debris as headlights filled the entrance and vehicles flooded into the site to form a semicircle. Kath struggled free and ran back towards the car at the same time as a group of grey-clad soldiers reached James' body.

The explosion that vapourised the German troops lifted Kath off her feet and moved her through the air, depositing her on a flat piece of ground amongst jagged shards of wrought iron.

~

"Then we waited for more to come and investigate. They had no clue that there were so many of us and we really let 'em have it. From the body count afterwards, it looks like it was the better part of a *Vergeltungskraft Batailon*."

"And all it cost was the life of one brave kid," Jones said, flicking ash into the cut-down howitzer shell Harry used as an ashtray.

"Don't give me that shit, mate."

He slammed his fist on the table.

"Was there anything left of him to bury?"

"That's where they managed to really put the fucking boot in," he said through gritted teeth. "Somehow, they recovered the body unharmed. You see, the explosive force of a bomb travels up and outwards. So, poor Jimmy Lynch, lying as he was, a few yards from where the car stood, well he wasn't *untouched* but there was a body. A body those fucking bastards strung up outside his old school in Mile End. They hung a sign around his neck that said, *Ich habe die Hand gebissen, die füttert!*"

Harry turned away, perhaps to hide a tear, ostensibly to open a drawer and rummage around.

"*I bit the hand that feeds...* they're bloody animals," Jones said, embarrassed by the display of emotion.

"And that's not all it cost; good men died and Kath, well she didn't..."

The door opened and in walked the beautiful former driver of Colonel von Schöenfeld herself. She wore high-waisted trousers with putties and her old boots, while on her top half was a beautifully tailored leather jacket and a Khaki coloured silk scarf that did its best to contain her wild brown curls.

"Hello, you must be Kath?" Jones said affably as both men stood and Jones offered his hand. When she turned to take it, he realised what Harry had been about to say. A livid pink scar dissected her right cheek diagonally, then before it reached the mouth it took a sharp turn to her jawline.

"Jones," he said. "How do you do?"

In that moment, he was truly grateful for that poker face he'd spent years perfecting.

271

"Hello, I've heard absolutely nothing about you, which is why I've been in the U-boat for the last hour, waiting to cut your balls off."

Her eyes narrowed, and for the first time in years Jones felt something akin to fear.

"That won't be necessary, love, he's passed all our tests with flying colours. In fact, he may well be the reason I'm still alive."

"I am glad," she said sardonically, the disappointment evident in the twist of her mouth.

Rat Catcher – 1916

Hauptmann Otto Kessler was hungry. His men were hungry, just as the entire occupying force was hungry. The fighting in their sector had been some of the easiest in the war, comparable even to France, but to men accustomed to the Ost front, boredom was deadly.

More than a few of the hardened veterans, men who had walked through Petrograd with him and seen the horrors of nuclear war, had taken their own lives. You could say what you liked, but Otto put it down to the tediousness of occupation. The men had too much time to think about the terrible things they had done and the things they would still have to do. In addition to the cancer epidemic that seemed to be ravishing only his company, ten of his men had hanged themselves in the last six months, leaving Otto's company undersupplied, undermanned and dangerously low on morale.

That was before the new assignment when Z company Fifteenth *Sturmbataillon Leibstandarte* Erik von Ludendorff was resubordinated to a new branch of the SB called the *Vergeltungskraft*: the retribution force. These new units were formed specifically to deal with the fierce British resistance, and each company was assigned a small detachment of former civil policemen to advise and lead investigations, help with arrests, and facilitate flying tribunals.

"The fact is, Otto... that we don't have any real fighting for you to do, not until we smash this resistance. The concentration camps are full and the SB is overstretched. Last week, and I tell you this in the strictest of confidence, last week Schöenfeld's driver, his personal live-in driver," he winked, smirking lasciviously, "stole his car in the middle of the night and lured him and his men into an ambush. Scores of good Germans were killed and Schöenfeld is on the brink... the brink."

He grimaced, rubbing his hands against the cold.

"Does this have something to do with the *Junge* hanging outside a school in Mile End?"

"Oh my, Otto, we are perceptive, and that's what I've been trying to say. We need experienced field commanders like you working counterinsurgency and when we find the rats' nest, we want battle-hardened men like yours to lead the charge. Think of this assignment as a promotion, and if you do well I will naturally take all the credit, get *myself* promoted, and make sure you get the battalion in my stead. How does that sound?"

"Herr Major, I'm flattered that you think me worthy... but you should know that the battle-hardened men of whom you speak are dropping like flies and I don't think that rounding up civilians for reprisals is going to help."

"Well, all I can say is work closely with your SB inspector and make sure the civilians you kill are actually guilty of something first."

"Perhaps then I could have some leave, Herr Major?" Otto ventured. "You see my wife, Brunhilda, is pregnant and the child will be born in the spring."

"First, let me say congratulations, Otto."

He stubbed out his cigarette and produced a bottle of Schnaps and two glasses from a drawer in his desk.

"Do you have a name for the child?"

"Armin for a boy and Emma for a girl," he beamed, producing a locket containing a photograph of Brunhilda.

"Beautiful woman, Otto, here's to beautiful children!"

"Prosit!" they said as the glasses clanked.

By now, Z company was made up of over three quarters conscripts. They weren't all bad and he still had a strong core of NCOs to support his three original platoon commanders from Russia. Nevertheless, the work was taking its toll, not physically, but Otto felt that he was giving away a small piece of his soul every time he ordered the execution of a group of farm boys or later in London, kids younger than his conscripts. No doubt they had done things to frustrate the occupation and delay their return to the Fatherland, but few of the truly dangerous ones were ever caught or even seen above ground.

The biggest mystery for the *Vergeltungskraft* was where they all came from, because with the scale of the operations they carried out there must have been over one thousand resistance fighters in London alone.

His attached Inspector, Helmut Curth, was a capable detective and pleasant to work with, but the task was beyond him. He often looked to the central SB for guidance as well as intelligence. The man in charge of the hunt overall was Colonel von Schöenfeld, and he often had good intelligence, but the resistance always seemed to be one step ahead.

One evening in early January, Otto sat in the officer's mess drinking silently in a corner when Curth and Schöenfeld approached the table. Formerly the Athenaeum, a prestigious private members' Club, it had been requisitioned early in the occupation for use as a mess for the Officers of the SB and related arms. Some men were used to this level of luxury, but Otto still felt out of place, ever the penniless orphan from Gütersloh. The neoclassical exterior was imposing in white stone with a Grecian portico adorned with carvings of the Gods and topped with a golden statue of Athena herself. Otto felt like an imposter as he ascended the magnificent central staircase, the thick carpet under his scuffed hessian boots unsettling and the art on the walls making him feel ignorant and uncultured.

"May we join you, Hauptmann?" Schöenfeld asked, sitting down before Otto could answer.

Otto tried not to like Schöenfeld because he did not agree with his methods and for all his talk of propaganda and killing with kindness, he still ended up torturing kids in the basement of Cannon Row. Despite this, Schöenfeld was charming and charismatic, always polite to his subordinates, and he smiled a lot so Otto felt drawn to the man.

Curth was a fussy character, nervous around men like Schöenfeld and always fiddling with his notebook or his wirerimmed spectacles. However, Otto knew that out on the street or even in a fight he was a different man – confident, commanding, and sharp-witted.

"Hauptmann, the Inspector and I have been sifting through the latest intelligence."

A waiter arrived, and Schöenfeld looked disapprovingly at the neat schnapps in Otto's glass before ordering two black coffees.

"It seems that the resistance is far smaller in number than we first imagined. We now believe them to be fewer than one hundred, and we have the location of their nest. Now *you*, my good Hauptmann, are the rat catcher. I need you to go in there and exterminate these vermin."

"Tonight, Herr Oberst?"

"Tonight," he shouted. "We must strike while the iron is hot."

He beat the table with a perfectly calculated blow, enough to emphasise his point but not enough to rattle the glassware.

"*Jawohl*, Herr Oberst. I will send a message to rouse my men and return immediately to discuss strategy."

He scrawled a note and with his spare hand and summoned a waiter.

"Give this message to the runner at the door and press upon him the need for expedience."

The waiter nodded and walked from the room.

~

"Harry?" Andy rapped on the door.

"Come in!" came the muffled reply.

Andy opened the door to be faced with Kath's bare, muscular back and broad shoulders. She was straddling her lover, but she turned to look Andy directly in the eye, one perfect breast visible and a mischievous grin on her face.

"Oh, shit, sorr—"

"Spit it out, Andy, can't you see we're fuckin' busy?" she demanded with mock irritation.

"It's happening tonight, the raid on the rats' nest!"

This was the accepted name for the South Kentish Town tube station, partly because it contained a rat and partly because they knew the Germans were referring to the resistance as vermin.

"Right, fuck off then, he'll be out in a minute," Kath said and turned away, resuming her activity as he closed the door.

~

Andy's brother Dave was sitting in the office of South Kentish Town tube station with Paul, Si, and Stiff Mickey when the phone rang.

"Hello, MacCulloch & Wallis?"

"Yes, I'm looking for a regimental necktie?" came the staticky voice.

"Which regiment?" Dave asked nervously.

"Guards."

The line went dead.

"They're coming! The Boche are coming!"

The colour drained from Dave's face as he looked around the room at the three men he would need to trust absolutely over the coming minutes and hours.

"This is it, boys, this is the beginning of the end. Harry says that this ambush will turn the tide of the war in our favour. Now, what are the names of McNairy's cronies? The ones he's been sending up with messages for the Kaiser?"

"Baxter, Collins, Jeffries and Parker," Stiff Mickey said confidently.

"We're gonna send a fucking message to the Kaiser tonight lads, and it's this: Don't mess with the Shoreditch firm," Paul said.

"Si, get the vest ready, you two come with me."

Paul and Mickey followed Dave out, beckoning Fred on sentry duty in the ticket box to join them.

Gleeson turned to see the four men emerge from the stairwell and whistled using his finger and thumb. A rifle fired and when Dave's eyes fell on the source, he was shocked to see that the round had exploded in the breach. Baxter was holding his bloody face, one hand over the other and screaming hysterically.

"Dovecot, shut him up!" shouted Si, a farmer from Surrey who had suffered the misfortune of trying to sell his produce in the city on invasion day and been with the resistance ever since.

"Paul, Micky, go and get the good bullets and start dishing them out in case the cavalry is late to the party."

Dave turned to see McNairy lowering himself onto the tracks by the rifle range.

"Get that fucking rat!" he roared, and to his relief, several men sprinted in his direction, jumping onto the tracks, and catching the fat old man easily.

"Bring me Colins and Parker!"

The crowds that had formed at the two accommodation tunnels parted as the men were frogmarched onto the wooden floor covering the section of track in the centre of the station. Dave looked at them both. He'd never liked Parker, labelling him a fat gobshite with no discernible qualities.

"Cut his tongue out, cauterise the wound and glue an unloaded rifle into his hands, he's on stag in the ticket office."

The men nodded, shocked to see such a brutal side to their usually placid leader.

Si appeared around the same time as McNairy was thrown down at Dave's feet, where his captors restrained him as Si fitted the explosive vest.

"See this, you treacherous mick bastard?" Dave dangled a coil of tough-looking string, "This is your lead. If you pull on your lead, you'll go bang, understood?"

"Right, Dave, the front door's rigged with a timer to blow ninety seconds after it's opened, the lads upstairs have shut Parker up and put 'im on stag."

Si nodded to Gleeson.

"He's primed, so be careful with that pull cord, and if you listen carefully," he craned his neck, "I think that's Harry and Andy coming down the tracks with the cavalry."

"Right, you lot," Dave shouted. "Paul's team go north towards Highgate and Micky's south towards Euston."

Gleeson was alone on the platform, gagged and tethered to his executioner. He could hear the trains approaching, and when they came into view he saw that each was little more than a hand-powered platform for a machine gun that he did not recognise before he saw the face of Harry Tench looking very pleased with himself.

He was toying with the idea of just yanking on the detonator cord when men began to drag corpses onto the platform, dozens of them, and each was given one of the terrible rifles he'd been trying to train those poor boys how to use all month.

As he began to understand Harry's plan, sick realisation hit him in the gut. Harry had played him *and* Schöenfeld, and he'd done it with finesse. He'd portrayed the moronic hard man so well that he had them all fooled, looking instead for the man behind the man. They had thought it was Sampson or Jones, *but who was he really?* This was going to be a blood bath, but worse still, Schöenfeld would see it as a victory and Tench would make his next move against an enemy that thought him defeated, decimated, and the evidence would be right here for all to see.

Well done, Sir. Well done indeed, Gleeson thought.

~

Otto rode in the front of the truck as the battalion rumbled through the snow-covered streets of London, and he went over the plan again in his head. X company was approaching from Euston, Y company from Highgate, and Z would storm from above. He was glad he didn't have to run along those tracks in the dark.

How many young men would go down with a sprained or broken ankle tonight?

The convoy grew smaller until it was only Z company, and when they reached South Kentish Town they dismounted. He walked among his men, some of whom he'd known through nearly two years of hard fighting and unimaginable horror, the punishment battalion, Petersburg, and the beaches on X-Tag.

This was not the time or place for speeches, so while they waited for H hour, Otto chatted with his men and made sure that the youngest and most inexperienced were as ready as they could be.

As H hour approached, they formed up ready to storm the station. First, a three-man team would enter via the service door, take out the guard and unlock the large public doors that opened onto the Kentish Town Road. Then Z company would assault the resistance stronghold and take a huge step towards going back home to Germany.

"*Ein, zwei, drei,*" whispered the Wachtmeister.

A month ago he'd been Feldwebel Weiss, but the new police regiments had the old *Feldgendarmerie* ranks. Ten months ago, this man who had been ordered to the parole battalion because he was an unrepenting sodomite, was now a Wachtmeister in the special police. Otto stifled a chuckle as they breached.

The traitor Parker gave a muffled cry and tried to raise his hand as they entered, but he involuntarily brought a rifle to bear and the assault team shot him dead. He slumped sideways onto the not inconsiderable amount of stolen hexogen rigged to blow on a delayed fuse.

Weiss' men heaved open the heavy door and picquet gate, allowing squad after squad of stormtroopers dressed as MPs to rush in. As the fourth squad crossed the threshold, the hexogen taken from a German convoy ambushed two weeks earlier exploded with devastating effect.

The shockwave tore through flesh and bone killing and maiming as the front of the ticket office disintegrated into violent projectiles blinding and slashing Otto's men indiscriminately. Immediately following the blast all was still and silent, burst ear drums and rattled skulls rendered every man dazed, prone and inert.

Then came the screams, moans and shuffling of two dozen injured men, crying out for help, for mother, and for home. Dust filled the confined space and coughing rose up, followed by the fit and walking wounded, men in awe of their miraculous escape dusted themselves off and made to help their comrades. The rallying cries of NCO's echoed about in the darkness and leaving the wounded to their fate the remainder surged onwards and down into the stairwell. Tossing a few stick grenades down ahead of them for good measure, but they landed among dead men who could not become any more so.

Otto had never seen a suicide vest before, and his mouth fell open in horror as he took in the implications and, tracing the command wire to a machine gun in the tunnel, he tried to recall his men, most of whom were on the platform by now losing momentum in the confusion, staring about at the countless corpses at their feet.

Two machine guns opened up, but no bullets came, and Otto realised they were firing up the tracks at X and Y companies.

These were the last thoughts of Hauptmann Otto Kessler.

The wall of smoke and debris moved in slow motion towards him. Fragments of Gleeson's skull penetrated Otto's torso at three thousand feet per second, but the shock wave had already caused so much damage to his internal organs that he was dead before he hit the wall of the tunnel like a rag doll. The roof began to fracture, and as large pieces fell away, earth began to fall too, smothering any of Z company that survived the blast and burying them alive.

Harry had asked two men on each gun to stay behind. He had shown them how to escape at the very last minute, and then led the rest of the group to safety via a parallel service tunnel. Two of these men were the traitors Jeffries and Collins.

Jeffries fired while Collins loaded as the hundred or so men of X company charged at their position, not because this was a chance at redemption, but because they knew it was their only hope of survival and their only chance of a clean death. The blast was not powerful enough to kill them, but it was sufficient to give their attackers the upper hand.

Bloody hand to hand combat ensued as trench knives and hatchets were produced and the tattered remnants of the police battalion swarmed the guns.

Schöenfeld picked his way through the rubble and debris in South Kentish Town tube station with Curth at his side.

"It's a damn shame," Curth said standing over Otto's limp form.

"It's a victory for Germany no matter the price, and we have struck a decisive blow this night, one that could change the course of the war," Schöenfeld remarked, surveying the carnage and wondering if Handbuch had escaped to safety before the attack.

"It will certainly make our job a lot easier if this is the end of the resistance," he added and as he spoke, Curth stooped to search the body. He found the locket and removed Otto's "*Gold gab ich für Eisen*" ring, wrapping them with his iron cross in a handkerchief and pocketing it.

"I'll have these sent to his wife," he said when Schöenfeld caught his eye.

The Boudicca – 1916

Bringer of victory

Charlie Baxter, the man whose rifle had backfired earlier that night, was shivering and alone in the U-boat. His painfully skinny wrists and ankles were tied to a metal chair, and he sat there completely naked, nervously eyeing the various instruments of torture while he awaited his fate. The door creaked open and a wedge of light grew to fill the room, where the shadow of a shapely woman appeared, followed by its master.

"Hello, dear, you must be Charlie," Kath smiled sweetly. "I'm Kathleen Lynch. Heard of me?"

He shook his head.

"How about my brother James?"

He shook it again.

"I want you to think back to the last time you ran one of McNairy's little messages."

Charlie gave a muffled scream, accompanied by a vigorously shaking head.

"Speak up, dear, I'm deaf in one ear these days," she said, pulling out the gag and smiling warmly. "What did you say?"

"I never run messages for that Kaiser loving bastard," he said, pleading in his eyes.

"Now, Charlie, I was in the middle of explaining something," her voice was calm and full of patience, like a mother speaking to a beloved child. "Please don't interrupt me again." She tilted her head to one side and smiled.

"Where was I? So, when you was running around London, doing whatever it was," she shrugged, "you may have seen a boy. Now, he was strung up from a lamppost with a sign around his neck that read *I bit the hand that feeds.*"

She turned away from him and picked something up, the object obscured by her body.

"Did you see it, Charlie?"

"Yeah," he said slowly, "I seen it, horrible it was."

With one swift motion, she turned, swinging a twelve-pound sledgehammer in both hands, and struck Charlie a bone-cracking blow to the chest.

"It was my fucking baby brother!" she screamed as Charlie gasped desperately for breath, while his diaphragm spasmed and contracted painfully, preventing his lungs from inflating.

She watched his struggle in disgust for some minutes.

"Be quiet, Charlie, there's a good boy," she told him as she ruffled his greasy hair.

Loud rasping breaths came suddenly as he regained control of his diaphragm. Kath produced a riding crop, whipping Charlie's face with it before leaning forwards and grabbing his jaw.

"You see this?" she said, turning her face to show him the angry pink scar that zig-zagged across her otherwise perfect young skin.

"LOOK AT IT," she screamed. "Open your fucking eyes and look at what you did!"

"I, I'm not responsible for that, Miss, I don't even know who you are?"

His voice imploring her to believe him. She let go of his face and turned her back on him. She looked good in the high-waisted trousers and they gave her confidence. She would stride purposefully around the complex of tunnels empowered and respected. Not as Harry's woman but as a resistance hero in her own right. Before, the pencil skirts she wore in and out of uniform hobbled her, and then she saw it for the first time. This was the patriarchy that Pankhurst was on about.

The men who designed these clothes wanted women to be constrained, unable to walk with purpose, unable to run. From little girls they had only been told what they *must* do, what they *couldn't* do and never what they *could*.

Well no more. She was Kathleen Lynch and she was going to wear trousers and drive cars, she would fight for the resistance and damn well enjoy sex on her terms when *she* wanted it. She was going to do what made her happy and talk to men as an equal or as a superior, but never as a subordinate again. If she had children, *if*, because it was *her* choice, then her girls would be brought up to believe that they could do anything, and she would find Pankhurst and Fawcett and join them on the picket line, shoulder to shoulder until all women had the vote.

She spun around fast and struck Charlie on the cheek again.

"Do you feel that, Charlie? Does it sting?"

"Y-yes, Miss," he said through rasping breaths.

"Good, because that feeling, that pain in your cheek is the first thing I feel every morning and the last thing I feel every night and every fucking second of every minute in between!"

She hefted the sledgehammer in one hand and he flinched. She allowed the riding crop to quiver beside her in her other hand and Charlie shuddered.

"Good," she said, smiling as she put both items down on a bench. "Now, Charlie dear, you're going to tell me everything you did for McNairy and everything you did to betray your country. I don't care why you did it and I promise that if you tell me absolutely everything," she smiled again, a genuinely sweet smile, the way she smiled before all this, before Schöenfeld and before Harry, before the war when she lived in a crowded house with three noisy brothers and her loving Irish parents. "I promise I will let you live and I won't hurt you anymore."

Charlie drew in another painful breath. He looked at Kath, then down at the floor, then back up at her.

"Alright," he sniffed. "When I joined the resistance, I wanted to fight the Boche, take our city back and maybe our countr—"

"BORING!" she shouted, not bothering to look at him from where she stood half leaning against the workbench and blew air through her lips.

"So, we got taken to this warehouse... it was dark, even in the day so you couldn't see properly," he said rapidly, risking a terrified glimpse at his captor. "There was about five of us, we got hardly no food and all we had to sleep on was these two mouldy blankets each."

All the time, he made furtive glances up at her as he spoke, scared she would get angry.

"No one spoke to us and we was there for two weeks, then more came until there was nearly twenty of us wandering round in the half-dark, angry and starving. That's when fights broke out over food and the guards would just fire over our heads."

"How did you know how many, Charlie?" she beamed.

"I counted us later, f-for McNairy."

"Okay, go on, love," she winked.

"Well, after the last lot arrived, they started to train us and those that did well got more food."

He looked at her pleadingly.

"Could I have some water, Miss?"

Out of nowhere the whip hit his cheek, drawing blood.

"You were telling me a story, dear?"

She nodded and smiled, encouraging him to continue.

"For the next week," he sniffed, tears streaming down his face mixing with the blood, "we trained. Marching, weapon handling and marksmanship theory, they showed us all sorts…"

"I know what the resistance teaches new recruits, darlin'," she said sweetly, and then sourly she snapped, "*get to the good bit.*"

"About a week later they woke us in the night and ordered us to gather our stuff, and we marched in a big circle around the warehouse for hours, until a truck came about midday and took us to South Kensington Tube station."

"And what happened?" She tilted her head sweetly to the side again.

"There was about twenty lads already there and we were given bunks and told that this was resistance HQ. Then McNairy arrived and they fed us the best meal we'd eaten in two weeks, a thin turnip soup with one stale roll."

"Tell me about McNairy?"

"He was kind, he knew a lot about war and weapons and bombs and how to fight like a guerrilla. They made him our instructor and Parker, Collins and me, we was all in the same part of the East accommodation tunnel."

"Good boy."

She threw water in his face, and he sniffed, his breathing still laboured.

"Then we got talking, talking about Ireland and home rule, how nice it was there since the British left. He would describe the brutality of the British soldiers, he reeled off all the massacres, usually around a hundred people shot. The most recent was 1914, Miss."

Kath continued to stare at the ceiling for a moment before whipping her head around to look him directly in the eye.

"What's my last name?" she demanded.

"Err, L-lynch, Miss."

"Errr, L-l-l-l-lynch, Miss," she mocked him, "Fucking Lynch, so don't sit there and tell me how badly *my* parents, my grandparents, my uncle, cousins and aunts have had it off the British."

She began pacing the room, thrashing her whip absentmindedly, apparently unaware of the anxiety in Charlie's face.

"This is not about Britain, you fucking moron, this is about survival. What the fuck do you think would have happened when McNairy's job was done? Did you think you'd all go home to Ireland with him and take turns fucking his wife?"

"I, I didn't..."

"No, of course, you didn't fucking think, boys like you rarely do. After McNairy was gone, you'd be left here, in a broken city under the boot of the Kaiser, bowing and scraping to the Germans whose laces you helped to tie."

"We didn't only talk about Ireland," he said obsequiously. "McNairy was in Africa during the Boer war, and he told us how the British used concentration camps, like what the Boche has done to us, he said we're no better."

"Don't you see, Charlie, it doesn't matter. You cannot fix past mistakes by selling your own countrymen up the river. Now move on. When did you start doing things for him, for the Germans?"

"The first time I did it, I didn't realise what I'd done until it was too late."

Just like me, she thought.

"What was it?"

"He gave me a letter, said it was for his family in Ireland, asked me to post it for him, but not in a post box. He had me post it through the door of a disused pawn shop, then chalk an X on the boarded-up window."

"And you just did that for him, no questions asked?" she said with mock incredulity.

"He had a hold over me… I don't know, I just wanted to do things for him, to make him like me, to be of use to him, I can't explain it."

Kath was reminded of her relationship with Harry, though the dynamic had changed somewhat since she'd moved in, and he had got her brother killed.

"You weren't… he wasn't buggering you?" she asked in disbelief.

"No," he protested. "he wasn't like that, he was kind and noble, a good man."

"If you say so. Just tell me what else you did for him, and I want a list of the dead-drop locations and the fill signals."

Charlie sang like a canary and Kath sporadically rewarded him with water or a biscuit. By the time the sun rose over the Docklands, Charlie was hers, and she had everything she needed, so she unbound his wrists and ankles, tossed him a blanket, and left him curled up in a corner to type up her report.

As she swaggered through the complex, head high and chin stuck out, the bulk of the resistance fighters were beginning to wake, emerging from storerooms or side tunnels, and greeting her like the queen she was. This scar, she thought, although a painful reminder of the night she had lost James, was better than any medal. It said to the two thousand other men and women down here that she had been there and done it.

It screamed '*Here stands the brave warrior queen of the resistance*' and it gave her carte blanche to do and say whatever to whomever, including Harry Tench.

~

"I want my own team."

It wasn't a question, there was no inflexion in her voice to even pretend that it could be. She had been typing for the last thirty minutes, each keystroke a hammer blow to Harry's aching head, and when he finally abandoned his efforts at sleep, he sat up in the bed and she pounced.

"What? No man will follow you; they're all programmed to think…"

"I want an all-woman team."

He made a pained noise. Perhaps it was his hangover or perhaps it was the thought of a gang of iron-willed five-and-a-half-foot Amazonians strutting around his underground lair.

"What for?"

"Less full-frontal attack and more reconnaissance and espionage," she said without looking up or ceasing her farriery on the infernal typewriter.

"Ahh, I still don't know."

It was too late though, he'd made the noise, the noise that acknowledged she was right.

"Look, you said it, none of the men wants a woman under their command unless they're trying to get in her knickers, and you don't want your officers trying to fuck their soldiers, no matter what the individual case."

"Fine, *handwrite* me a list of potential recruits and outline what stores you'll need, and the duties you hope to perform."

"I want all the women fit enough to fight and when I have them, I'll figure the rest out."

She said this more to avoid doing paperwork than anything else. The typewriter dinged and she rose from her chair, stalking towards her prey, peeling away, and discarding garments as she moved, until finally naked, she pounced and devoured her quarry whole.

Nine mismatched, bedraggled women stood in an *almost* straight line in a seldom-used section of the labyrinth of tunnels that had become resistance HQ. Ostensibly these women *were* soldiers in that they all had a uniform of sorts, they all had a weapon, they could hit what they aimed at and most importantly, they were here! They had left their safe life on the surface to fight, fight the Boche, fight oppression, and fight the patriarchal narrative that women were too weak, too sensitive, and too pretty to get stuck in where they were needed, in the mud and blood and the flying steel and lead.

"Women are not helpless. We are not too emotional, and we are not hysterical. We're fucking *angry!*" Kath announced.

She looked at her new team. Some wore variations of Kath's tailored uniform trousers, a couple had acquired jodhpurs and one had a sort of khaki jumpsuit that Kath secretly coveted. Brown leather jackets seemed to be the one thing that everyone in the resistance either had or wanted, and she suspected that Harry had obtained a large consignment of them after the invasion and the latecomers had assumed they needed one too.

"This war, this invasion, this occupation, has affected *us* as much as any man. We are still occupied, we are still patriots, and we are still standing!"

She paced up and down the single rank slowly, her hands on her hips.

"My name is Captain Kath Lynch," she announced, promoting herself on the spot, "and I've been given command of a special unit. For this, I need strong women, women who are not ruled by the will of a weak man, a man who must control those around him to feel safe. If this is you, go now, deal with that man, and return an empowered woman. A woman I can use."

No one moved, so she assumed that if they were down here, then they were probably in charge of their own shit.

"Some of you may have heard what happened in Kentish town the other night and what that means? It means that the Boche think we are through, that we're defeated and the city is theirs. Well, for the next three weeks, we're gonna let them believe it. We are gonna stay down here and out of sight while they celebrate and divert their forces elsewhere, and in that time, we are going to train, we are going to drill, and we are going to sweat! At the end of it, we will be *unstoppable*."

Murmurs of approval rose up.

"Shut up!" Kath snapped. "This unit will be disciplined, it will be strong, and it will be deadly. Now I didn't spend the last six months playing nice with a fucking slimy Hun Colonel, laughing at his jokes, letting him and his cronies make eyes at me while stealing his secrets, and risking my life to get them to the resistance just so I could die because one of you can't be quiet when you're supposed to be.

"Now, the Hun is vicious, the Hun is primitive, and the Hun *is* a rapist. I know, I've been in the basement under Cannon Row, and I came this close."

She held up a thumb and forefinger to demonstrate how close she had come to being raped.

"It is because they are primitive and because they are rapists, because they will not think twice about killing a child or shooting an innocent family in the street to send a message, it is because of all these things, that we are going to send a message back! We are going to kill every last dirty fucking Hun we see."

She stopped to take a breath and gather her thoughts, eyeing the women under her command.

"Nearly two thousand years ago another empire came to our shores with eagles and technology and assumptions of conquest! The Britons then responded much like we have, some betraying all for the favour of Rome and others like the fierce warriors of the Iceni, stood and fought to the last. They kept the Romans at bay for nearly twenty-years. We will learn from their mistakes while taking their name for our own. The Boudicca was merciless, slaughtering all who stood for Rome with impunity. Like her, we too will hunt the Boche, we too will find the Boche and when we catch him, we too will be merciless! And through our relentless brutality the Hun will know us, they will see who we are, they will see what we have done, and they will fear us! We will become the Iceni of British legend, feared and respected, God-like in our power and ruthless in our justice!"

She looked from one woman to the next, the hairs on her neck and arms rigid as tears threatened.

"Want to join my tribe?" she shouted.

"Yes, Ma'am," they chorused.

"That's what I thought!"

For three weeks the Iceni trained, they ran, they boxed, they learned to fight with knives and brushed up on their shooting.

297

They practised lying and stealing from the two thousand strong population in the tunnels and they ran some more. Harry showed them how to use explosives and a few moves he'd picked up on his travels.

At the end of three weeks they were transformed from mediocre soldiers into reasonably fit soldiers that stood a chance of not dying, if they were careful.

"Ladies, we have a problem. I only need eight of you," Kath announced, letting the statement hang in the air for a moment. "One of you has got to go, only question is, who?"

She looked each woman up and down, pacing the line with the occasional click of her tongue to break the atmospheric silence.

"I propose a battle royal, each loser facing one another until only the weakest remain in a fight to the death."

The Iceni erupted in protest, collective gasps, before they began eyeing their comrades up, trying to figure out who was the weakest.

"Silence!" Kath bellowed. "If you can't figure out who the weakest in the team is, it's probably you. Which is absolute bollocks, we all know who the weakest is and if she steps forward now, I'll call the whole thing off."

Silently, the women continued their search, until all eyes fell upon Sadie, a match girl from Wapping with match-like limbs and flame red hair. She was the weakest, but she had other talents. Talents that would be immensely useful to Kath in the coming war, and Kath realised that what she was doing would only damage her, make her look unhinged, she felt unhinged, but was this now beyond her control?

Only one thing for it, she thought, before erupting into a maniacal laughter that reverberated around the enclosed space, enveloping the Iceni in an audible manifestation of her madness.

"You can't think I was serious? Killing one of our own? Not a fucking chance. I want you to remember who you imagined to be the weakest and think about how *you* might work to help them and what strengths they bring to our number."

With her newly formed, untested team now questioning her sanity, Kath felt lost, at a loss and unsure of what to do next.

"Let's have a scrap anyway, not to the death just a bit of sparring, I'll take you all on one at a time," she suggested, while rummaging in her jacket, "winner gets these."

Kath tossed a set of sergeant's stripes onto the floor at her feet, before dramatically removing her jacket and adopting classic boxing stance, a frenzied look in her piercing green eyes.

She was fast, faster than most, but not Blau. Blau was lightning, and when she landed one on Kath's nose and popped it, Kath hit back a little too hard. Blau took it in her stride, smiling as they shook hands, white teeth showing through the flowing blood. Kath handed her the stripes and, producing a bottle of whisky, she passed it around the group of bruised and bloody women, who each took a swig.

Kath looked around at the ragtag bunch of women from every corner of Britain and her empire. She should feel pride, or accomplishment, but all she felt was an overwhelming desire for revenge and that these women were the tool with which deliver retribution.

Command – 1916

Oberst Reinhardt Freiherr von Schöenfeld luxuriated in a high-backed leather armchair. A fine single malt burned pleasantly in his throat, warming his insides and lowering the thinnest of veils over his mind. He afforded himself the indulgence of a third measure tonight of all nights because this marked three weeks since the decisive victory at Kentish town. He was once again the *Wunderkind* of local command and enjoyed the full confidence of his SB masters. This, in turn, would allow him to proceed unhindered onto the next phase of his plan for the subjugation of the British people and the smoking out of the last pockets of resistance.

Schöenfeld planned to reward the remainder of the London populace with increased rations, wages, and free time. He would organise entertainment and concentrate his cheap labour on the building of new homes, hospitals, and community centres. When this was done and the people were comfortable, content and most importantly of all, distracted, he would introduce the new enemy, the resistance fighter. It did not matter who they were really, but they would assume the blame for any shortcomings of the occupational government.

Food shortages? The resistance stole the shipment.

Longer working hours? The resistance blew up a similar factory in another sector.

This new bogeyman would soon be the focus of the Londoners' discontent instead of the occupiers, then he would have succeeded in convincing them to hate their would-be liberators and look to the Germans for safety, warmth, and comfort.

When this was achieved the new regime of work in return for food and housing could begin, with troublemakers branded the now universally despised resistance and ousted by their neighbours and friends. Soon the youth would see the attraction of joining the German army auxiliary to escape the life of slavery that would be the only alternative, and they would be used to take the rest of the island. Schöenfeld chuckled mirthlessly to himself at the thought of sons and brothers waging war with fathers and uncles in order to give their homeland to the men who enslaved their mothers and sisters.

As he enjoyed a fourth whisky, Schöenfeld rose from his chair and strode confidently to the window of his study on the third floor of his Belgravia mansion. His men were plastering the new posters all over the city, posters decrying the resistance and honouring those who laboured to rebuild London, using children to tug at the heartstrings of the populace.

One poster read: "Will you rebuild London's homes and hospitals for your family, or blow them up for your own selfish pride?"

The muscular man wielding a hammer was surrounded by his adoring family while caricatures of rats in leather jackets cowered in the shadows waiting to detonate an unseen device. He had designed that one himself and he was very pleased with it, imagining that Bernays would have been proud.

He tried to cry out as he felt the cold steel drag across his bare throat, but nothing came. His hands flew to the eight-inch opening at his neck through which fresh, hot blood was gushing. He sank to his knees and watched his life flowing through his fingers, his panicked face staring back at him in the glass of the window.

His last image was of Kathleen Lynch using the curtain to dispassionately wipe the blood from her knife, and she caught his eye and smiled sweetly as his world went dark and he felt his body hit the floor.

Outside the door to the study stood Ruth Blackett, originally from Cumbria, she towered over Kath whose eyeline was only level with the fall of Blackett's auburn hair. Both women moved silently down the hallway to the servants' stairs and into the kitchen were they found Blau with Mrs Higgins.

"Come with us," Kath said, her hand outstretched to the distraught cook.

They moved carefully past the half-concealed pile of dead guards to a manhole cover in the courtyard, where the rest of the Iceni were waiting for them below. Reunited, they set off down the tunnel, the unsteady yellow light from their lanterns flickered on the concave walls. After walking for about ten minutes the file of women stopped.

"Walk that way for about forty-five minutes and you should come to a sentry. Tell him what happened, and they will look after you."

Kath placed a reassuring hand on the old woman's upper arm, handed her a lantern and smiled that winning smile. Mrs Higgins did as she was told until soon she was little more than a dim light dancing on the tunnel walls.

As the team moved north to the home of their next victim, the tunnel walls shook and dust fell as an almighty blast reverberated through the city.

"That'll be that treacherous bastard Charlie," Ruth said to murmurs of assent.

Kath cast her mind back to the previous afternoon spent preparing Charlie for his mission. Si had built the device and helped fit it while Kath spoke to the lad, encouraging him and making sure that he was going to go through with it. Charlie was distraught, reluctant, and terrified.

Then there were the moral implications of this act but Kath was resolute; satisfied that she was doing something tremendously important for the cause. Harry, however, had distanced himself from the operation. He was clearly uneasy with using suicide bombers, just not enough to veto the move and lose out to the tactical advantage of taking out so many key officers with one decisive blow.

"I know it's scary, Charlie dear, but you're doing something so brave and important for a cause that you worked so very hard to undermine less than a month ago."

She spoke in her caring, motherly voice, but both knew that the sadist lurked just beneath the surface, ready to strike if Charlie stepped out of line.

"I know, and I want to help, but I'm just so scared. What if it doesn't go off? I'll be captured and tortured," he shot her a glance before saying, "again."

"Oh, Charlie, my sweet boy." She took his face in her hands. "If you think that was torture, try fucking this up tonight because then I'll show you what torture is. Now, let's go over the plan once more."

"I'll go topside wearing the Boche clobber and carrying the satchel, then make my way to the Ritz hotel. When I'm there I'll start the two-minute timers, run into the lobby and give one of my bombs to reception. Then I'll burst into the main lounge and shout: *Ich habe eine dringende Nachricht für den Oberst Schreiber* when I'm in the most crowded area, and I'll put down the satchel and run for the door."

"Very good," Kath said. "Your accent is impressive, have you been practising?"

"Yes, Ma'am," he said, basking in the praise. He'd spent hours over the last weeks memorising the phrase: *I have an urgent message for Colonel Schreiber.*

"But remember, you must not run because if you do, they will know something is up. You have to walk calmly from the room, then you can run."

Brigadier Sir Gerald Clive surveyed his men, a rag-tag bunch for sure, but brave without question. Well trained, well equipped, and well fed, their collective breath formed a cloud above their heads. He was pleased with himself and amazed at the sheer numbers; the ranks had swelled, and as word got around about the Hun's food and supply issues, and more and more men came forward to help drive them into the sea.

Bored and frustrated Tommies had deserted their idle commanders to find a new home in the kinetic ranks of the resistance, and with them came the experience and discipline that hitherto were lacking in Gerald's outfit.

This immense army had advanced south from Bury St Edmonds into the northernmost reaches of London meeting little resistance until the first major battle was fought over the grounds of Wrotham Park, a stately home just north of Barnet. The Second Battle of Barnet was bloody for both sides and many of the newer resistance fighters saw their first and last action that day. As the tide turned and the Germans began a fighting withdrawal, Sir Gerald chose to ride into battle himself on a dun gelding. A carbine in one hand and sabre in the other, cutting down the malnourished *Sturmtruppen,* slashing at their backs as they fled his Hussars. They harried the enemy as far south as Hendon, where they regrouped and set up camp for the night.

The next day the army marched further south to Hampstead Heath, where they assembled for a final stand against the depleted German Imperial forces.

Now over a thousand men and women of the uprising stood, parade fashion, hanging on this charlatan's every word and he had plenty for them.

"You men who stand before me today are the finest I have had the honour to serve with. Today the stakes are higher than ever before. Fight now for freedom, for failure will condemn those who survive us to generations of slavery. Let this not be another Wattling Street or Hastings, but an Agincourt or a Waterloo."

He took a deep breath and basked in his own importance, mistaking the groans and sighs of his despondent troops for the restless fervour that comes before battle. He droned on, oblivious and monotone, inspiring only boredom and *Weltschmertz*. Gerald would not have cared for this was *his* finest hour, his Waterloo. The troops were here only to facilitate that, and a rousing speech was part of his unassailable self-image.

"Young Tommy Atkins," he continued. "This is Britain's hour of greatest need and she needs *you*, whose guts are iron and whose mettle is granite, to charge snarling into the teeth of the Hun. I know you worthy of your forebears, so prove it this day, upon this heath. Show that limp-wristed King of Huns that he cannot just march in here with impunity and subjugate this great nation of ours. Go now as our guns pummel the German positions to find the Hun and spill his blood on this ancient heath...but know this...if you fall here today, you will be immortalised in glory, forever remembered as one who stood up to the occupation and made the ultimate sacrifice to protect your country."

The columns of soldiers gave a lacklustre roar in reply, prodded, and poked into compliance by their officers. Gerald wheeled his charger around to face the enemy, sabre to the sky. When he let fall his arm, the great guns began their preparatory barrage and the first wave of infantry began their advance. They marched past Gerald in the direction his sword pointed up to the line of departure as the smell of cordite and churned earth filled their nostrils.

Alf Grant had not matched Sir Gerald's trajectory having found his ceiling in the post of Company Sergeant Major. The most experienced soldier in the company and in charge of discipline and administration for about two hundred men, he was father, martinet and shining example to all but the most senior of his NCOs. Alf still wore the leather jacket of earlier times, now with a large crown stitched in gold on the right sleeve near the cuff. He never bothered with the battle bowler, sticking instead to his old, green, woolly hat.

Now he brought up the rear of Audley Company of the First Battalion of the Anglian Resistance, part of the Eastern Resistance Division which formed one third of the English Uprising. They did not run but marched quickly. The men carried only weapons, water, and iron rations. Alf had secured their heavy equipment inside Kenwood house with the rest of the baggage train.

Audley Company were in the first wave of the attack, following the creeping barrage as it tore up the lawns of the ancient heath, hurling the brown London clay into the air and leaving small craters for the men to traverse or use as cover should the need to retreat arise. Of the original men Alf had trained, only Gerald and Michael had left for anything other than the undertakers. Gerald still had his adjutant, the bombardier with the maimed hand was now a major and had led men in battle with distinction on several occasions, but he always returned to the side of his patron when the action was over.

The sound of the guns was deafening. The men of A Company had the almost constant boom of the gun at their backs and the less frequent but equally harrowing whistle and bang of the shells to their front. The experience, although comforting on some level, frayed the nerves and wore down one's courage, such that Alf and his small section had the unenviable task of chiding the men whose proclivity for shock and stress was already sated.

Few bullets found their way through the barrage and Alf lost more men to twisted ankles and shell shock than lead or shrapnel. He simply allowed them to rest in a shell hole or limp back to the line of departure, saving the stretcher bearers for the gruesome wounds that were certainly on the horizon. When the barrage, about a hundred feet ahead of the line suddenly ceased its advance, the men were ordered to seek cover in the nearest shell hole. What followed was a further five minutes of intense bombardment on what was thought to be the enemy line. This was confirmed when equipment, weapons and horrifying chunks of German soldiers began to land in and around Alf's position.

Just as abruptly as they had begun the guns fell silent, and the air was filled with the sound of whistles and shouts of '*Attack!*'

Alf echoed these and his NCOs took up the cry. Men rose from the muddy earth and charged on as smoke eddied around them, both providing cover and obscuring their vision—a double-edged sword. When all his men were moving, Alf ran ahead, although this was counterintuitive, because one of his primary roles in battle was the organisation of casualty extraction and this could only be done from the rear. Nevertheless, he charged, half afraid that a squad of Germans would appear behind a working gun ready to tear him and his boys to shreds.

The plan was always to advance behind the barrage and clear the hastily dug enemy positions, fighting through to the other side and regrouping behind them. They did this with Alf leading the charge. He sprayed bullets from his MP40 into the writhing form of an injured German and ran on, kicking in the balls any he suspected of still living just to make sure. He was directing his men into an all-round defensive position – a rough circle, with every man and woman facing outward in the direction of the enemy threat – when the staccato rattle of at least three maxim guns filled his ears.

He looked on in horror as the men of his company were torn to shreds from three directions, thrown to the ground gurgling blood, or crying out in pain and confusion. He fought the urge to take cover and began to direct some sort of counterattack, collecting uninjured soldiers and giving them tasks when yet more Germans arrived and the rain of lead intensified.

Alf's ear started to burn and he felt blood running down his neck soaking his shirt. Another tore through his guts causing him to double over, and he fell to his knees still able to witness the carnage unfolding around him. Men and women lay still, staring up with unseeing eyes or worse as they lay writhing in agony, calling out for help, for their mothers, or for the sweet release of death. As the ground slid out of view and the grey morning sky took centre stage, he turned his head to the side just in time to see a wife, desperately, futilely, trying to reassemble her husband's entrails while his blood-soaked hand searched blindly for hers and for a small piece of comfort in this life before passing through to the next.

Alf's vison faded and the screams of his comrades filled his consciousness; the rattle of the guns muted and distant. As his breathing became shallow he could still smell war; smoke and blood, iron and lead, powder and shit. The last sound he heard was the British great guns. When he drew his final breath, a shell threw his lifeless body into the air as the ground around him was churned up, burying the soldiers of A company both dead and alive.

~

Harry Tench, another general in another part of London gave another speech. Not vain enough to promote himself to anything and known universally as Harry, he stepped up onto the raised platform in the cavernous intersection of tunnels that he always used for gatherings like this. The crowd shuffled and stamped their feet against the cold, impatient to get to the relative warmth of the surface.

"Heroes of London, Liberators of Britain and fighters for peace, freedom, and justice, I come before you 'umbled. You 'umble me. You brave men and women with your tenacity and unwavering commitment to what at times has felt like a desperate, unwinnable war. These words are nothing. Nothing compared with the sacrifices you lot have made and the risks you have taken to get us here. Today we launch what I hope will be the final offensive in a long and bloody campaign. A campaign of brutal and undeserved reprisals by men that would see you and your families in chains, slaves to Kaiser Bill and the German Empire, was it not for those what stand among us today, those what stood up and said no, not in my fucking country, not my kids, not my brothers and sisters!

And we're nearly there, we've given the Hun the run around and beat him at his own game. As I speak, Kath and her Iceni are sweeping through London via the tunnels, killing all the higher-ups, including that bastard Schöenfeld, the one what tortured, butchered, and strung up so many of our boys. The slag what sent that mick spy to bring us down from the inside. He'll be dead by now, bleeding out on his posh rug in the drum he stole from an Englishman."

"Yeah, some fucking Englishman," a voice called from the crowd of nearly two thousand armed men and women. "Where is he now? Hiding on his country estate?"

"That's right, brother," Harry said, pointing at no one in particular. "That's right. *When*, yeah, *when* we win the war there are gonna be a few changes around here, starting with a bit of truth and reconciliation. The next time some toff comes out with that bollocks about being bred to lead us in war, you can ask them, 'Where were you at the Battle of Westminster? Or the Battle of Shipton Street? How about the Battle of the Nine Bridges?' and he'll bluster an excuse and you can smile and say, 'Well, son, I think you'd better be moving along then, don't you?'

"Today though, today is about blood. *German* blood. I want you to spill it, I want to see it flow through the streets and I want the Thames to run red with it. Today you have the chance to become immortal, to be lauded as the men and women what drove the Hun from this land once and for all. Them what saved Britain from generations of servitude, oppression, and tyranny. So, go from this place, noble Englishmen, proud Londoners, and fierce warriors. Go from this place of hiding and stand firm on the streets of your city, breathe the air and roar with pride. As you charge into battle cry out…"

"For England, Harry, and Saint George!" came multiple voices from the crowd, quickly becoming a collective roar as the troops were led above ground, hopefully for the final time.

These were guerrillas, insurgents, cold-blooded killers who had discarded childish notions of mercy and honour long ago. The moment they hit the dawn's early light, they melted away into the scenery. This was not going to be conventional war on the Hun's terms, this would be dirty and violent and they weren't going know what had hit them. Central London teemed with nearly two thousand efficient life-takers, no Hun was safe, no collaborator, no-one who looked a bit foreign.

Revolution – 1916

When patrols stopped reporting at the appointed time, the hauptmann in charge of security in the docklands sector grew anxious. Until now he had been a logistician organising the supply chain and distribution of rations and ammunition, his combat training was years ago and he was out of his depth. Hauptmann Ludwig sent out more patrols to discover what had happened to the others and when they did not return, he sent more. Finally, when only he and his radio operator remained, he called down the sentries to help.

They did not answer.

"Herr Hauptmann?" *Unteroffizier* Liebig asked, a seasoned *Zwölfender* from Frankfurt.

"Go, man, don't make me tell you twice."

Ludwig's voice betrayed him, and the experienced corporal pressed his advantage.

"Herr Hauptmann, we must stay together," he implored. "Someone is out there picking us off, we should barricade the guardroom and prepare for an attack."

The captain thought silently for a moment.

"Perhaps you are right, Liebig… go and look for things to block the door."

The light from the low winter sun struggled to penetrate the thick cloud overhead and the smog that engulfed this eerie city. The two men were sitting with their backs to the enormous desk in the guardroom, while a filing cabinet formed the foundation of a sturdy looking barricade made from tables, chairs, and even mattresses from the cells.

"Five hundred and twelve rounds, Herr Hauptmann," announced Liebig, casting a furtive glance at the door.

Outside the insurgents worked, silently picking off soldiers in ones and twos. After the work of the Iceni the night before there was no-one experienced enough left alive to give orders and men like Hauptmann Ludwig struggled to deal with a situation that was far outside their competence. By lunchtime the streets were littered with the bodies of dead Germans, their throats cut, and as predicted, the sewers glut with the putrid red of blood and entrails. Afterwards, those who bore witness that day swore that the Thames took on a similar hue.

In Deptford, south of the river and a world apart, signals officer Major Joachim Stuber had realised what was happening and had spent the morning desperately scrounging for men. A resourceful man if not a tactician, he'd managed to gather a few hundred by lunchtime and was marching them west towards Tower Bridge. The Jacks avoided forces of this size, choosing instead to track their movements using the network of police telephone boxes to report back to HQ.

Doctrine dictates that troops in hostile territory should follow a strict course of action when crossing a bridge but Major Stuber was ignorant to any of this. Since Kath had blown up every officers' mess in the city, only the officers on duty that night had seen the dawn and they were not around to argue. Most were similarly ignorant or already dead but to his credit, Stuber sent four scouts across first. They were overweight,

314

logistical types whom he considered expendable. The field telephone rang at the southern end of the bridge.

"Herr Major," came a breathless voice through the receiver. "The sentries at this end are dead, their throats cut... it's... it's *everywhere*."

"What is?"

"What is what?"

"What is what, *Herr Major*!"

"Apologies, Herr Major."

"What is everywhere?"

"Blood, Herr Major...blood."

Stuber found this distasteful because he had been shielded from the gruesome reality of war and now found himself wishing that the opportunities afforded to him for frontline experience had not been squandered in brothels and on 'supply runs.' He was useful in the niche that modern warfare had created for him, but as an officer he might as well have stayed in bed that day.

While his corpulent blanket stackers searched the bridge, Stuber read the directory in the modest guardhouse and noticed that they were also connected to the Tower of London. He dialled the number and listened to it ring as he stared across the river at a window in the tower where he imagined the handset to be, but there was no answer so he called the northern bridge phone again.

"Is it safe for the company to cross?" demanded Stuber.

"Ja, Herr Major," crackled the voice.

"They're gonna find 'em."

"No, mate, look at the state of it," the man pointed. "They ain't proper soldiers, not what you'd call your *Sturmtruppen*. Those fat coves are storemen or clerks. The officer probably thought sending those oxygen thieves was smart, 'cause no one'd miss 'em."

"He'd be wrong though, wouldn't 'ee, Sam?"

"That's right, Sonny," Sam agreed. "You want your sharpest pair of eyes on a job like that."

"So, they ain't finding our angry playdoh then, are they Sam?"

"Not a chance."

The phone rang.

"You gonna get that?" Sonny asked.

"Depends," Sam said. "How's your German?"

"What German?"

"Exactly, now get that flare gun ready."

"I've 'ad it ready for the last six hours."

Sam and Sonny watched as the sweating men beckoned their comrades across the bridge.

"I don't believe it! He's gonna send the lot across, all together!" Sam sang with the unconcealed glee of a man moments away from revenge against the pitiless regime who had murdered his family.

Sure enough, all three-hundred and sixty-seven men of Stuber's cobbled-together force made for the bridge. They were packed tightly, apparently scared to separate themselves from

316

the press. Sam watched intently as the last men set foot on the bridge.

"Fire!"

Sonny raised the flare gun above his head and, arm outstretched, he let it fall in an arc. As the gun drew level with the open window, he squeezed the trigger and with a muted pop the flare sizzled through the sky over the Thames.

The head of the demolition team received his signal, and grasping the T-shaped handle, he plunged it into the blast machine. Sam and Sonny watched in slow motion as each charge blew in succession and the iron beams of the bridge twisted violently as the concrete crumbled into the filthy river, taking Stuber and his men to their watery deaths. Smoke hung with the smog on the river as the screams and desperate thrashing of those still alive in the water echoed off the stone and brick of the ancient city.

Three miles to the west another flare was fired. This signalled Harry Tench's personal retinue to break cover in Saint James' Park and to run. They ran past the empty sentry posts and through the gaps in the barbed wire. They ran past the Victoria Memorial and through the smouldering gate posts where two dead guardsmen lay, blood congealing in their Busbies, the black fur matted to their pale faces. These giant men had remained loyal to a king who had abandoned his country for a life of comfort under the German yoke. They had taken four resistance fighters down with them, their prostrate forms dwarfing those of the wiry young Cockneys.

With Harry at their head, the forty-strong force stormed through the central arch and fanned out into the quadrangle to be met by sporadic small arms from several upper windows. As Dave's brains exploded, covering Harry with blood and skull fragments, the force pulled back into the arches, and someone fired a rifle grenade into the offending window. A man in royal livery tumbled down into the courtyard, dead before he hit the ground, while thirty-nine men stormed through the grand entrance of Buckingham Palace, meeting further resistance from royal servants. Harry found a ceremonial sword and began hacking at the poorly armed footmen, he grabbed a scullery maid in her late teens by the throat, a blonde curl escaping from under her mobcap as she screamed in horror.

"Show me where the King is," he demanded.

"Please, don't hurt me," she pleaded, tears streaming down her face.

"Hurt you? We're here to set you free, love!" Harry said, releasing his grip and allowing the blood-soaked sword to fall to his side.

"Why are you killing us then?" she wailed.

"Self-defence, now take us to the King!" he demanded again.

"Fine," she sobbed, walking quickly ahead, putting some distance between her and this vile man.

All over the Palace scenes like this were repeated as brave, stupid boys in royal livery stood up to hardened men with sharp knives and clean consciences. Harry had given strict instructions not to kill anyone that didn't offer resistance, but these kids were brainwashed. Indoctrinated at a young age to believe that the lives of this fat old man and his family were more important than the lives of millions of so-called commoners.

"They're in there," she jerked her head at a set of ornate white doors inset with patterns in gold leaf. Harry tutted at the opulence and burst through the doors theatrically.

King George V sat at the head of a breakfast table, with a piece of scrambled egg in his bushy beard and a colourful parrot perched on his shoulder, and he stared in disbelief at the scene unfolding before him.

"Your Majesty," Tench gushed, bowing low as his entourage flanked him, weapons raised.

"It is high time for me to put an end to your sittin' in this place which you have dishonoured with your contempt for the people of this great country," Tench recited the words of Cromwell with a broad smile on his face.

"Did you know that England has been invaded by your cousin Willie?"

The King opened his mouth to speak but Harry continued over him.

"You wouldn't think so from in here," he said, looking about at the obvious comfort and abundance the royal family still enjoyed.

"We have all made sacrifices—"

"I don't want to hear it, George! *Us lot*..." he gestured around the room at his men, "...we've been living underground, like rats. In fact, that's what the Boche have been calling us. Rats!"

"You'll be pleased to know, though, George..." Harry held up a hand to silence protests against his disregard for royal protocol. "You'll be pleased to know we've done for that lot out there. The fucking Huns, I mean."

The queen gasped aloud at Harry's use of profanity.

"And what have *you lot* done?"

He picked up a chipolata and eyed it with disgust before shrugging and pushing the whole thing into his mouth with two grimy digits and spoke as he chewed.

"Eat. Fucking. Sausages. Do you know how many of your subjects have been tortured, killed, strung up in public for fighting against this invasion? An invasion that you so readily accepted. No, neither do I, numbers was never really my game, so let's just agree that it's a lot. Far more than you…"

He pointed at George V accusingly, summoning up his full title.

"As By the Grace of God, King of the United Kingdom of Great Britain and Ireland and of the British Dominions beyond the Seas, Defender of the Faith, Emperor of India, ever bothered to do! Except that's wrong, isn't it? It's just King of Great Britain now, not Ireland or the Dominion beyond the Seas and don't get me started on the fucking Faith! You, old son, are just a vassal. And you're not even that now."

"Now see here," the king exclaimed, rising to his feet. "I can't imagine how you got in—"

Harry casually raised his pistol and shot the bird from his monarch's shoulder. Feathers filled the room accompanied by screams from the queen and her children, while the king recoiled, one hand clasped to his ear.

Harry smiled down at his king to reveal a set of teeth that had not known the luxury of modern dentistry and were probably beyond its powers anyway. He drew himself up and, holding his looted sword aloft, he shouted.

"George Frederick Ernest Albert of Saxe-Coburg and Gotha, you've been weighed and measured by the people of London and have been found wanting. Wanting in spine, in courage, and in loyalty. Your capitulation to your cousin Wilhelm was an act of treason and as such, you shall be taken from this place and hanged by the neck until you are dead. Dead. Dead."

He paused between each 'dead' and looked at each of the king's children; sixteen-year-old Henry, fourteen-year-old George, and the sickly young Prince John. At the realisation of what was happening, the ten-year-old began to have a seizure and he died right there in the royal apartments, his mother and sister crying out for their little Johnnie.

The eldest princes, both of whom would one day be king, were away. Prince Albert aboard HMS *Collingwood* and Prince Edward was somewhere to the north with the Grenadier Guards.

"You lot will be allowed to choose one of the royal residences. You will go there today with whoever decides they want to go with you. I'd suggest Balmoral."

"You can't do this," Prince Henry shouted, striding forwards to confront Harry. Andy took one step towards him and landed a gentle blow on the boy's jaw. Tears welled up in his eyes as he clasped his face with both hands and cowered backwards.

"This *is* happening, folks, so don't just stand there. Get your shit and get out of my house!" he roared, causing the Queen and Princess Mary to wail in despair.

"As for this slag," he waved a hand at the forlorn looking monarch, "take 'im to Banqueting House and string 'im up with the rest of the collaborators. I want a sign that says, 'I sold my subjects into slavery'."

Harry Tench smiled, he had deposed his King and taken the first steps towards moulding the empire in his own image, but he needed the proletariat to know their king was truly dead.

"And don't forget to mark him out as the King. Make sure His Majesty has a crown or summin'. In fact, dress him up in one of those ridiculous uniforms with the rows of unearned medals."

Tench turned on his heel and his retinue parted to let him leave as George V was led from the room and his family erupted in protest. The queen and princess wailed with grief both over Johnny and George V, but remained kneeling over the child. The princes however, moved to save their father, hurling themselves in a fit of wild rage at the hardened men of Tench's personal guard. While voluble, the attack was ineffectual.

"Stay down son, if you get up, I'll 'ave to really hurt you," Andy warned Prince Henry after punching him hard in the stomach.

Stiff Micky was not so generous, as the butt of his rifle struck Prince George's face with a sickening crack, launching the boy backwards through the room until his head connected with the marble fireplace. He lay unmoving in the grate as blood pooled around his head.

Gerald rode south at the head of his personal guard with Michael at his right flank. The uprising's forces were much depleted after the Battle of Hampstead Heath, and most were left to recover at Kenwood House. As they entered Trafalgar Square the atmosphere of jubilation and victory was palpable. His squadron of Hussars in their brown leather jackets was received with cheers and shouts of, "No gods, no masters!" and, "Freedom from slavery, freedom from monarchy!"

It was their brown leather jackets marking them out as resistance that saved them. A file of Hussars in traditional uniform, or heaven forbid, ceremonial dress, would have been surrounded and pulled to the ground, never rising from beneath the boots of the proletariat. They rode on, under Admiralty Arch and along The Mall.

"What's that flying over the Palace, Michael? It looks black," Gerald asked as they trotted along the tree-lined Avenue.

"I'm not sure, Sir Gerald, perhaps it's still the *Reichskriegsflagge,* that does appear black from a distance."

"No, I don't think so, it looks like it is a black flag. Get Holford up here, he's got eyes like a shithouse rat."

Michael turned and beckoned to Holford.

"That's a plain black flag, Sir Gerald, no mistaking," Holford said after standing upright in his saddle for a moment.

"Huh, how very ominous," chuckled Gerald. They trotted on, eager to liberate their King and give him the good news as Gerald pondered his reward for saving the Empire. A barony or earldom, perhaps even a marquisate.

"What the fuck is that?" Harry asked through a mouthful of chicken leg. He was standing at an east-facing window of the Chinese Dining Room. Since his expulsion of the royal family, he had stripped to the waist and a mantle hung about his shoulders with one of Queen Mary's tiaras nestled securely amongst his wild ginger curls.

Kath and her Iceni had joined him some time ago and each had occupied one of the seven-hundred and seventy-five rooms. It was Harry's intention that every member of the resistance would be invited to live in the Palace, much as they had done in the tunnels, as a community supporting one another and working together for a better Britain. Kath and Harry had enjoyed victory sex in the royal bed and now they were enjoying a royal meal, in royal clothing, Kath wore a beautiful silk dressing gown that had belonged to Queen Mary and a pair of slippers that had cost more than all of the houses on her old street.

"What's that Prasutagus?" she said as joined Harry at the window.

"Very funny, and I suppose that makes you Boudicca: Bringer of victory?"

"Of course," she chuckled. "Actually it's my being Boudicca makes *you* Prasutagus, wife of the Boudicca."

"That sounds about right," he said, trying to kiss her with a mouthful of chicken but she pulled away in mock disgust.

"That's a squadron of Hussars, they must be part of The Uprising, the ones who fought today at Hampstead Heath,"

Kath said as she brushed a piece of chicken from the snowy white fur of Harry's mantel.

"Oh, here we go, they've probably come to free the King and collect their reward. Yeah, look 'ere, that's Sir Gerald Clive. I know all about him, he's a territorial captain with no service who pretended to be a colonel then got a load of his men killed and the officers' mess ran him out. Now he calls himself *Brigadier* Sir Gerald Clive. What a fucking prick! Do me a favour, get dressed and warn Andy that we might have some trouble very soon!"

He shrugged off the mantel and jabbed the half-eaten chicken leg into a glass of wine before marching from the room purposefully.

Kath found some riding clothes in Princess Mary's rooms and dressed hurriedly. She rang the guardhouse from the King's study and instructed them to invite the brigadier and his men to stable their horses at the Royal Mews, then join her and Harry for a meal in the grand dining room.

"Surely you mean my officers and me?" Gerald asked at the gate.

"All of you," the guard said flatly.

"How…" he said, pausing for the right word to present itself, "*unconventional.*"

The Jacks had done a pretty good job of tidying up after the earlier violence, so Gerald and his men enjoyed a pleasant walk through the grounds back to the Palace. They found tables to seat over two hundred in the Grand Dining Room and more than enough food for each diner to feel satisfied, if not actually full. Harry now wore similar clothing to Gerald, except that he didn't and never would wear badges of rank, because he was, after all, an anarchist. Gerald took his assigned place at the right hand of Harry who sat beside Kath at the focal point of the room.

"When will the King and the royal family be joining us?" Gerald asked.

Harry winked at him as he rose from his seat, glass in hand.

"Brothers and sisters of the resistance. This is it. We have driven the Hun out of London and into the sea. Now, there may be those of you among us who would like things to return to the way they were. Lords and masters, class war and mass suffering for the benefit of the few..."

This was met with jeering and table thumping until Harry placated his followers with a calming gesture.

"Now what's all this?" demanded Gerald, making to stand, but Harry placed a hand on his shoulder and easily forcing him back into his seat. Gerald's face darkened and his skin turned scarlet as Michael began to issue inaudible instructions to his men.

"As I was saying," Harry continued.

"Eat the rich!" called an Iceni named Jean.

"Yes, thanks, Jean," laughed Harry as he tousled Gerald's hair. "That sums it up perfectly. This land no longer belongs to the likes of Lord Fauntleroy here, it belongs to us, and them like us what fought for it. And if the parasitic aristocracy of this country wants to try and restore the status quo after hiding in their country mansions while we fought another fucking war on their behalf? Well, they've got another think coming!"

The diners roared, including many of the Hussars. Michael, Gerald, and the handful of other officers began to feel the eyes of the room upon them.

"Where's the King?" Gerald demanded again, and this time Harry allowed him to stand.

"He's swinging from a lamppost on Whitehall with the rest of the collaborators!" came an anonymous voice.

"That's high treason! It's *regicide*!" exclaimed Gerald, his face draining of all colour.

"Sit down, son," Harry said, his voice quiet but firm.

"I will *not*!"

He turned to face his men.

"We're leaving. I will not break bread with traitors!"

Gerald felt a vice-like grip on his shoulder which compelled him to sit again.

"Anyone willing to follow Mr Clive out of here to whatever bootlicking future he has planned for them can leave now unmolested," Harry announced, his hand still resting firmly on Gerald's shoulder. Michael and two other officers stood, their chairs scraping noisily in the silent hall.

"Three men and one of those has a fucked-up hand. The future don't look too bright for you, old son."

Harry removed his hand allowing him to stand.

"Go on then, run along. Andy here will take you to the stables and see that you have what you need."

Harry waited for Gerald to reach the door before he presented his final ultimatum.

"Know this, though. If I ever lay eyes upon you again, you're a dead man. Understood?"

327

"Hah," Gerald scoffed. "I'm a hero of The Uprising, and I'll come and go as I please!" he said, sticking out his chin defiantly.

"No, you're a chancer, a charlatan. You have no respect for the lives of the men you command and most abhorrent to me, you're a proponent of the old ways. The ways that would have the likes of us working fourteen-hour days, eating shit, and living in a hovel. All to keep the likes of you in the manner to which you're accustomed."

He bared his teeth at Gerald, and if any of the assembled diners had not been listening intently to Harry Tench before, they were now. His voice reverberated around the huge room.

"Millions living in squalor, dying young and for what? For a few thousand of you to be able to live lives of leisure in the lap of luxury. Occasionally playing at soldier or farmer, even statesman. Don't it make you sick?" Harry spat.

"Now, I ain't gonna kill ya, much as it would please me. No, out of respect for what you done, I'm letting you go home to Broadlands. Now, fuck off."

Harry sat back down and resumed his meal to roars of approval from the crowd.

Sir Gerald rode out of London with Michael and two subalterns under a dark cloud, realising that they'd swapped German occupation for popular revolution.

These ungrateful plebs would see his great country ruined, a grotesque parody of republican France. Images of the guillotine and baskets filled with the heads of his friends danced around Gerald's mind, with their cold unseeing eyes and gaping mouths. If he did nothing, this *would* happen. He resolved to find the government in Birmingham and warn them of this new threat and the coming civil war.

"Oi, Clive!"

The voice of a young man caused all four men to turn in the saddle to see where it had come from. They found to their horror that they were surrounded by armed men in the battered and mud-caked uniforms of the Suffolks.

"What is the meaning of this?" demanded Sir Gerald.

"You don't remember me, do you?" the man asked, walking slowly towards Gerald.

"Why? Should I?" he scoffed, turning to his retinue for support.

"Something funny, Captain Clive? Is the impersonation of an officer holding a King's commission a matter for light-hearted witticisms? I am sure that when this is over and the nature of your egregious crime is common knowledge, there won't be much laughing and joking, and until then, until you have learned that preservation of morale and the lives of your men is all, you will not laugh, you will not smile. In fact, I wouldn't be surprised if you were reduced to tears over the coming months. I sincerely hope that your time at the top was worth it, Captain Clive."

Private Savage looked up into the eyes of his former CO and Gerald and sighed.

"I find you guilty of the charge. You will be taken from this place and subjected to Field Punishment Number One for a period of ninety days. Do you accept my award?"

"What, what do you mean, boy? I am a General Officer of The Uprising. You will not be taking me anywhere. Now, kindly stand your men down!"

"Very well. RSM, get this man out of my sight," he said with a wink at the old soldier, one he knew he'd pay for later.

The actual RSM of 1st battalion Suffolks, the man who had marched Savage to the gun that day all those months ago, stepped forward. With a lightning movement of his knife, he cut the leather thong that suspended Gerald's left stirrup. Grabbing his left boot, he forced it upwards, causing Gerald to fall off the horse's right side.

"Stand up, you 'orrible little man."

He dragged him bodily to his feet and a soldier with a rifle introduced his bayonet to the small of Gerald's back.

"A-bout turn!" bawled the regimental sergeant major. "Quick march, left, right, left, right, left!"

The streets and buildings reverberated with the sound of the RSM's unique drill voice.

Gerald was marched into the market square where to his horror, there stood a pillory. The RSM, Savage, and his assistant secured Sir Gerald inside the wooden stocks and walked away.

"See you in ninety days, *Sir,*" the RSM called. The laughter of the soldiers echoed around the square as they left to return to the horses.

"Come on, Wanker, let's take care of those other Ruperts," he said, using Savage's nickname.

Epilogue – 1951

At the end of the Trinity term of Carla's third year, Sir Gerald and Henry travelled up to watch her graduate with a first class with honours in modern history and a full blue for both lacrosse and fencing. After the ceremony Sir Gerald took his family, as he now enjoyed calling them, for a private dinner in a pub once frequented by Oscar Wilde.

It was at this dinner that Rudi announced he was ready to attempt building the time machine over the summer. Carla was confused, not that Rudi was attempting something so outlandish, but by everyone else's apparent complacence over the words *time machine*.

"Is there something I don't know?" she laughed; her German accent barely noticeable by then.

"You know all those dreams you have? Dreams of things that didn't happen, or could not happen?" Sir Gerald was drunk, something becoming a regular event at Broadlands. Carla swallowed as her eyes widened in interest.

"I do?" Carla said, her mind racing.

It all made sense somehow. The dreams, the memories of experiences that could not be true. She felt betrayed and angry but her overriding emotion was excitement.

"It's because this one keeps on inventing time machines and these two go around meddling," he used a fork to prong in the general direction of the accused. "Aren't you going to deny it?"

"No, Father, it's true. Carla, it's why I helped you all those years ago and it's why we are all here," confessed Olga.

"When were you going to tell me?" Carla asked, indignant about being left out of a secret that her baby brother was privy to.

"When Rudi actually invents the time machine. You see, we wanted you to finish your studies and not to be biased towards any particular course of events. This way, you can provide us with the impartial advice we need," Henry said.

"Advice about what?" she demanded.

She would have separate conversations with each of her family alone, Carla knew that she would get nowhere in this setting, so she decided to act like she was fine with it. Alone she would get the information she needed and get to the bottom of this betrayal.

"We want to know the best way to save the twentieth century, to prevent all of the bloodshed, the genocides and the suffering," Olga said.

"Perhaps you could do your master's degree on the subject, a sort of, 'What caused fascism' or 'How did we end up with men like Hitler and Stalin?'" Henry cut in.

"You want me to tell my supervisor that I want to write my masters dissertation on the causes of World War One?"

She held her stony expression for as long as she could before it broke into a smile.

"What an interesting concept, there are so many angles. The Black Hand, the brinkmanship, Mittleurope and German militarism."

She produced a notepad and began scrawling.

"Imperialism, Bethmann-Hollweg, Wilhelm II and France's losses in 1871."

"Carla, Carla!" Henry had to raise his voice to get her attention.

"Oh, I do beg your pardon, this can of course wait. Rudi, tell me more about your time machine?" she said, writing one last thing as she held the notebook in mid-flight to her pocket.

"Well, err, to keep it simple, I hope to use quantum entanglement to transport matter through…"

"Can we just have a nice family meal without harping on about how clever we all are?"

Sir Gerald found it all quite boring. He'd attended Oxford as a Victorian gentleman and Victorian gentlemen were not there to learn about quarks and Einstein Rosen bridges.

"Capital idea, Father, we have the entire summer to discuss this," Henry declared as he looked around the table at the family he had created from the ashes of World War Two.

"I think a toast is in order to the next generation of Clives!"

They raised their glasses in response and drank the delicious champagne.

While Rudi worked on his time machine in the converted stable block, Olga, Henry, and Carla trained. The previous night the two women had stayed awake into the early hours devising a plan to prevent the Great War. While Olga threw herself into the task, Carla carefully manipulated the conversation to glean as much information as she could. The betrayal had left her feeling paranoid and she knew she wouldn't shake it until she had the facts.

"Right, so first of all," Olga said, speaking to Henry over breakfast, "I need to know that you want to come with us."

"Of course, I mean you and I are the only people we know that can actually jump."

"Good, just checking,"

"What about me?" Sir Gerald asked from the far end of the table. Olga paused with a fork full of kedgeree halfway to her mouth.

"Err, well it's a long-term mission, Sir Gerald, and..." Olga stumbled over her words, desperately trying not to offend the old man.

"And I'm too bloody old?"

"I wasn't going to put it quite so bluntly."

"There's still fight left in the old warhorse yet, girl."

"I don't doubt it for one moment, but it's not that kind of mission. We've been training for years to do this and it's highly specialised work." She looked pleadingly at Henry, who cleared his throat.

"Why don't we hear the plan first, Father?"

"Yes, yes, go on, dear," he said, waving a butter knife at her.

"Well, Rudi has a theory about who can and can't jump and it sounds promising, but first I'll give you a basic outline."

She paused to gulp coffee from a bone china cup.

"This plan, though more effective with four, could work with two. So, assuming that only Henry and I jump, Henry will jump back to 1900, adopt the identity of a captain of line infantry whose file we have. He's an orphan who died ignominiously on a remote colonial outpost somewhere in the South Atlantic. He will turn up in South Africa apparently shipwrecked and join in with the Boer war. With an established record and dozens of officers who now believe him to be Captain..." she checked her notes, "Captain Roberts, he will attempt to insinuate himself into the foreign office and eventually the government. All the time working to calm tensions between the Entente and the Central Powers. If Rudi were able to jump too, he would perform a similar task from Berlin.

"That's a good plan. It plays to my strengths and gives me time to really get my claws into Westminster. I wonder though..."

"Go on?"

"I wonder, Father, do you think that the twenty-five-year-old Gerald Clive could be induced to stay in the Transvaal if, say..." he waved a skewered sausage around, "your mine was successful?"

"I hate to admit it, but I was highly motivated by money in those days, and I dare say that if the mine had been a success I would have stayed, but what if that means I don't meet your mother and as a result, you don't come into being?"

"Well, I am, that is to say, I *was* born in this reality, and you *did* meet my mother and when we jump, this reality will cease to exist except in our memories and only then if you come into contact with someone from outside of this reality. So, what I'm saying is, yes, I may not be born in the new reality, but I will still exist in it because I already *do* exist."

"So, what you're suggesting," Olga said through a mouthful of toast, "is that we make sure your father becomes wealthy and

335

stays in the Transvaal, so you can be him in England, with all the benefits of being landed gentry? I assume you look enough like one another at that age?"

"Precisely. Well, I'm not quite thirty and he would be in his mid-twenties in 1900. I think that that, coupled with a knowledge of future events and my particular skills, will be sufficient time to develop enough of a position to have rather more influence by 1913."

"We want you to be able to influence the wording of the Anglo-French Naval Convention," Carla said. "Make it easier for Britain not to support France in a war, or better still make sure it doesn't happen, then the Germans won't feel threatened on all sides, something they called encirclement." She checked her notes. "More importantly, Germany needs to understand that as long as they do not violate Belgian neutrality, Britain *will* stay out of the war. Failing that, leak it to the press, make sure Germany is in no doubt that Britain will only enter the war if Belgium, not France, is invaded."

"Understood, but what do you plan to do, Olga? You can't expect, as a woman, to be doing something similar?" Sir Gerald asked, almost scared of tongue lashing.

"My job is a lot more fun, either on my own or with Carla." She smiled wickedly across the table at her.

"I will move undetected around Europe, assassinating a carefully compiled list of key players. Would you like to read it?"

Carla produced a sheet of paper and unfolded it.

"I should say that these will be silent kills in most cases, made to look like an accident. Dragutin Dimitrijević AKA Apis. The man behind the Sarajevo assassination."

Carla shuffled her notes.

"I also have a list of his key supporters to take out."

Looking up to check she had her family's attention, she continued.

"Franz Josef I, the emperor of Austria. His death will pave the way for his heir, Franz Ferdinand, a well-documented advocate for peace and a third, Slavic crown. French Prime Minister Raymond Poincaré, a well-documented Germanophobe and a proponent of three-year conscription. A move of military aggression towards Germany, this we want to blame on a Russian, weakening the Franco-Russian alliance... Vladimir Purishkevich, a Russian right-wing politician, a real nasty piece of work, he organised the pogroms of Jewish Russians that drove them from their homes, and he's been described as the first fascist. Make it look like a Frenchman did it, and while you're there, get Stalin too."

"What about the Kaiser, bloody limp-wristed warmonger?" Sir Gerald suggested.

"Who takes over if he dies?" Olga asked.

"His son," Carla said checking her notes. "Crown Prince Wilhelm, a militarist, just as keen for war as his father if not more so, and latterly a supporter of Hitler, who when approached, refused to support the July plot on Hitler's life."

"Speaking of, obviously we do Hitler," Rudi said, looking up from a journal and receiving enthusiastic nods all round.

"Oh," Gerald said. "Who's next in line after him?"

"Prince William, a child, and eventual Wehrmacht officer, if not an actual Nazi."

"Better the devil you know then, what?" Gerald conceded.

337

"Can I suggest that while still planning to take over my father's identity in 1909, I spend a few years building a network of contacts and laying the groundwork that will assist both of us when time is tight?" Henry offered.

"Write that down," Olga said enthusiastically. "Any more on the kill list?"

"I think that's quite enough to be going on with, don't you?" Carla reproached.

"Now, Rudi, something that's been bothering me," Henry said.

"What's that then?"

"Olga was told in 2036 that she would only be able to time travel seventy-five years into the past..."

"That's easy," Rudi interrupted. "Yael, what remained of Yael's life, was used as a sort of booster, allowing a further sixteen-years of time travel."

Rudi looked a little bit too pleased with himself as he took a bite of toast.

"Okay, so what about time travel for people other than Olga and Henry?" Carla asked.

"Funny you should ask that," Rudi answered, a toast-filled grin spreading across his face.

"I've been working on an entirely new approach, it's called phasing and if it works, there will be no constraints whatsoever."

He took a sip of coffee and looked around at his adoptive family and the woman he loved as they hung on his every word.

"Essentially, I will generate an Einstein-Rosen Bridge that will appear to the naked eye like a rip in the fabric of time. The traveller will simply step through the tear and into the past, or future if so desired."

End of Book 2

Continue the zeitkreig in Altered State 3: *The Sarajevo Hypothesis*

J. G. Jenkinson is a father, engineer, history nerd and a sailor. He emerged from the burning wreckage of his scholastic career unscathed, but with very little to show for it. This led him to the recruiter's office and over a decade with the British army. As promised, he saw the world, just not the bits of it you might find on a mood board. The army taught him to sail, ski and fence – badly. After a couple of trips to Helmand, the novelty wore off and he sort a living on the Canadian Prairies as an agricultural mechanic. He wrestled steers, drove trucks and fished on frozen rivers. After an interesting year running a farm, he returned to England and took up surveying to fund his writing habit. Now he splits his time between a wind farm in the North Sea and his home in Worcestershire which he shares with his wife and daughters.

jgjenkinson.weebly.com/

instagram.com/author_j.g._jenkinson/

facebook.com/paperbackwindfarmer

·

Printed in Great Britain
by Amazon

31303120R20198